On Everything I Love
By Jimmy DaSaint

Published By:

PO Box 97

Bala Cynwyd, PA 19004

Website: www.dasaintentertainment.com

Email: dasaintent@gmail.com

ISBN: 978-0-9823111-7-2

Acknowledgements

First I would like to give thanks to my Lord and savior Jesus Christ. Thanks to all the people that stood by my side while I was in my darkest moments: my mother Belinda Mathis, sisters Dawn, Tammy, and Tanya, and my brother Sean, my three sons Marquise, Nigel, and Jaiden, my ICH rap camp: SC, HH-SPADY, REEK IVAN, CHARLIE HEAT, K.WALKER, CHEESE, YOUNG SAVAGE, BOSSMAN, SPORT, JEEKY, SHORTY RAW, and SCARFO.

I want to give a special thanks to Tiona Brown (author of *Ain't No Sunshine*) for all the help and support you have given me since day one. Tiah "DC Book Diva", TLJ, Tiff and Zahir from The Firm Publications, Black and Nobel, and all my friends in the publishing industry. Sorry, but I have too many to name.

To all my fans who continue to support me, thank you very much.

Last but not least, I can't forget all my incarcerated brothers and sisters doing time in the Federal and State prisons. Keep y'all heads up and never give up on your dreams!

ONE
March 2, 1979
Philadelphia, PA...

Holding a small bag of groceries in her arms, Penny left the supermarket that was only a few blocks away from her house on 51st and Westminster Avenue. In a rush to get home and watch her favorite rerun of the sitcom, *Good Times*, the naïve 15-year-old girl decided to disobey her mother's rule and take the shortcut home. Many times her mother, who was paralyzed as a result of a car accident, would warn her and her older sister Vanessa about the dangerous young men who lingered around on the corners waiting for the opportunity to harass young, immature girls who were somewhere they should not be alone. Only two weeks earlier a young woman had been brutally raped and strangled just a block away from the same supermarket.

Usually both girls would go to their neighborhood supermarket together, but on this particular night Vanessa was sick with a temperature of 101°. Therefore, Penny had to go food shopping alone. Before she left her mother instructed her to go straight to the supermarket and back; no shortcuts and to take no rides. But the stubborn Penny had other plans, and getting back to watch her favorite TV show at 7 o'clock was definitely one of them.

The sky was pitch black on this cold March night and no one seemed to be outside as Penny began walking down 49th Street. The abandoned street full of decrepit row houses was indeed a scary sight, but it was a shortcut home that Penny took many times; disobeying her disabled mother's constant warnings. At the end of the block, Mercy Mental Hospital was situated, which housed some of Philadelphia's most unstable and mentally disabled citizens. Sometimes the patients would even manage to escape this minimum security facility only to be caught walking up and down the streets of Philly half naked, not knowing if they were coming or going. Mercy Hospital had been built before the turn of the century, and it was rumored to have been the last residence of a few children of former United States Presidents. Still, the eager and naïve Penny showed no fear as she took her precious time walking down the dark and abandoned street. Looking at her Timex wristwatch, Penny noticed the time was 6:50 and her TV show would soon be coming on.

Gripping the bag of food tightly against her chest, Penny looked back and noticed someone dressed in all white quickly approaching her from behind. Instantly, the feeling of fear crept into Penny's young body as she began to walk faster down the gloomy, haunted ghetto street. Then, out of nowhere, another man also dressed in all white suddenly appeared in front of the now scared and terrified teenage girl. Before she could scream and call out for help, a large hand covered her mouth entirely. As her bag of groceries hit the pavement, both men dragged Penny into a dark, secluded alleyway.

While one of the men firmly held her down, the other began removing her clothes but Penny would not go down without a fight as she tried to bite, kick and scratch her way to freedom. Yet, the young 110-pound frightened female was no match for the two full-grown men. Soon her aggressive attempt to free herself became meaningless. All she could do was give into this demented pair of evil and heartless men. Men that would take turns raping this once proud young virgin female, over and over again, till they finally decided to spare her life and run off; leaving her laying half naked, exhausted, bloody, and alone on the cold, dark, and abandoned street.

With both men vanished into the darkness, Penny finally opening her tearful eyes. She was disorganized but regained her senses and put her pants and sneakers back on. Quickly getting up off the cold ground, she grabbed her bag of groceries, and although scared stiff she began running down the dark street. Still in a state of shock and fear, Penny ran as fast as she could, never once looking back. When Penny finally made it to the safety of her loving and warm home her sister and mother were both inside their rooms.

"What took you so long?" her mother yelled out from the back room.

"The supermarket was packed, Mommy", Penny shouted as she wiped away the tears from her terrified face.

"You missed *Good Times*" her mother called out.

"I know. It'll be back on tomorrow", Penny said, walking into her bedroom.

Taking off her bloody and dirty clothes, Penny grabbed her robe and hurried into the bathroom before anyone could see her horrible condition. As the warm water hit her bruised and sore body, her tears escaped the confines of her eyelids and fell down her beautiful face. The blood from her vagina also fell and was slowly sucked into the drain of the tub. Both Penny and Vanessa were two attractive girls, but on this night, Penny felt like the ugliest person on earth. *"If only I had listened to my mother"*, is what Penny thought as she tried to wash away the filth that would now stay with her forever. She just couldn't believe she had become a victim of rape and that the first time, her first time being touched by a man was by someone whom she had never known.

An hour earlier
Mercy Mental Hospital...

John Williams and Peter Smith were two of Mercy's most unstable patients. Diagnosed with sociopathic personalities and psychotic disorders, both men were hiding inside of a small closet on the first floor of the hospital's left wing. From there they were able to see everything and anyone who came and went down 49th Street from an inside window.

"Put on this" John said, passing Peter a white nurse's uniform. "We have to hurry back" he said, as he put on a similar white uniform. The wide-eyed Peter said nothing, as he just obeyed every word of the much bigger man.

"She will be right back. Her and another girl always walk down this street, but today she was alone", John said as he opened up the window and started to climb out. Peter quickly followed behind him looking like a crazy pit bull following his maniac master.

John Williams stood around 6'3" tall, weighing 220 pounds. He had been a patient at Mercy for four years. In 1975, he had strangled and suffocated his younger sister, believing that she was the devil and had been sent from hell to kill him. Only 14 years old at the time, John was sent to Mercy's Mental Hospital where he would spend the rest of his life, one of only eight Afro-American patients that Mercy housed. John was also considered the hospital's bully, manipulating most of the other patients to help him with his many devilish acts. Because of his size, many of the patients feared him, and so did most of the staff.

Peter Smith was the complete opposite. A quiet, timid white man standing about 5' 10" tall, with a large scar that went across his neck -- which was self-inflicted. Peter had tried to hang himself after being raped as a child by his own father. This was something that went on for many years inside his suburban household until he finally got fed up and stabbed his sleeping father seventy-seven times in the face and chest as he laid drunk in bed one night. On June 3, 1972, a day before his 15th birthday, Peter was committed to Mercy's Mental Hospital for psychological and suicidal treatment. Once, Peter was asked by his doctor, "Why did you stab your father seventy-seven times?" His answer was "Because that's how many times he raped me."

Without even knowing by raping this young girl Peter became the one thing that he feared most -- a replica of his own father. Luckily today Penny's life, although forever scared, had been spared by the men. Both were capable of murder yet they didn't kill her. Still, both men were unstable and very dangerous individuals and should have been locked behind bars for life.

~~~

After a long, relieving shower, Penny dried herself off and went into her bedroom. Posters of the Jackson 5 filled the walls of her bedroom. On the back of the door was an even larger poster of "J.J." -- actor Jimmy Walker – of her favorite show *Good Times*. Roller skates, dolls, and clothes were all scattered around her bedroom floor. After putting her soiled clothes inside of her laundry hamper Penny did what she would do every night. She got on her knees and said her prayers. Closing her eyes, nervously she began, "Please God, take away this pain and continue to watch over me. Please don't let

9

my mother find out Father...and please, get those bad men that did this to me. Amen."

Cutting off her bed lamp, Penny got into bed and lay under her blanket. All kinds of thoughts began to enter her confused and terrified mind. Though she could not remember what either of the men looked like, there was one thing that she couldn't forget -- the long horrible looking scar that encircled the neck of Peter Smith.

Reaching under her pillow she pulled out her favorite good luck charm, a small gold angel that was given to her on her 10th birthday by her mother. Her mother would constantly say, "The angel will always protect you and keep you safe." Today, however, she forgot to put her good luck charm in her pocket. Something Penny never forgot to do and she felt her negligence had brought this bad luck upon her.

With her eyes closed, the tears once again began to travel down her gorgeous brown face, and now her once peaceful dreams had now begin the cycle of frightening nightmares.

TWO
Three months later...

While Vanessa and Penny were both in school, Mrs. McDaniel would have to do things for herself until one of the girls came home to help her. Usually, Vanessa would get home first since her high school was much closer to the house, but for the last three months, Penny's strange behavior caused Vanessa to realize something was wrong with her younger sister. Now Vanessa would wait for Penny every day after school.

Since that tragic night, Penny would not walk alone and began to act very strangely, distancing herself from her family and friends. At first no one paid her strange behavior any mind, but Vanessa knew something was wrong when one day she walked into Penny's bedroom and found her crying on her bed. Vanessa asked, "What's wrong?" But Penny just brushed her off saying, "Nothing, I'm okay." However, Vanessa knew something was bothering her little sister. Fright was written all over Penny's face.

Vanessa was eighteen years old and a senior honor roll student at Overbrook High School in West Philadelphia. She had an attractive brown complexion and slim petite body, with the brains to go with it. Not only was she the class president, but Vanessa was also the head cheerleader, making her mother very proud of her college-bound daughter. Ever since her mother's accident, which left her paralyzed from the waist down, Vanessa was expected to make sure everything was taken care of; such as paying the bills, buying and preparing the food, as well as washing the clothes, in addition to all the other tasks a household needs. These were all a part of Vanessa's responsibilities. She was the head of the household and she ran it very well.

Though her number one priority was her mother, Vanessa made sure she was seen as a positive role model for Penny, helping her with homework and other things that big sisters do. But now her once boy-crazy, hard-headed younger sister appeared to change overnight. And if no one was taking heed, Vanessa was. Penny had been very moody, barely ate and lately she'd wake up from her sleep dripping with sweat and Vanessa was determined to find out why.

On the corner of 50th Street Vanessa waited for Penny to show up. After fifteen minutes Penny finally appeared, walking around the corner.

"What took you so long?" Vanessa asked in a sarcastic tone.

"I was in the bathroom", Penny said with a sickly look upon her face.

"Girl, what's wrong with you? You ain't been right the last few weeks."

"I'm okay. I just feel sick", Penny said as they both began walking home.

"Something is wrong with you and you need to tell me what's going on. Why have you been so tired lately and now you sleep with your bedroom light on?"

"I just haven't been feeling good", Penny answered.

"Okay, you don't have to tell me... I'm through asking you."

As they continued to walk up the street Penny quickly grabbed her stomach, throwing up all of her food on the sidewalk.

"Girl, are you okay?" Vanessa calmly asked, passing her a few napkins from her pocket. "Tell me what's wrong with you, Penny!!!?"

After wiping around her mouth Penny stood up and tearfully looked into her big sister's eyes.

"I'm...I'm..."

"You're what?" Vanessa asked.

"I'm pregnant! I'm three months pregnant, Vanessa!"

"What! By who? Oh, my God!"

Seeing a vacant porch step both girls sat down.

"Who's the boy? Is it your boyfriend, Stanley?"

"No, it's not Stanley."

"Who then? That's the only boy you ever talk to."

"Well, it's not Stanley", Penny said, wiping her tears.

"Who is it then?"

"I don't know!"

"What do you mean you don't know? Stop playing and tell me whose baby you're carrying."

"I don't know, Vanessa!"

"How come you don't know, Penny?"

"Because I was raped!"

"What!" Vanessa said, not believing what she had just heard.

"I was raped three months ago."

"By who?" A shocked Vanessa asked.

"I don't know. It was dark and there were two of them."

"Two of them!" Vanessa shouted. "Oh, my God!"

"Yeah, two men raped me that night I went to the supermarket by myself, that time you were real sick and couldn't go with me!"

"Why didn't you tell me? You could have told me!"

"I was afraid. And I didn't want you and Mommy to find out."

"Where did this happen?"

"On 49th Street, down the street from the crazy hospital."

On Everything I Love

"On 49th Street? You know not to go down there alone. So many things have been happening around there, and mom warned us about it so many times."
"I know, but I didn't want to miss *Good Times,* so I took the short cut... And that's when it happened."
"You don't know what they look like?"
"One had a long scar on his neck but that's all I can remember."
"Who said you were pregnant?"
"I just know. I've been feeling sick for awhile now, and my period hasn't come on."
"We need to tell Mommy this."
"No! No! Please don't tell Mommy. She will kill me", Penny cried.
"She needs to know, Penny. You need to be checked out."
"I'm fine. Please, Vanessa, I'll get rid of it."
"How? How will you do that?"
"I heard about this girl in North Philly who took her baby out and flushed it down the toilet."
"Girl, are you crazy? You can kill yourself doing that! We are going to tell Mommy, and that's it!"

With a scared look on her face, Penny knew Vanessa was right and that telling her mother would be the best thing to do. Vanessa reached over and hugged her little sister, knowing she was scared and had no idea what to do. Being the big sister Vanessa would be there for Penny every step of the way.
"I'm sorry, Penny. I love you, lil' sis. Everything will be okay", Vanessa said as a flow of tears traveled down her face. "Thanks, Vanessa. I love you too", Penny said as she remained embraced in Vanessa's loving arms wishing she could stay there forever. After wiping away their tears the girls stood up from the step and continued their journey home.

Twenty minutes later...

Entering their street on 51ˢᵗ and Westminster Avenue, the girls both noticed a red medical ambulance in front of their house. A small crowd was also gathered around outside. As both girls began running towards their home two paramedics walked out carrying their mother on a stretcher.

"Hold up, young ladies. Where do y'all think you're going?" A big, white muscular man in a blue uniform said.

"That's our mother!" Vanessa yelled.

"What's wrong with our mother?" Penny asked as the men began placing her inside the waiting ambulance.

"She had a bad accident", the man said. "She was found by your neighbors at the bottom of the steps inside the house."

"It appears she lost control of her wheelchair", another man added.

"Is she okay?" Vanessa tearfully asked.

"She was unconscious when we arrived. The doctors at the hospital will be able to tell you more. Please, get in ladies. We must hurry up."

Vanessa and Penny both jumped inside the ambulance which quickly sped off after one of the paramedics shut the door behind them. Inside the ambulance Vanessa and Penny both sat on the side of their unconscious mother, more frightened than they've ever been in their young lives. Seeing their mother's condition, both girls knew it was serious; and there was nothing they could do because their mother was now in God's hands.

On Everything I Love

Two days later
Misericordia Hospital...

The painful tears of both girls began falling like pouring rain after just being told their mother died from the serious head injury she sustained in the tragic fall. The doctors did all they could do to save their mother but the impact to her head was too severe for her to handle. Inside the waiting room, both girls could do nothing but cry and pray to God to watch over their mother's soul.

Ever since their father ran off with another woman their mother was all the family the girls had ever known. Their young mother did her best to raise her girls and the three of them had been very close. Now, all they had left was each other.

Later that day...

Inside a doctor's office, Vanessa and Penny sat beside each other still crying from the loss of their mother. After signing hospital papers, the girls were ready to leave and go home when Penny fainted on the floor and went into a convulsion. The doctor quickly ran to Penny's side, helping her up. A short, older nurse entered the office and began helping the doctor lay Penny in a nearby chair.

Moments later two more nurses arrived with a rolling stretcher. Vanessa remained in shock as everything around her seemed to be moving so fast. Too fast.

"This doesn't look good", the doctor said to one of the nurses who was now rolling Penny out on the stretcher.

"Doc, what's wrong?" Vanessa asked in a worried voice.

"I'm not sure, but a few tests will let us know what's going on" he said, rushing out of his office.

Vanessa followed closely behind the doctor and nurses as they hurried down the hall. Entering a large room with Penny on the stretcher, the doctor asked Vanessa to wait outside as he shut the door behind him. As she waited Vanessa could do nothing but cry. Still dealing with the loss of her mother, Penny's situation made her worry even more. The worst part about it was she had no one to call, no family and no friends. All she ever had was her mother and little sister. Now, in less than three days, her loving mother was dead and she had no idea what was wrong with Penny.

Forty-five minutes later...

The doctor walked out into the hallway where Vanessa was still crying and impatiently waiting. "Is everything okay, doctor?" she asked concerned, yet scared to hear any bad news.
"Yes, everything is fine. Your sister scared us for a minute there", he smiled. "But everything is fine now. She and her baby will be okay."
Vanessa's eyes lit up. She had forgotten all about Penny being pregnant.
"What happened?"
"Your sister had a mild seizure."
"Will she be okay?"
"Yes, she's fine but she needs to take better care of herself. She needs to eat more if she expects to have a healthy child. I'm really sorry about your mother but if she doesn't take better care of herself and her child things can become very dangerous for her as well."
"I'll keep an eye on her", Vanessa promised.
"She'll need it. Your mother's passing has brought on stress that can really complicate matters. I gave

17

her instructions on what to do for the next six months. And I'm a little worried that the baby isn't growing at the normal rate of a child of twelve weeks."

"I'll help her, Doc. Can I see her now?"

"Sure. She's still up, but we'll keep her here tonight for observation."

"Thank you doctor, very much", Vanessa said, walking into Penny's room.

Lying on the bed, a smile appeared on Penny's face at the sight of Vanessa walking through the door.

"Don't you scare me like that anymore", Vanessa said, noticing all the tubes attached to Penny.

"I'm sorry, Vanessa", Penny said as she began crying again.

"I'm so scared. My body feels so funny."

"The doctor said you'll be okay and that you need to eat."

"I know. He told me to start taking better care of myself but I can't help it because all I can think about now is Mommy."

"Mommy is gone, Penny... She's in heaven. We need to worry about you right now; you and your baby."

"What are we going to do?"

"The same things we've been doing and the same things Mommy taught us. Take it one day at a time."

"What about money?" Penny asked.

"Mommy had life insurance and she wanted to be cremated to make sure we had enough left over...We are both her beneficiaries."

"What about school?" Penny questioned.

"I'll be graduating soon and everything should be in order by then. You just take care of yourself and that baby. I'll make sure everything else is taken care of. I learned from the best", Vanessa smiled.

"I love you, Big Sis."

"I love you too, Penny. Now you just rest. I have to go home and make some important phone calls. I'll be back to take you home."

After kissing Penny on her cheek, Vanessa stood and walked out the door. Walking down the hall of the crowded hospital, Vanessa broke down into tears. Everything appeared to be slowly crumbling around her. She had nowhere to turn and no one to run to. In just three days, her entire life had tragically changed. But Vanessa would do what she had to do. She would do what her mother had taught her and showed her ever since she was a little girl-take it one day at a time and never break.

THREE

Vanessa had done everything she was supposed to do. Though the loss of her mother affected her dearly she understood now more than ever she would be counted on to raise her younger sister. The life insurance company paid a seventy-five thousand dollar check to each of the girls for the death of their mother. Vanessa immediately paid all of the bills for the next six months, leaving the remainder of the money in the bank. After cremating their mother's body the ashes of her flesh were put into a white vase and placed inside the living room china closet.

A week later...

Penny sat alone in attendance of her sister's high school graduation wishing her mother could be there. Seeing her sister become the first in the family to receive her diploma brought tears to her eyes. Vanessa had kept the promise she made to her mother before she had passed -- that she would graduate and make her proud. Receiving her diploma became the proudest moment of Vanessa's young life, but without her mother right there to share in that moment it also became the saddest.

As for Penny, her stomach was now beginning to show more. Vanessa made sure she was eating and taking better care of herself like the doctor asked her to.

One evening while both girls were sitting in the living room watching TV, they were startled by a loud knock at the door. Getting up and looking through the small peephole in the door, Vanessa was very surprised to see the person who was standing outside on the porch. For a moment, she thought she was hallucinating, but after another look she knew she was not seeing things, that he was real.

Seeing the tall, handsome, full-bearded, middle-aged man instantly brought a lonely tear to her eye. Though it had been fourteen years since she had last seen him, she never forgot her father. The last time she had seen the man who helped bring her into this world she was only four years old. At that time, he had meant the world to her. Then, Penny was just one year old and had no idea who the strange man that would occasionally hold her in his loving and caring arms was. But Vanessa knew who he was. She was his first child. She could never forget the days when he would come home from his construction job at night and she would run and jump into his lap, never paying any attention to the dirty jeans and sweatshirt he would have on. All she knew was this was her daddy, and to her that's all that really mattered. Until one night she waited by the door like she would always do, and the man she had always looked forward to seeing walk through the door never showed up again...until today.

"What do you want, Reggie?" Vanessa said, opening the door.

"Hi, Vanessa. How are you and your sister doing?" he asked in a sickly voice.

"I know you didn't wait fourteen long years to come ask how me and my sister are doing! Don't act like you care now!"

"Please, Vanessa, can I talk to you and your sister? Please!"

Looking into his face, Vanessa could plainly see that her once loving and caring father was very sick. The big muscular man she had always known was now as frail and skinny as she was. Only in his mid-30s, he looked as if he had doubled in age during his 14-year absence.

"Who is it?" Penny yelled from the living room couch.

"Nobody", Vanessa calmly yelled back.

"Vanessa, please! Please, Vanessa, can I talk with the both of y'all?"

"Reggie, why do you show up on my mother's step after all of these years? Why did you wait until after she died to come? Is it money? I'm sure that's why you're here. Are you looking for some money? What? What is it you want? We have been doing fine without you. Why show up now? Why?" Vanessa said, losing the battle of holding back her tears.

"I just wanted to say I'm sorry and tell y'all something."

"Fourteen years have passed and you finally got the nerve to want to tell us you're sorry. You walked away from us -- me, Mommy and Penny and never turned back. Now we're supposed to let you back into our lives because you said you're sorry? How dare you!"

"No! No! Because I'm dying, that's why!" he said in a heartbreaking tone.

"I know you might not care but I felt as though y'all needed to know."

"Who are you talking to?" Penny yelled again, unable to pull herself from her favorite TV show *Good Times.*

"A Jehovah's Witness", Vanessa quickly answered.

"Well, hurry up. You're missing J.J." Penny said, laughing out loud.

"I'll be right there. He's almost finished", a sarcastic Vanessa yelled back.

"So we're supposed to feel sorry for you? Show you sympathy, huh?" Vanessa asked, turning her attention back to the man standing in front of her.

"No, I didn't come for your sympathy. I came to give you this", he said, passing her a small white box. "What's this?" she said, grabbing the box. "When you read it you'll understand everything. All of your questions will be answered about me... about your mother... about everything."

"What do you mean?"

"Just take your time and read what's in the box."

"So that's it. Just read what's in this box?"

"That's it, Vanessa, and know that I always loved you and your sister. And never once forgot y'all."

"Okay, fine, Reggie, I'll read it."

"Thank you. Bye, Vanessa", he said, walking away with his head held low.

"Hold up, Reggie. You said that you were dying. What is it that you're dying from?"

"I'm not sure", he answered, raising his head slightly. "The doctors said it's a rare form of cancer that only a few people have been diagnosed with. Said it's slowly killing me. I was told I only have less than a year to live", he said as he began to loudly cough.

"What's it called?" Vanessa asked in a now concerned voice.

"They are calling it A.I.D.S", he said, then continued walking away. "That's all I know. Read what's in the box and y'all take care."

Watching her sick father walk slowly down the street, Vanessa knew in her heart it would be the last time she would ever see him again. Wiping her tears away, she watched him until he finally disappeared into the night. Now, just like that, both her parents were gone forever. Walking back inside the house, she shut the door and went upstairs to her room. After setting the small white box on her dresser, she went back downstairs and sat next to Penny so the two of them could finish enjoying their favorite TV show, *Good Times.*

On Everything I Love

Later that night, after Penny had gone to sleep and everything was quiet, Vanessa sat on her bed and opened up the white box that was between her legs. Inside laid a pile of neatly stacked papers. On top was an old handwritten letter that was addressed to their mother.

Dear Lillian,
January 13, 1967

It's been a year since I've last talked to or heard from you. The pain that you caused still affects my weakened heart whenever I think of what you did to me. How could you mislead me like that after all of the years I gave you my deepest love? How could you go on living with a lie that you knew would eventually come to light one day?

First of all, I want you to know that I will always love Vanessa, even if she's not my daughter. Though you disgraced me, I understand it's not Vanessa's fault. Your unfaithfulness is and will always be the reason why I left. Why did you? Why? Tell me why my own brother? To make me believe that Vanessa was my daughter when she was actually my brother's child is pure evil. I trusted you! I gave you my heart and you ripped it apart. How do you think I felt finding out my first child was actually my niece? Can you imagine my pain? I could never look at you the same for this. You made my love turn to hate. You destroyed me. Why did you sleep with my brother behind my back? Were you coming around with me just to get close to him? Is that it? When you found out you were pregnant, you knew whose child it was. Why lie? The two of y'all had been sleeping with each other for months. Was I not man enough at the time? He was older and very handsome before he

24

died, so I can understand the attraction. But why use me? Is that why you cried so much after hearing he had been killed in Vietnam? I never saw a woman cry so much over another man's brother. You cried more than his own girlfriend. Now I know why. You were pregnant with his child. So why did you tell me it was mine? Why lie? Is it because you would have looked like a whore to our families? Whatever your reasons for doing what you did, you will have to live with it for the rest of your life. And one day, you will be judged for it, though I thank you for my daughter Penny, who I know is mine.

I no longer have any love in me to share with you. Maybe this will hurt me one day for walking away, but to me, it's the best thing to do. As far as the girls, I will make sure they are taken care of just like I always did. Every two weeks you can count on receiving a portion of my check. I will make sure they have everything they need. Both of them! My daughter and my niece.
Sincerely,
Reggie

The stunned Vanessa could not believe what she had just read. Realizing that her mother had been lying to her and Penny for so many years, making them both believe their father had left her for another woman, was shocking. And even worse, the man she had always thought was her father was actually her uncle. Looking through the box, she found similar letters all stacked inside. Underneath the letters were a large stack of checks and money orders, each from Reggie, each dated two weeks apart for the past fourteen years with the last money order coming just a week before their mother's tragic death.

On Everything I Love

In the bottom of the box, the tearful Vanessa noticed a small, white card. Taking out the card, she opened it up, and a small gold angel identical to the one that Penny owned fell into her lap. Noticing some handwritten words, Vanessa began to read them.
"Lillian, please give these gold angels to my daughters."

The card read:
An angel will protect you...An angel will bring you light...An angel will make things better when nothing seems to be right...An angel will hear your cries...An angel will wipe your eyes...It will be an angel that will change your life forever... One sent from the heavenly skies.

Putting everything back in the box, Vanessa closed it and placed it underneath her mattress. Then, she cut off her light and softly cried herself to sleep.

FOUR
A few months later...

A strange letter from an anonymous sender wrote Vanessa informing her that Reggie had died.

Dear Vanessa,

I am writing to let you know that Reggie McDaniel recently lost his battle to his illness. I was asked by him a few days before his death to write and let you know of his passing. Reggie wanted me to tell you that he always loved you as his own, and in his heart you were and will always be his first child. He also said revealing the truth to you about him and your mother helped take some of the stress off of his fading mind. From all of Reggie's large medical bills, he eventually died a broke man. And from all the stories he told me of your mother, his first true love, he also died a brokenhearted man.

Before he died, he told me that after seeing your beautiful face one more time and seeing how you had grown and matured into a beautiful black woman, he was now at peace and ready to leave this cruel world behind him. He said seeing you, his angel, was one of the happiest moments in his unhappy life. Please do not try and reach me. This situation has affected me in more ways than you can imagine. But this was his final wish, to notify his two daughters and tell them that an angel will watch over and protect them.

Reggie's gravesite is at the Preston Cemetery in West Philadelphia.
Blessings

After reading the letter, Vanessa sat alone in her bedroom and prayed for God to protect and save Reggie's soul. Then, she cried the whole day, mourning the loss of the only father she had ever known.

One day after eating dinner, Vanessa finally told Penny the whole truth about Reggie and their mother. She told Penny about all of the lies that their mother had been telling them over the years and how she had used Reggie just to get to his older brother. Both girls cried together, realizing Reggie had been taking care of them ever since they were little girls and was indeed the only true father they had ever known.

After Vanessa found out that Reggie died a brokenhearted and broke man and didn't even have a memorial headstone on his final resting place, she and Penny purchased a large tombstone for his grave and held a special ceremony in honor of their father. The words on his headstone read:

Reggie McDaniel
Sunrise: 1945 Sunset: 1979
Thank you for everything, Daddy, the father we
will always love

Vanessa also bought two small gold chains for their gold angels to go on. Now, Penny and she could both proudly wear the piece of memory that their father left them.

In an effort to contact the anonymous sender of the letter, Vanessa's efforts fell short. Vanessa believed that the person who sent the mysterious letter would know more about their father and could possibly help them find other living relatives. But all attempts failed.

After deciding to put her college education on hold until Penny gave birth to her child, Vanessa got a part-time job working at a hair salon in Center City. Doing hair was something that Vanessa had enjoyed ever since she was young and she would experiment with her younger sister's hair.

On the weekends, Vanessa and Penny would sometimes go to Wildwood, New Jersey to enjoy the nice hot weather and the beautiful Atlantic Ocean. This was something the girls had always looked forward to while their mother was still alive, and the three of them would enjoy spending summers at the Jersey shore. This peaceful time away also seemed to help Penny through her pregnancy.

However, as the hot summer quickly passed and the fall soon approached, Penny's moods suddenly changed. The pregnancy had begun to take its toll on Penny, causing her much pain and agony through the nights. Many nights, Vanessa would sit beside her little sister and rub her stomach to comfort her and make her feel at ease.

Sometimes she would even lay in bed next to her because Penny had become afraid of the dark and afraid to be alone. So, Vanessa would stay with her scared and frightened younger sister until she would fall asleep, doing everything she could to make her comfortable. Until one night when that all changed.

October 30th, Mystery night...

Mystery night is always the day before Halloween and in Philadelphia, it was considered the scariest day of the year. So many strange and unusual things would occur on this day. Most people stayed in the house because of panic and fear.

Hearing Penny's loud cries, Vanessa suddenly jumped from her bed and quickly ran into her sister's bedroom that was just across the hall. The sight of a bed full of blood brought on an instant fear. Penny's screams were so intense that they could be heard throughout the entire house. The sound of an extreme degree of pain exploded from this young girl's mouth, a pain she never knew existed until that night.

"Hold on, Penny. Everything will be okay", Vanessa voiced, trying to comfort her tearful young sister as well as she could. "It hurts, Vanessa. My stomach feels like it's ripping apart", she said, crying out loud. "You'll be fine. Just hold on till I get you dressed", Vanessa nervously said. "Why am I bleeding? What's wrong with me? Vanessa, what's happening?" "You'll be okay. Stop worrying. I'm almost done", she said, removing all of Penny's bloody clothes. "Ohhhhhh", Penny continued to scream out loud.

Vanessa knew the situation was bad, but she also knew she would have to keep her frightened sister calm if she wanted to save her child. The more Penny panicked, the more the baby was at risk. After calling 911, a police car was dispatched to the house, and both girls were immediately driven to the hospital.

Vanessa sat alone in the hospital's waiting room. A few other people were also there waiting to hear news from doctors about their loved one's situation. All she could do was wait and pray that everything was okay with Penny and the baby.

The seconds quickly turned to minutes and the minutes into hours as Vanessa cried in fear of her sister's painful condition. Finally, after waiting nine long, disturbing hours, Penny's doctor appeared. From the somber look on his face, Vanessa could tell that something was wrong, and an immediate fear entered her soul.

Rising from her seat, Vanessa nervously approached the depressed looking doctor. His eyes were saying so much, but his mouth said nothing. "Doctor, is everything okay?" Vanessa tearfully asked.

"I have good news and bad news", the doctor said in a distressing voice.

"What's wrong? What is it?" Vanessa hollered into the halls.

"Calm down! Calm down! This is very hard on me!"

"What doctor? What are you trying to tell me?"

"Your sister died from complications of the pregnancy!"

"No! No! No! Please tell me you're lying! Please, Doc!" Vanessa screamed, falling to her knees. "No! Why is all of this happening? No! God, why are you punishing me?" she cried.

"Why? Why?"

"I'm sorry. I'm so sorry. My staff and I tried all we could to save them both, but only the baby survived", he said desolately.

"The baby survived?" the tearful Vanessa said, looking up at the doctor.

"Yes, a 5 pound, 6 ounce baby boy. A little premature, but he's doing fine."

Wiping her tears away, Vanessa stood up and regained her composure.

"Can I see the baby?" she asked. "Please, can I see him?"

"Sure, the baby is with the nurses. I'm so sorry about your sister. I really wish we could have saved her."

"Doc, I'm sure you and your staff tried", a shaken Vanessa replied.

"I'm glad you're taking this well."

"I'm not. Inside I'm dying slowly, but for my sister's child, I must live. I must be strong. I was taught not to break, Doc. But much pain rests inside of me right now. So much pain", Vanessa said, looking into the doctor's eyes.

"Maybe the child will help heal your pain? Sometimes life is the only thing that can heal death."

"So far, my life has not been good to me. All I've ever known were losses and pain, though I understand that God does not put in our path what we cannot conquer. Maybe this child will help ease some of my pain. Only God knows the answer. Soon I'll find out", Vanessa said in a low voice.

Holding the baby in her arms, a nurse walked out of a room into the hallway where Vanessa and the doctor were talking. "Here's your nephew", she said, passing the small bundle of joy to Vanessa.

Uncovering the small blanket that hid his head, Vanessa's eyes lit up.

"Whoa!" she said in a surprised voice. "What the..."

"What's wrong?" the doctor asked.

"He's white! Where's my sister's child?"

"That is her child", the doctor said.

"What! Oh, my God! I can't believe this!"

"Is there a problem, ma'am? Something you want to tell us?"

Shaking her head in total disbelief, "No, Doc, it's fine."

"Are you sure?"

"I'm sure. Everything is okay."

Staring down at the dark, curly-haired, green-eyed baby boy, Vanessa could do nothing but smile. He was gorgeous and had many of his mother's features. The rest of his features were from his unknown father. Still, the child was one of the most beautiful babies Vanessa, the nurse, and the doctor said they have ever seen before.

"What are you going to name him?" the nurse asked.

"I have the perfect name for him", Vanessa said, kissing him on his rosy red cheeks.

"What's that?" the curious doctor asked.

"I'm going to name him Angel", Vanessa said, smiling.

"Angel?" the nurse asked with a smile on her face as well.

"Yes, Angel Reggie McDaniel, after our father."

Sitting on an empty bench, Vanessa continued to hold Angel in her loving arms. Though the pain of her sister's death would always remain in her aching soul, the life of this new beautiful child slowly began to ease some of her pain and misery. The day was October 30th, 1979, and Vanessa's Angel had finally come.

A few days later...

Being the only living relative to Angel, Vanessa was easily granted legal guardian by the State of Pennsylvania's Family Welfare and Child Services. After signing all the proper documents, Vanessa sat back and cried, thinking about how her whole life had drastically changed in less than one year. Losing her mother, her father, and then her sister and becoming an unexpected mother, something she was never prepared for and had no knowledge of being, were drastic changes indeed. And now she would be raising a white baby on top of it.

On Everything I Love

A week later...

Penny Camille McDaniel was buried in a grave next to her beloved father. The ceremony was small with just a few friends and teachers from her school. Vanessa, who held Angel in her arms, said a final farewell to her sister and made a promise that she would take care of Angel as if he was her own.

"Don't worry about nothing, Sis. Everything will be alright. I will take care of Angel like he's my own and give him the best life I can. You could never imagine the pain I'm going through standing here in front of your grave. I thought you would live to be one hundred years old, but God had other plans. And I will never question His motives. What's done is what was supposed to happen. I'm going to miss you, though, Penny. I feel like a part of me has gone with you. I feel lost and everything seems dark to me. One day God will bring me into the light, but now I'm a blind woman in a dark world. I don't understand why everything's happening to those who I love most. In time, my pain shall vanish, but my memories will stay forever. I love you, Penny. I love you, Lil Sis. May God bless your soul. Amen."

"Live each day to the fullest because no one knows what tomorrow will bring. Thank you all very much for coming and showing your support", Vanessa expressed, speaking to the small crowd before walking towards the waiting limousine.

"Vanessa, is everything okay...Where are you going?" the preacher asked. "I'm sorry, Reverend Jones, but I don't want to watch as dirt is poured on my sister", Vanessa answered as she continued to walk away holding baby Angel in her arms.

FIVE
Two years later...

Angel had grown up fast in the last two years, and his temper and bad behavior were becoming too much for Vanessa to handle. He would cry all night and throw his toys from out of his crib onto the floor. He also would bite anyone who picked him up and tried to hold him except Vanessa. One day after buying a baby kitten for him to play with, Vanessa left the room for a moment. When she returned, to her horror, the kitten's neck had been broken and Angel was throwing the dead kitten around inside his crib.

Vanessa even took Angel to see a child psychologist who told her that Angel, like any other two-year-old, would grow out of it. He was wrong. Angel's bad and violent behavior just continued. He would throw his dirty diapers everywhere and sometimes just start screaming for no apparent reason. He became so bad that no one even wanted to baby sit him. No matter how much money Vanessa would try and offer one of the young girls around the neighborhood, no one wanted to deal with Angel. He was considered two things around the neighborhood: the most gorgeous baby and the worst headache.

One evening....

While Vanessa was sitting on the porch enjoying the warm weather with Angel inside of his crib, the sound of the telephone caused her to quickly run into the house. While talking on the telephone, Vanessa kept her eyes on Angel the whole time.

Walking down the street at that exact same time, a young lady holding her child saw Angel in his crib crying very loudly, so she stopped. Looking at the gorgeous white baby with his watery green eyes, she smiled.

"Hey, handsome", the young lady said, walking up to Angel's crib. "You are such a beautiful child." Looking through the screen door, Vanessa noticed the young girl on her porch about to put the baby inside of Angel's crib.

"No! No! No, don't do it", she screamed out loud to the young lady. Vanessa knew that Angel would have no mercy for the innocent child. Dropping the phone, Vanessa quickly ran to stop the naïve young girl who had no idea of the terrible mistake she was about to make. But it was too late!

Walking out onto the porch, a bewildered Vanessa could not believe her now tearful eyes. Inside of Angel's crib, he and the beautiful baby girl, who was about the same age as he, were actually playing and laughing with each other.

"I'm sorry, but he was so cute", the young lady said, smiling at both of the children as they continued to play. "He is gorgeous. Are you his mother?"

"No. I'm his aunt. His mother died", Vanessa answered while wiping her tears.

"Oh, I'm sorry."

"It's okay. I'm his legal guardian now. What's your name?"

"My name is Sandy. I just moved around here. I'm from North Carolina."

"What part?"

"Charlotte, North Carolina. What's your name?" she asked.

"My name is Vanessa", she said as the two ladies shook hands. "What's your daughter's name? She is so pretty."

"Oh, her name is Alexis. What's cutie's name?"

"His name is Angel."

"Oh, that is so cute, a lil Angel. Is he mixed?"

Vanessa just shook her head, calmly agreeing.

"Look at them. They really like each other", Sandy said, smiling.

"Yeah, I see."

"What's wrong?"

"You may not believe this, Sandy, but that's the first time I've ever seen my nephew smile or happy."

"No, he's so cute. How could it be? He is going to be a heartbreaker."

"I'm serious. He never smiles. I don't believe this. He is actually happy and sharing his toys."

"What's that around his neck?"

"Oh, that's a gold angel. It was his mother's. He cries whenever I take it off. So, I just leave it on."

"Oh, look at him. He's sharing his bottle with Alexis. That's so cute", Sandy said.

"I just don't understand", Vanessa whispered to herself, shaking her head. "Well, if you don't mind, I would like to give you my phone number. Maybe you and Alexis can come by sometime."

"Sure, I would like that. I'm new in Philly, and I don't have any friends. I'll give you mine, too."

"I still can't believe my eyes", Vanessa voiced while reaching into her purse to pull out a pen and piece of paper. "Here, Sandy, this is my number", Vanessa said, passing her the small piece of paper with her number on it.

After the two women exchanged numbers, Sandy said, "I'm sorry, but I have to go. I was on my way home."

"Where do you live?"

"I live around the corner on Folsom Street."

"Are you busy tomorrow?"

"No, my husband works all day. I'm usually home alone with Alexis watching my soaps."

"I'm going to call you tomorrow. Maybe we can all hang out."

"That would be fine for us. The city is so big, it's scary", Sandy commented, smiling. "So many people and tall buildings. And everybody seems to be moving so fast."

"Well, I'll show you around town. You'll get used to it after a while."

"Just call me, Vanessa. I'll be ready."

Reaching into Angel's crib, Sandy picked up Alexis. A sad look appeared on Angel's little face, and then tears and loud screams soon followed.

"Don't cry, handsome. She'll be back", Sandy consoled, squeezing Angel's cheeks. But Angel continued to cry. "Say bye-bye, Alexis", Sandy said. Waving bye, the two babies stared at each other as if they did not want to be separated from one another.

"Oh, that is so cute. Look at both of them, like they're in love already", Sandy said, smiling. "Maybe they are", Vanessa replied, smiling as she took Angel out of his crib. "Bye, Vanessa. I'll see y'all tomorrow." Sandy waved as she walked down the street. "Bye, Sandy", she said, waving back as Angel continued to cry while watching Alexis being carried away. Vanessa could not understand the sudden change in Angel's attitude. And she did not care. As long as Alexis made Angel happy, she was happy. Now she had a new friend in Sandy and a savior in little Alexis.

As the next few weeks passed...

Sandy and Vanessa became very good friends. While Angel and Alexis became inseparable, the two babies became so close that Vanessa would have to wait till Angel fell asleep before taking Alexis out of his crib or else he would throw a tantrum.

After a while, Angel's behavior did get better as he was now able to walk and say certain words. The first word he said was Mama. "Mama" is what he would call Vanessa and she loved it every time he said it. His second words surprised everyone when one day he yelled "Lexis, Lexis", while they both were playing in the living room. The girls knew then that something was very special between these two young children. Something very strange and mysterious that only these two innocent babies understood. And no one could figure it out.

For the next few years...

As the children quickly grew, things mostly remained the same. One day, Vanessa met a young man named Howard, whom she had seen before. The 6' 1" Howard was a very attractive man. His dark brown complexion and chinky eyes would drive any woman crazy, and Vanessa was no exception. The two met at the neighborhood playground one day while Vanessa was playing with Angel. Howard had noticed her while playing basketball and politely introduced himself. The attraction was instant and the two of them began seeing each other seriously weeks later.

Howard was a known hustler and had plenty of respect around the hood. At twenty-four years old, he already owned his own house and car and had bought it all with money he earned from the streets. Vanessa eventually found out that the money Howard possessed was from selling cocaine and marijuana, but she never involved herself in Howard's street business. She was in love and so was he. And Angel liked Howard, too. This made

On Everything I Love

Vanessa even happier. For the first time in years she felt like she had a family, something she missed so much and had always wanted.

SIX
1986...

"Angel, get off of him before you kill him!" Alexis cried out.

"No, he shouldn't have touched your butt", Angel yelled, choking the skinny little boy whose face was red as a rose. The classroom full of kids all stood around looking on.

"Please, Angel, stop! Please!" Alexis pleaded, grabbing his arms.

"No, I'm going to kill him for doing that", he angrily said.

Walking back into the classroom, the teacher saw what was happening and quickly grabbed Angel off of the crying and scared young boy.

"What are you doing, Angel? Didn't I tell you one more fight and you would lose your seat next to Alexis? Why are you so violent? How many times must your mother come up here for you?"

"But it ain't my fault, Mr. Conly. Ricky touched Alexis on her butt."

"Is this true, Alexis?" he asked, looking at the tearful Alexis.

"Yes Mr. Conly. It's the truth."

"I will handle Ricky, but still, this does not get you off the hook, young man. You cannot continue to hurt people. I'm going to inform your mother that you are still being a class bully and recommend you get transferred to another room. Your behavior is getting out of control, and this needs to stop now."

"Is Alexis going to go with me?"

"No, Alexis is staying! Until you can prove to be a better student, the two of you will be separated."

"Please, Mr. Conly, I won't fight any more. Please don't put me in another classroom."

On Everything I Love

"No young man. Maybe this will teach you a lesson."
"I'm sorry. Please. I'm sorry."
"Tell that to Ricky."
"Ricky, I'm sorry", Angel said.

A tearful Ricky just walked away, taking his seat back at his desk.
"I'm sorry, Angel. You are one of my smartest students. I've had you in my class since kindergarten, but you need to stop being so violent. I think it's best that you and Alexis be separated for a while. I'll tell your mother when she picks you up."
"How long will I have to go away?"
"You're only going to another second grade class. Probably Mrs. Riley's room down the hall."
"How long?"
"However long it takes for you to understand that fighting is not tolerated in this school. I understand that you and Alexis are very close, and your mothers are best friends, but you need to be disciplined or someday you'll be an uncontrollable menace."
"What's a menace?" a tearful Angel asked, looking at Alexis.
"It's a bad person that everybody's afraid of and nobody likes."

Walking over to Angel, Alexis whispered into his ear.
"I told you to stop. Now see what you've done."
"Okay, class, everyone get back into their seats and get out your homework from last night", Mr. Conly instructed.

Sitting in her seat next to Angel, Alexis smiled. Although she didn't like Angel's violent attitude, she knew he was only making sure she was okay. And deep down inside her little soul, she loved it. She would just never let him know how much.

The next day, Angel was placed in another class, but every chance he got he would run down to check on Alexis and make sure she was all right.

Angel had gotten his point across. If you touched her, boy or girl, you would have him to deal with, and the whole school knew this now.

Sitting on the step one day with Howard, Angel noticed him fiddling with a pair of dice in his hands.

"What are those for?" a curious Angel asked.

"They are dice. They're for making money, young buck."

"That's how you buy all of those gold chains and stuff?"

"Yup! That's one of the ways."

"Well, can you teach me, Howard? I want to buy Alexis a gold chain one day."

"Okay, little man, but don't tell your mama."

"I won't. I promise."

After showing Angel how to play and shoot dice, Angel had become very good in just a short time. The two of them would play for fun whenever Vanessa was at work or away from home. After a while, the fast learning Angel was beating Howard on a daily basis. Luckily, they never played for money, Howard thought. Angel looked up to Howard, because this was the only man he had ever known.

Secretly, Howard had shown Angel all the ghetto tricks and cons. Dice, three card monte, even pick-pocketing were all some of the things Angel had quickly learned at his young age. Howard would even let Angel count large stacks of money for him, and every time Angel would get the count right, Howard would give him ten dollars. Angel would put every penny into his piggy bank that was inside of his closet. Sometimes, Howard would even let Angel watch porno flicks with him, and laugh as Angel kept shifting his green eyes back and forth between the T.V. and his small erection popping from his pants.

At seven years old, Angel was very wise and mature for his age. Howard had shown and taught him everything; things that eventually he would regret in the years to come.

"Now what are those words that I taught you to always remember?" Howard asked Angel one day after picking him up from school.

"You said, 'Hustlers hustle and get that doe. Pimps pimp and control they hoe. Gangsters kill and let they pistols go. But a hustler is smarter than them all, because he only controls that money and kills when his back is against the wall.'"

"That's right, lil man, and don't you forget it", Howard said with a large Kool-Aid smile on his face. "You're going to be the man one day, Angel. I can see it. All the men will fear you, and the women will love you."

"I'm going to be just like you, Howard?"

"No, lil man, you're gonna be better than me. You're gonna be one of the best. I think I created a monster", he laughed.

Sitting back against the leather seats of Howard's brand new 1987 Lincoln Continental, a smile appeared on Angel's face. He knew what he wanted to be now. And a policeman or lawyer wasn't one of them. Already, at just seven years old, he knew he was going to be only one thing.., a hustler.., and nothing could change his mind.

1987...

A year later, Vanessa and Howard had a 6 lb., 6 oz. baby girl they named Chyna. A few months afterwards, the two were married in a large beautiful wedding where Angel was Howard's best man. Eventually selling her mother's house, Vanessa moved in with Howard, who owned a house on the other side of town. Even though Angel and Alexis no longer went to the same school, the two would still talk to each other every day on the phone and remained close. On the weekends, one would usually spend the night over the other's house.

1990...

Howard's street business had quickly blossomed into a major drug operation. He was now bringing in over $100,000 a week. Life was going real well for him and his family. Everything they could imagine or wish for, they had and more; money, cars, jewelry, clothes. Howard even bought Vanessa her own beauty salon, which employed six girls, making sure the love of his life would never have to work again.

For awhile, things were all good, until one unexpected night when things fell apart. While leaving her beauty salon one night with Angel, who she had picked up from school earlier that day, Vanessa had just locked up the shop and was about to get into her brand new, custom painted pink Mercedes Benz 300E. Suddenly, two masked gunmen approached them from behind, forcing them both into a waiting dusty grey Chevy Nova. Both had been schooled by Howard on what to do if anything like that ever happened. So, calm and collected, Vanessa and Angel remained silent. Vanessa knew it was only one thing that these thugs wanted, and that was money.

After a bumpy half-hour ride, the car finally stopped on a small back street. Parking behind a waiting minivan, the masked men then forced

Vanessa and Angel into the empty van. After another forty-five minute ride, the van pulled into an open garage. Still, Vanessa and Angel remained calm. They knew that the men would be stupid to harm them if they ever expected any money at all from Howard. Stepping from the van, the men removed Vanessa and Angel, walking them into a small dark room that only had a few wooden chairs and a telephone. After seating them, one of the men then passed Vanessa the phone.

"Okay, you know what it is we want", he said in a hard deep voice. "Call that nigga and tell him $500,000 in an hour or both of y'all gonna get it. Shorty, you be quiet and don't say a word."

"Fuck you! You coward!" Angel angrily shouted out at the man.

"What did you say, you little bastard", the man growled, smacking Angel across the face with the back of his hand and knocking him to the floor.

"Please don't hit him anymore!" Vanessa shouted.

"Well keep that little bastard quiet then, or the next time it'll be worse."

"I'm not afraid of y'all. Only cowards hide behind a mask", Angel said loudly.

"You didn't learn, did you, you little punk", the other man spat, kicking Angel in his stomach. "We got ourselves a little tough guy here", he laughed.

Holding his stomach, Angel angrily stared at the two masked men, but neither knew this was all a part of Angel's plan to keep them talking so he could recognize both men's voices, something that he was very good at doing.

"Shorty, you're lucky we need you or else you would be one dead little Shorty."

"I ain't afraid to die. I ain't scared of nothing, especially no cowards."

"That's it! Keep that little bastard quiet or I'm going to say the hell with the money", one of the men angrily said.

Angel's plan was working. He could tell by the way the two men were talking they wanted to get him out of their hair as soon as possible. "Angel, that's it! Be quiet and let's get this over with", Vanessa voiced sternly.

Still holding his stomach, Angel remained quiet while Vanessa made the call. After two rings, Howard picked up his cell phone.

"Hello."

"Honey, it's me."

"Where are you? I've been calling your cell phone for an hour now, and I called the shop."

"They got us!"

"What! Who are they?" Howard said in a concerned tone.

"Two guys. I don't know. Angel is here with me."

"Oh, shit! Are you okay? Did they hurt y'all?"

"We're okay. I'm just scared."

"Remember what I told you."

"I will. I'm calm."

"What do they want?"

"They want $500,000 in one hour."

"Okay. Ask them where they want me to bring it."

"Where do you want him to bring it?" Vanessa asked the men.

"Tell him the T.G.I. Friday's men's bathroom on City Line Avenue. To have it in all small bills. Inside the bathroom will be a large brown paper bag. Put all of the money inside it. It will be sitting behind the black trashcan in the corner."

"He said..."

"I heard him, baby. Are you sure y'all are okay?"

"We are fine. Just hurry up."

"Ask them how will I know they won't harm y'all."

"He wants to know how he will know we'll be safe."
"As long as he follows directions, you two will be alright. As soon as we make sure the money is where it's supposed to be and is all there, y'all will be released into the T.G.I. Friday's parking lot. Any foul play and both of y'all will be killed."
"He said..."
"I heard him. Tell them it will be there in an hour. And there better not be one scratch on either one of y'all, or I swear with every dollar I have I'll personally track them down and kill them both with my bare hands."
"Okay, baby. I love you", Vanessa said, hanging up the telephone.
"What'd he say?" one of the men asked.
"He said it will be there in an hour."
"Smart man", he said, laughing. "Let's hurry up and get Shorty out of our hair", he added, looking at Angel.
"This is sweeter than I thought", the other man said. "Five hundred thousand dollars in an hour. Bill Gates, eat your heart out. Didn't I tell you a sucker is born every day? So, every day I go looking for one." Both men began laughing loudly.
"See, pretty, that wasn't all that hard. As long as the money's all there, you and Shorty will be okay. But y'all better hope money man don't try nothing foolish", one of the men snarled, pointing his loaded .357 Magnum at Vanessa's head. "And, Shorty, you better hope and pray everything goes right, or you'll be the first to get it. Do you hear me, tough guy?" the man said, now pointing his gun towards Angel.
"Leave Shorty alone before he starts cryin and shit", the other guy said.
"I ain't gonna cry!" Angel shouted.
"You little mother fucker, didn't we tell you to shut the fuck up!" shouted the man with the .357 Magnum.

Before he could voice what he really wanted to say, the sound of a cell phone started ringing. "Hello", he answered after removing the phone from his pocket. "Yeah, everything so far so good. An hour...behind the trashcan like we said. Five hundred thousand. One penny less and I'll personally kill both of them", he said loudly. "We'll all be waiting outside. Everything is fine, just like I told you it would be. We're on our way. Peace out", he said as he hung up the cell phone. "He's ready. Let's go!"

Standing up, Vanessa and Angel began walking towards the door as both men followed closely behind them holding their loaded guns.

"Nothing stupid Shorty."

"We're okay. Let's just get this over with", Vanessa said, walking out the door.

Vanessa's only concern was to protect Angel and keep the situation as calm as possible. She knew that Angel's temper could easily make matters worse. But if she had to, she would take a bullet before letting anything happen to him.

SEVEN

Opening up the large steel safe that was carefully hidden in the basement of his house, Howard pulled out five large stacks of hundred dollar bills. Each stack was a bundle of $100,000. After placing the money inside of a Gap clothing/shoe bag, Howard locked the safe back up that still contained stacks of money and grabbed his loaded 9mm from off a table.

The thought of calling one of his close friends entered his confused mind, but Howard knew how men would look at this as a sign of sloppiness and weakness on his part where the predator can easily become the prey. He decided to go it alone and take his chances. His main concern was his beautiful wife, Vanessa, and lil Angel. Walking up the stairs into the living room, Howard told Tisha, his teenage niece who was babysitting Chyna, he would be back soon. While Chyna lay asleep on the couch, Howard quickly rushed out the door.

After getting inside his midnight black 1990 Acura Legend, Howard drove off. On the empty passenger seat, the Gap bag full of $500,000 in cold cash laid alone. Under his large white t-shirt, the loaded 9mm was tucked safely inside of his jeans. All Howard could think about was the safety of his family while at the same time wondering who in their right mind had the balls to disrespect him. Sooner or later he knew he would find out, and whoever had the heart to do this would eventually be a few dead men.

Forty-Five minutes later...

Howard entered the large parking lot of T.G.I. Friday's. Saturday night was one of its busiest days.

So many people were about, getting in and out of their cars. Howard looked around trying to notice anything strange, but everything seemed normal and time was steadily ticking. Realizing his hour would soon be up; Howard snatched the large bag of money from the seat and exited his car. With his 9mm still safely tucked inside his jeans, he cautiously walked inside the popular and very crowded restaurant.

Inside the large restaurant, it was packed full of people. The loud music playing in the background was barely audible as most of the customers booed and cheered a boxing match that was being shown on HBO.

Walking through the hysterical crowd, Howard noticed the men's bath and walked inside. Looking around, there were a few men using urinals and a few more guys were fixing themselves up in front of the large mirror. Howard noticed the black trashcan in the back and began walking towards it. Seeing the empty brown paper bag behind it, he effortlessly placed the Gap bag full of money inside of it. By looking around he thought no one had noticed what he had just done, but someone was definitely watching his every move. Howard took another quick glance at everyone who still remained then he walked out.

After walking back out to the parking lot, Howard returned to his car and patiently waited. So many thoughts entered his mind, but only one made him mad...the thought of Vanessa and Angel being kidnapped. With his eyes moving in every direction, Howard began to get a little nervous as the time quickly passed and Vanessa and Angel were still nowhere in sight.

After waiting another ten minutes, Howard decided to go back inside the restaurant. Going back into the bathroom, Howard noticed that the trashcan had been slightly moved. Looking behind the trashcan, Howard noticed the brown bag had been taken, with all of the $500,000 that was inside of it gone as well.

Howard then rushed back to his car and got back inside to wait. Looking through his rearview mirror, a smile finally appeared on his face at the sight of Vanessa and Angel walking towards the car.

After Vanessa and Angel got inside, a shaken Vanessa began to nervously speak. "They watched you, baby. They watched your every move", she said.

"Are y'all okay?" Howard asked as he began hugging his frightened wife.

"We're fine. I'm just happy it's all over."

"We saw you when you drove into the parking lot. We were parked right over there", she said, pointing at an empty phone booth.

"How many of them were there?" Howard asked as he started up the car and slowly drove out of the crowded parking lot.

"I think it's three of them, because the two masked men stayed with us and kept mentioning something about another man already being inside. I guess once they saw everything was okay, and the money was all there, that's when they released us and said we were free to go. It was definitely more than two of them who set this whole thing up."

"Are you sure you're okay?" Howard asked in a concerned voice, looking her and Angel over.

"I'm fine, but I can't live like this, baby. I can't go through this again. Next time, we might not be as fortunate."

"I'm sorry, baby. I'm so sorry for putting you and Angel's life in danger. Things will definitely be different after today, I promise! There won't be a next time. Angel, what's wrong with you? You ain't saying much", Howard asked.

"I'm gonna kill em! I'm gonna kill those cowards for what they did me."

"What is he talking about, Vanessa?"

"They hit him and kicked him in his stomach."

"They did what?! Why did they do that?"

"Angel kept calling them cowards, telling them only cowards hid behind masks. Angel was not afraid of them, and they did not like that he wouldn't back down."

"Don't worry, Angel. They'll get what's coming to them. The streets talk, and I have plenty of listening ears on my payroll."

"But I want to get them! Nobody ever smacked me before!"

"Calm down, lil man, calm down", Howard said as he continued to drive home.

Looking at Vanessa's face, Howard could tell that his beautiful wife was still very much shaken. For the rest of the ride, no one said a word. Angel sat in the backseat with an evil look on his face. Howard noticed a cold stare through his rearview mirror. Looking in Angel's eyes, he could see anger and rage all built up. At that moment, Howard knew Angel was not your normal 10-year-old. He knew this kid did not fear anything and that one day Angel was going to be a problem.

Later that night, back inside the safety of their home...

While Howard slept with Chyna snuggled in his arms, Vanessa sat on the bed wrapping up her hair. After tapping on the door, Angel walked inside of their room and sat next to her on the bed.

"Mama, can I ask you something?" he asked, with a serious look on his face.

"What is it, Angel?"

"Why don't you ever talk about my mother?"

"What! What are you talking about Angel?"

"Why don't you ever talk about my mother?"

"I told you that she died."

"I know, but you never told me how. You never say much about her or my father. Why? What is it that you don't want me to know?"

"Because you wouldn't understand."

"You said that when I was seven. Now I'm ten. What is it that you don't want me to know, Mama? Please, I'm a big boy. I can take it."

"Angel, it hurts me even to think about it."

"What? What is it that hurts you? Why can't you tell me?"

"Angel, please! Please don't make me do this."

"Mama, please tell me, please! Why am I so much lighter than everyone else? Why do I have green eyes? Why am I so different?"

"Okay, Angel, okay. I'll tell you everything. Come with me. Let's go downstairs", Vanessa said, walking out of her bedroom.

After walking downstairs, the two of them sat side by side on the couch.

"Now, what is it that you want to know?"

"Everything, Mama, tell me everything. How did my mother die?"

Looking into Angel's gorgeous green eyes, Vanessa said, "Your mother died having you, Angel."

"What!" Angel said in shock as his eyes widened. "Your mother died when you were born. She couldn't handle the pregnancy. One night, she started bleeding and I rushed her to the hospital. After going into labor, she continued to bleed. The doctors did all they could to save her life, but it was just too much for her to handle. She just couldn't pull through."

"So she died because of me?"

"No, she died for you, and never forget that."

"Who is my father?"

"I don't know."

"What do you mean you don't know? Everyone has a father."

"Angel, your mother was raped!"

"What! Who raped her?"

"I don't know. She was raped by two men one night on her way home."

"Two men raped my mom!" Angel screamed as the tears began rolling down his face.

"Yes, Angel. That's what happened to her."

"So is one of those men my father?"

"Yes, Angel! Yes! One of them is your father."

"Were they white?"

"Your father is. I don't know what color the other guy was."

"She never said what they looked like?"

"It was dark and she was too scared to try and look at their faces. Oh, hold on! She did tell me something once."

"What's that?"

"She told me that one of the men had a long scar that went across his neck and that's all she could remember."

"So am I white?"

"No, your mother is black, so you are black. You look just like your mother."

"Where did my mother get raped?"

"It happened a few blocks away from our mother's house when we lived in West Philly. It happened on a very bad street my mother would warn us about."

"What street is that?"

"Forty-Ninth Street. The only thing still remaining on that horrible block is that crazy ass hospital. Are you okay, Angel?" Vanessa asked as he sat quietly with his arms crossed.

"Yes, Mama, I'm fine. Thank you for telling me."

"I'm sorry, Angel. I'm so sorry you had to find out what happened to your mother. I knew one day you would want to know. I just didn't expect it to be this soon. I'm so sorry."

"I'm okay, Mama. I told you I'm a big boy. I can deal with it. I'm just glad I know now. I needed to know who I am, and now I know. I'm Angel Reggie McDaniel, the child of a beautiful black woman who died to bring me into this world."

Reaching over, Vanessa hugged her tearful nephew, and the two of them cried in each other's arms.

EIGHT
The next day...

    Word quickly spread throughout the city that a $100,000 reward would be paid to anyone who had any information about the kidnapping. Howard decided it would be best to let people know what had happened because that was the only way people would begin talking when money was involved. And a quick $100,000 was plenty of money for somebody to make just for supplying a little information. Also, Howard made sure one of his street workers checked on Vanessa every hour to make sure she was okay. Then, at the end of her workday, they would wait until she closed up the shop and follow her halfway home. The reason behind them only following her halfway is because no one knew where they lived. Howard trusted nobody. Not even his close friend, Kevin, who had been working for him the past five years. Kevin and Howard both grew up down "The Bottom", which was considered the worst section of West Philadelphia, a place where young boys became men at early ages since they had no fathers and no choice. Crack dealers and smokers both roamed the streets. Death constantly filled the air as a young life was taken away every day. Young girls became mothers before they were in junior high school. And grandmothers were in their late 20's and early 30's. Police patrolled the hood like a small army, but even they respect this deadly section of West Philly called "The Bottom."

    Kevin, a chubby dark-skinned man, standing 5'11" tall and weighing close to 300 pounds, was Howard's right hand man. Kevin would make sure all of Howard's street business was taken care of and things stayed in order. Finding out what happened to Vanessa and Lil Angel was a shock to Kevin, because he knew Howard was very street smart and thorough when it came to dealing with the game of hustling. Even Kevin had no idea who would do such a crazy thing like that and not fear the consequences they would face once they were caught. Howard had many friends, even a few cops on his payroll that would keep the heat off of him and his operation. Sooner or later, the truth would come out.

The next few weeks...

Howard waited patiently for any kind of information that would help lead him to the kidnappers of his family. His friends on the police force could not even help. After no information was provided, he upped the reward another $50,000. Still, after a few more weeks, no one had come to collect the reward money.

Since the kidnapping of Vanessa and Angel, Howard began wearing a bulletproof vest. He understood the game very well and knew that a rat comes back for cheese, especially when he got away with no problems the first time.

One night...

Lying across his bed dressed in his pajamas, Angel's telephone rang. Hello, he said, already knowing who it was--the same voice he heard every night before he went to bed.

"Hey, Angel", a beautiful voice spoke in the other end of the phone.

"Hey, Alexis, what's up?"

"Nothing. Me and my mom went to the mall today."

"Oh yeah, what did you get?"

"I got a new pair of shoes and a summer outfit. What did you do today?"

"I was with Howard all day. He took me out to the park and was showing me how to drive."
"You're too young to drive."
"I know, but he still wants me to learn, so when I turn sixteen I'll be ready for my license."
"Howard loves you. He'd do anything for you."
"Yeah, he says I'm like his son. I love him, too. I miss you, Alexis", Angel whispered, changing the subject.
"I miss you, too. It's not the same anymore since y'all moved."
"We still see each other every weekend."
"I know, but it's just not the same."
"Oh, you miss my face? You miss seeing me every day?"
"Don't get conceited on me, boy. You already think you're God's gift."
"I don't think that. I know I am", he said, laughing.
"Angel, being cute ain't everything. It's what's inside that counts."
"I know, but being cute surely makes things easier", he laughed again.
"Plus, look at you. Alexis, you are the prettiest girl in your school. Everybody likes you."
"So what! I don't care about that. And I don't pay any of those knucklehead boys any mind anyway. They are so stupid. And besides, they are afraid of you."
"Why? I moved."
"So what, they're still scared of you. Ever since you came up to my school and beat up that boy."
"That was last year though."
"People don't forget, Angel, especially when somebody gets stomped in the ground."
"He shouldn't have called you a bitch."
"I wasn't worried about that. My mom says a bitch is a female dog."

"Shit, he called you one!"
"Angel, you can't go around and beat up the world. You can't always run to my rescue. One day you're not going to be around."
"Never! Whenever you get into trouble, I'll be there. And that's on everything I love!"
"On everything you love?"
"Yup. You hear me", Angel said.

At that moment, a big smile appeared on Alexis' glowing face. That's all she had wanted to hear. She loved the fact that Angel would always protect her. She just would never let him know.
"Angel, I'm about to go to bed now. I'll call you tomorrow", Alexis said.
"Okay, Alexis. Call me tomorrow after school."
"I will, Mr. Conceited."
"I'm not conceited. I'm convinced."
"Bye, Angel."
"Bye, Alexis. Goodnight", Angel said as they both hung up the phone.

Two days later
12:15 a.m...

Inside a house on Girard Avenue in North Philadelphia, Howard, Kevin, and three of their most loyal workers were all talking.
"What's so important, Howard, that you wanted to see us this time of night?" " ' Kevin asked.
"I wanted to let y'all know things will be down for a while." "Why? What's wrong?" Mitch inquired. Mitch was one of Kevin's trusted lieutenants who had been working with him and Howard for two years.
"My connect out in Miami got busted. Shit doesn't look good either."
"Awe, man! How long do you think it will be?" said Joey, another one of Kevin's top street lieuten-

ants who had been a close friend to Kevin since junior high school.

"I'm not sure, Joey, maybe a few weeks, maybe even a few months."

"Damn! Do you want us to close down shop?" asked Anthony, another street lieutenant who would get guns, cars and anything else they needed to run the illegal drug operation. Anthony had only been down for seven months. He had been introduced to Kevin by Mitch. He and Mitch were cousins.

"No. We still have enough for a few weeks, but after that, I might have to find a new connect. I wanted to let you guys know what was going on, so no one would be surprised if we ran out of shit."

"Thanks, Howard. Now I'll save my money and tell my girl to chill out on that shopping shit for a while", Kevin laughed. "Did any of y'all hear anything about the kidnapping?"

"No, nothing", Mitch answered, shaking his head.

"Not a word", Joey said also.

"I told everyone about the $150,000 reward, but no one has heard anything, not even my homeboy, Rasheed, the cop down at the 29th district", Howard said.

"Don't worry, Howard. We'll hear something soon. Somebody will talk", Kevin reassured.

"I just don't understand how nobody on the streets don't know anything. Not one clue. For that kind of money, people should be knocking down my doors", Howard said in an angry tone.

"Maybe it was some crooked cops. I read in the newspaper yesterday about how internal affairs just busted a bunch of dirty cops", Anthony said.

"No. I doubt that very seriously. Rasheed would have told me. He and I go way back. Before he became a cop, I paid for his daughter's operation. I would have been the first to know."

"Man, you can't trust nobody these days, not even family", Mitch commented, shaking his head.

"Don't worry, Howard. Just chill, dawg. We'll find them. Stop stressing", Kevin said, placing his arm around Howard's shoulder, trying to comfort him. "I just don't understand. Not one clue. Whoever it was knew exactly what they were doing and executed the whole plan perfectly."

"They knew exactly what time Vanessa closed the beauty salon. They must have been watching her for awhile", Howard uttered in disgust.

"Just chill, Howard. Something will pop up soon", Mitch said.

"I hope so. I really hope so", Howard sighed as all the men walked out the door.

The next day...

Inside of her beauty salon, Vanessa and a few of the girls who worked there were all talking.

"So are you coming to the cookout next Saturday, Tawanna?" Vanessa asked.

"Girl, you know I'll be there. I haven't missed one of your cookouts yet. Last year's cookout was the bomb", she said, smiling as she washed a customer's hair.

"What about you, Gloria?"

"I'll be there, too. I'm not missing any free food and all of those fine ass hustlers who are gonna be there."

"Is it at the same place as last year?" Tawanna asked.

"Yeah! We are having it again on Lemon Hill out in the park", Vanessa confirmed.

"Then I'm going to have to go get me a new outfit to wear", Tawanna said smiling.

"Girl, you've been going shopping almost every day. I must be paying too much", Vanessa teased.

Vanessa, Tawanna, and Gloria had all been friends since high school. All three of them were also cheerleaders for basketball teams. Ever since the shop opened, Gloria and Tawanna had been working for Vanessa.

"Yeah, this heffa been spending money like it grows on trees", Gloria shouted out.

"Don't be mad because my man takes care of me", Tawanna shot back.

"Well, he must be whipped, because that nigga bought you diamond earrings and a new car", Gloria said.

"You're just jealous. I can't help it if my shit is the bomb", Tawanna responded as all of the girls burst out laughing.

"Well, when can we meet this new man of yours?" Vanessa asked.

"He doesn't like to be all in public like that. He keeps it on the low."

"Well, you should bring him to the cookout."

"He hates crowds."

"I think she's scared he might see something else he likes", Gloria implied.

"I ain't worried about no chick ever taking anything from me. I know how to keep my man."

"Well ask him to come to the cookout", Vanessa said, walking across the room.

"I'll ask him, but I know he's going to say no."

"Does he have a brother?" Gloria asked.

"No! He's the only child", Tawanna answered quickly.

"Damn, girl, what are you hiding?" Gloria said.

"I don't want everybody sweating my man, that's all."

"Is that all? Sounds like you're hiding more than that", Vanessa said, turning on the radio.

"Yeah, it ain't like you not to introduce us to your boyfriends. You introduced us to Peanut", Gloria smiled.

"Peanut is old news. And plus, he's broke. I was paying for that nigga's gas."

"So now you found a man with money and we can't meet him, huh?" Gloria said.

"I'll ask him to come to the cookout, but like I said, he's low profile."

"Well, it will be nice to meet this guy who's spending all of his money on you. Maybe he knows Howard", Vanessa said.

"No, he doesn't know anybody. He's from Chester."

"Oh, that's where the ballers live, huh?" Gloria smiled.

"Stop messing with her, Glo", Vanessa said as she sat down to listen to her music.

Tawanna was a tall, dark-skinned woman who was Vanessa's best stylist. Though her looks weren't too appealing, her body was the total opposite. With her 38-26-38 figure, she had no problem making any man do a double-take when she walked by. Even back in high school, she had a body to die for. Some of her teachers would even get caught staring at her perfect form. Back in school, she was known as Miss One Night Stand. Almost the entire basketball team had slept with her, everyone except the coach and the water-boy.

Gloria was a short, pretty, light-skinned woman with light hazel eyes and a nice body also. Though it wasn't as fully developed as Tawanna's, it was just as nice. Her 32-24-34 figure blended well with her 5'5" height. Gloria and Tawanna had been best friends since junior high school. But unlike Tawanna, Gloria would never disrespect herself or her body. Since junior high, Gloria had only been with two men and both had been long-term relationships.

The two of them met Vanessa in high school when they all tried out and made the cheerleading squad, and had been close friends ever since.

At times, Tawanna would show signs of jealousy because she never had a true relationship with a man like her two girlfriends. As she got older she realized it was her youthful mistakes she made by sleeping with all types of men that would forever haunt her and cause her to learn the hard way that men fuck whores, but never marry them.

Now it appeared that Tawanna had finally met her Mr. Do Right, but for some strange reason, she didn't want anyone to know who he was.

NINE
On this hot Tuesday afternoon...

Howard had just dropped Angel off at Alexis' house. After telling Angel that he would be back in about a half hour, he drove off, leaving them both on the step.

"Hi, Angel", Sandy said, looking through her screen door and seeing him on the steps.
"Hi, Mrs. Sandy"
"Where's Vanessa?"
"She's at work. Howard dropped me off, but he'll be right back to get me."
"Okay, I'll leave y'all two love birds alone", she said, smiling and walked away.
"Mom!" Alexis shouted out in embarrassment.
"What? You don't ever want to admit it."
"Admit what?" Alexis asked, knowing exactly what he was talking about.
"That you love me", Angel said.
"I don't love you. I just care about you a whole lot."
"Oh, you don't love me, huh? Well, why when I was sick that time you called every five minutes?"
"Because I was worried, that's all."
"And why do you get mad when your girlfriends say I'm cute and stuff?"
"I don't get mad."
"Yes, you do. Stop lying. You know you love me, girl."
"Angel, you get on my nerves", Alexis said, scrunching up her face and crossing her arms.
"You don't have to tell me. I know you love me."
"Okay, whatever."

Reaching over, Angel surprisingly kissed her on her lips.

"Boy! Why did you do that?"

"Because you love me, that's why. And you're gonna be my wife one day."

"No, I'm not", Alexis frowned.

"Yes, you are."

"I am not going to marry no thug."

"I ain't no thug."

"You are so. All you do is act like you're so hard."

"What's wrong with that?"

"Everything."

"You know you like it."

"I do not."

"Yes, you do."

"What are you going to be when you grown up, Angel?" Alexis asked, waiting for an answer.

"A hustler."

"See what I mean. A thug. You are a thug."

"So what are you going to be?" Angel asked.

"I'm going to be a lawyer."

"A lawyer! Girl, you're crazy! Ain't no black girls lawyers."

"There are so, and if there ain't, I'm gonna be the first."

"I'm going to be somebody when I grow up. Just like I thought you were."

"I am. I'm going to be somebody, too."

"What? Tell me what you are going to be?"

"A hustler", Angel said, smiling. "The best hustler ever!"

Alexis didn't think it was funny as she stood up. "Okay, hustler, here comes your ride", she said, seeing Howard coming down the block.

"I'll call you later", Alexis said, wiping Angel's kiss away with her arm.

"What time?" Angel asked, smiling.

"The same time I call you every night, boy, before bedtime."

67

"Okay. I told you, you love me", Angel said, walking towards Howard's car and getting in.

"You still get on my nerves", Alexis responded, waving as the car drove away.

Once Angel was safely inside the car, Alexis went inside the house.

~~~

"What's up, little man?" Howard asked, rolling up the window and turning up the radio.

"Women!" Angel huffed, turning down the radio in a distressing voice.

"Already? You're too young to have girl problems", Howard said, smiling.

"Yeah, that's what I say, but I still got 'em."

"What's wrong? Tell me. Maybe I can help."

"It's Alexis. She's trippin'."

"What's wrong with your girl?"

"She thinks I'm a thug."

"Oh, yeah? Why does she think that?"

"I don't know. She said I think I'm hard."

"Well, what did you tell her?"

"I told her that I was going to be a hustler when I grow up. But she got upset when I said it."

"Never tell a female that", Howard said.

"But that's the truth. I'm going to be a hustler like you, Howard."

"Still, you can't tell no girl that. They get scared when a man says stuff like that."

"Why? You're a hustler, and Mama loves you."

"Yeah, but deep down inside your Mama hates that I'm a hustler. She might never say it, but she hates me being what I am."

"But why? You've got all the money, cars, jewelry and you always buy Mama stuff. You even bought her a hair salon. Why would she be mad that you are a hustler?"

"Because, lil man, hustlers live a fast life, and sometimes a fast life isn't good."

"Why not?"

"Because a hustler's life can be good one day, then bad the next. One day you'll understand. You'll see what I'm saying. See, deep down inside every woman wants a hustler, but they just don't want the problems that come along with 'em."

"Like what?"

"Like staying out late, getting locked up and going to prison, stuff like that. See, women love bad boys. They love everything that is associated with us, the fame, the popularity and especially the money. They don't want a corny 9 to 5 working man whose life isn't exciting, but they will act like that's what they want."

"Why not? Why don't they want that?"

"Because he's predictable. They know all of his moves. Bad boys are unpredictable and it drives them crazy, but they still love it."

"Then why doesn't Alexis like it?"

"She does. She loves you. She's just playing hard to get. They all do until they decide they want you to catch them."

"What happens when we catch them?"

"You won't have to worry about that. They'll show you", Howard laughed. "Just remember, it's not good to tell a woman you're going to be a hustler, even if that's what you're gonna be. Even though most men are hustlers, that word drives women nuts."

"Okay, I get it."

"You understand, lil man?"

"Yeah. I got to make 'em think I'm something else, but really I'm a hustler."

"Yeah, that's it. Make them think you're something else. How do you feel about Alexis?"

"Huh?" Angel said, with a confused look on his face.

"You heard me. How do you feel about Alexis?"

"I love her. She's my girl. She's always been my girl."

"How does she feel about you?"

"I don't know. She always seems to be mad at me, but I know she loves me. She ain't never said it, but I know she does."

"How do you know?"

"Because she gets jealous when other girls show interest in me, and she calls me every night just to hear my voice."

"Oh yeah?"

"Yup. One day she's going to tell me. She's just scared. She has pictures of me and her posted all over her bedroom."

"She does?"

"Yup, since we were both little kids."

"Oh, since y'all were little kids, huh?" Howard laughed out loud.

"Yeah. She's just playing hard to get, that's all. I know now", Angel said turning the radio back up.

As Howard continued to drive, all he could do was laugh seeing Angel already going through his first love stage, knowing that many more were not far behind. Driving through the poverty stricken area of North Philly, Angel stared out the car's windows. The sight of homeless women and children made him wonder how people got to that point. The torn down buildings and graffiti-filled walls were everywhere. Angel began to ask questions.

"Howard, why do people live down here? It's horrible."

"They can't help it, lil man. That's all they got."

"But it's real dirty and everybody looks scary."

"This is how it is for some people, lil man. Everybody's not as fortunate as you and I."

"Why doesn't anybody help them?"

"They don't care about people like them", Howard said, pointing at an old drunken man.

"Why? He's a person, too", a sad Angel responded.

"It doesn't matter. He's black and probably has no education, so there's no escape."

"What do you mean he's black?"

"See, lil man, his complexion will hurt him all of his life. It's real hard for him to make it in this country."

"Bill Cosby and Michael Jordan are rich, and they're both black!"

"Oh yeah, once in a while they throw us a bone, and it's always with sports or entertainment. See, lil man, there's something you need to know."

"What? What's that?" Angel asked, wondering what it could be.

"That every black man must go through misery and punishment before he reaches paradise. Never forget that", Howard said with a serious voice. "If you do right, your complexion will bring you everything you ever want in life."

"But I'm black like you."

"I know you are black, but you look white. Do you understand what I'm saying?"

"No, not really", a confused Angel said, staring at Howard.

"See, look over there", pointing at two police officers who had three black men up against a wall.

"What, the cops? I see them all the time."

"Yeah, do you see who's in control?"

"The cops", Angel said. "They got guns."

"Yeah, two white cops. And the men up against the wall are all ..."

"Black", Angel quickly interrupted.

"That's right, lil man. Remember that prison movie we watched a few weeks ago?"

"Yeah, I remember."

"What color were all the guards?"

"They were all white, even the warden."

"And what color were all the prisoners?"

"Black and Puerto Rican."

"What color is the president?"

"White."

"What color are your teachers and principal?"

"White."

"What color are all the men whose faces are on money?"

"White."

"Now you see who is in control? Do you understand what I'm telling you, lil man?"

"Yeah, black people are not as smart as white people."

"No, no", Howard laughed. "We're just as smart. We are just not in control and they are, but you are one of them and one of us. You can get some control. See, you can fool them. Many of us can't because of our skin."

"How can I fool them?"

"You look like them, but you are one of us. They can't tell."

"Oh, like Batman! He's really Bruce Wayne."

"Yeah, see nobody knows who Batman really is when he's got on his mask."

"But I don't have a mask."

"You don't need one. Your complexion is your mask. Now do you get it?"

"Yeah, I get it now. White people think I'm white, but really I'm black like you."

"Right. Now you get it", Howard smiled.

"Oh, that's why they treat me so different, so nice all the time."

"Right! See what I mean?"

"Yeah, I can be the president and help the poor people."

"Yeah, you can be whatever you want, but remember you are always ..."

"I know, black", Angel said, smiling.

"Look at my eyes, Angel. What color are they?"

"They are brown."

"What color are your mama's eyes?"

"Brown, too."

"And what color are Alexis' eyes?"

"Brown."

"What color are yours'?"

"Mine are green. People in my class say I'm different."

"You're not different. You're special, and don't you ever forget that. You have beautiful green eyes and dark black curly hair. No one looks like you because you are special."

A big smile appeared on Angel's face, and from that moment on he understood the power of his complexion and the difference between being white and black.

TEN
Saturday afternoon...

The temperature was in the mid 80's. Over three hundred people showed up for Vanessa and Howard's annual neighborhood cookout at Lemon Hill in Fairmount Park. The two large speakers loudly played rap music as the sounds could be heard all throughout the park. Females dressed in their best summer outfits, walking around checking out all the brothers who were out flexing their muscles and playing basketball and volleyball. Ten large grills, all lined up next to each other, filled the sky with grey smoke from all the hotdogs and hamburgers that were cooking. Cases of beer and sodas sat chilled inside the large metal trashcans full of blocks of ice. The old heads were all playing chess, while the older women played cards and talked about what had happened on their favorite soap operas. Children ran around kicking beach balls and throwing Frisbees.

On this beautiful day, everyone seemed to be having fun. Even a few homeless people showed up for the free food. Sitting on top of his parked Acura Legend, Howard and Vanessa held each other like the lovebirds they were. Everyone was here, all the street workers who worked for Howard and Kevin, and all the females who worked or got their hair done at Vanessa's beauty salon. Angel was sitting on a milk crate passing out sodas, while all of the pretty little girls admired his handsome looks, teasing and flirting with him like little girls do. Just a few feet away, Alexis stood behind a large table full of food passing out hotdogs and hamburgers, while the whole time keeping her eyes on Angel's every move. Every time a girl would flirt with Angel, she wanted to grab her as hard as she could and throw her to the ground. But when Angel would look over at her, she would turn her head as if she paid him no mind at all.

Sandy walked over to Vanessa and Howard who had now gotten off the car and sat on a long beach chair cuddled up.

"Hey, y'all, this is nice. Just like when we would have them back home in North Carolina", she said, smiling.

"I'm glad you're enjoying yourself, Sandy", Vanessa said.

"Yeah, but I can't say the same for Alexis. Look at her", Sandy said, laughing. "She's miserable over there watching all of those little girls flirt with her Angel. I'm gonna have to hear it all night long."

"Yeah, he got them all around him like flies on shit", Howard laughed.

"That boy is too much", Vanessa commented, looking at her handsome nephew.

"When are you doing the raffles?" Sandy asked.

"Later", Howard said. "That's later tonight."

"What are the prizes?"

"Third place is five hundred dollars, second place is one thousand, and first place is fifteen hundred", Howard answered.

"Well, I'll leave y'all two alone. I got to go get my husband off that basketball court. I don't want to hear any of his excuses tonight about him being tired", Sandy said as they all started laughing.

Walking up next to Alexis, Angel stood beside her.

"What's wrong with you?"

"Nothing is wrong with me", she snapped in an angry voice.

"Why aren't you talking to me? What did I do now?"

75

"You didn't do anything. Ain't nothing wrong, boy."
"Well you sure are acting funny."
"Aren't you having fun with your friends, Angel?"
"What are you talking about, girl?"
"You heard me. You and all of your girls."
"They aren't my girls. You are."
"No, I'm not. We're just friends. You have too many girls."
"I don't care about any of them. You're the only girl I care about. Why do you act like that all the time?" Angel sadly said.
"Act like what? What do you want me to act like, all of those other girls?"
"No, I just want you to act like my girl."
"I'm not your girl. I'm just your friend."
"Okay, friend, then don't get mad because other girls are around me."
"I told you that I don't get mad, boy."
"Look, you're mad now. No matter what I do you get mad."
"Stop saying I'm mad", Alexis said.
"Okay. Okay." Angel said, smiling and throwing his hands up in the air.

At that same moment, a group of men who had just finished playing volleyball approached the food table. Alexis and Angel stood beside each other with their white aprons on ready to serve the starving young men.

"Hey, Shorty, can I get two hotdogs with mustard and a cold Pepsi?" one of the sweaty young men asked. "Yeah, you can hook me up with one of the cheeseburgers when you finish", a man with a deeper voice said.

As Alexis was getting the sweaty young men's orders, Angel stood there frozen in his tracks. "Are you going to help me or not?" Alexis said, tapping Angel on his shoulder, bringing him out of his momentary daze. "Yeah, I'm sorry, you said a cold coke?" Angel asked. "No, Shorty, I said a Pepsi", the man replied. "You can give me one of those Heinekens", the deeper voiced man said.

Reaching for a Pepsi and a Heineken, Angel passed them to each man. "Anything else?" Alexis asked politely. "No, pretty, that's all. You and Shorty took care of us", the man said as he and his friend walked away. "You act like you just saw a ghost. What's wrong with you, boy?" Alexis asked. "I didn't see one, but I did hear one. A ghost from the past", Angel said. "Can you finish this for me, Alexis? I'll be right back. I have to tell Howard something." "Okay, hurry back", Alexis said, wondering what was bothering Angel. "I will. I'll only be a few minutes", Angel yelled over his shoulder as he ran away.

Running through the crowds of people, Angel spotted Howard sitting alone with a handful of red raffle tickets. Tired and out of breath, Angel took a seat beside him.
"What's up, lil man? Slow down!"
"I got something very important to tell you, Howard", Angel panted in a half-frightened voice.
"What is it?"
"I can't tell you here", Angel said, looking around.
"What's wrong, lil man? Is everything okay?"
"Please, let's go somewhere else. It's very, very important."
"But I have to get these raffles ready. Can you tell me in my ear?"
"Yeah. Okay", Angel said, putting his hands together in secrecy covering Howard's ear.
"You sure?" Howard asked in an angry tone.
"What two guys is it?" Howard said, now standing up and looking around. Also looking around, Angel

spotted the two men talking with a group of females.

"There they go, those two right there", Angel pointed out.

"Are you sure, lil man? You sure it's those two?" a surprised Howard asked.

"I'm positive, Howard. I never forget a voice."

"Them two guys right there?" Howard asked, again unable to believe his eyes.

"Yes, Howard, I'm telling you it's them! That's the guy who kept calling me Shorty."

"Okay, lil man, I believe you. I'll get to the bottom of this. Don't say anything to anybody else. You hear me, not anybody!"

"I won't. I'll keep my mouth closed like you taught me", Angel smiled.

"Thanks, lil man. Thanks a whole lot", Howard said, still staring at the two men.

"Just finish enjoying yourself and have fun."

"Okay. Howard, I hope I helped you out."

"You did, lil man. You helped me more than you could imagine", Howard said, staring at the two men as they continued to talk to the group of infatuated females. Walking back next to Alexis, Angel took a seat.

"Where'd you go?"

"I had to tell somebody something real important."

"Your girlfriends asked about you."

"What girlfriends?"

"Them", Alexis spat, pointing to a group of young girls who had been waiting for Angel's return.

"They aren't my girlfriends. You are!"

"No, I'm not. I told you I'm not going with no thug or hustler."

"Oh, I didn't tell you."

"Tell me what?" Alexis said with her arms folded across her chest.

"That I'm not going to be a hustler anymore.
"You're not?" Alexis asked with a big smile on her face.
"Nope, I changed my mind."
"What are you going to be?"
"The President! The President of the United States. Well, I'm gonna be the first black President, just like you're gonna be the first black lady lawyer."

With a big smile covering her entire face, Angel knew he had made Alexis' day, and realized that what Howard told him was true. The words hustler and thug are two words that women are afraid of. Even though, deep down inside, that's all they really want. A man who pays the bills, a man who brings the thrills, and a man who keeps it real.

An hour later...

After everyone had received a raffle ticket, a large crowd quickly formed around the small stage that was built in front of the D.J. equipment. The D.J. then turned the music down as Howard got on stage and grabbed one of the microphones. Looking down at the happy energetic crowd, Howard began to speak. "Is everyone enjoying themselves?"

A bunch of cheers and whistles erupted from the cheerful crowd. "Okay, I'm glad everyone's having a good time. Now is the moment you all have been waiting for", Howard said, holding a box which contained everyone's matching raffle ticket in his hand.

The crowd got real quiet. Vanessa and her girlfriends stood at the front of the stage. Angel and Alexis remained by the food table looking on. Sandy had finally found her husband, Leonard, and the two of them also stood close to the crowded stage.

On Everything I Love

Reaching into the box, Howard pulled out the first winning ticket. "The winner of five hundred dollars is ticket number 12!" Howard shouted.

Everyone looked at their tickets to see if they were the lucky winner. "Oh, that's me!" an older fat lady began yelling in excitement. "Oh, my God! I won", she said, jumping from her card game and running up to the stage.

Everyone began to clap as she finally reached the stage, shocked and out of breath. Looking at her ticket, Howard made sure it was the winning ticket.

"Here you go, Mrs. Mary", Howard said, passing her five crisp one-hundred dollar bills. "Oh, thank you so much, Howard. I needed this! Thank you so much", she said, accepting her money and leaving the stage. The happy crowd got quiet again as they all waited for the next winner to be called.

Reaching into the box again, Howard pulled out another winning ticket. "The second place winner of one thousand dollars is ticket number 18", he announced, holding the ticket up in the air.

Once again, everyone looked at their tickets to see if they had won.

"I won! I won!" Sandy shouted, jumping in her husband's arms. "I have number 18", she said, with tears running from her eyes. Vanessa smiled, seeing her good friend happy for being the winner of a thousand dollars. Running to the stage, Sandy showed Howard her winning ticket. "Here you go, Sandy", Howard said, passing her ten crisp one-hundred dollar bills. "Thank you, Howard. I will put this toward Alexis' college tuition", she said leaving the stage. Walking to Vanessa, the two of them hugged each other.

"And now, ladies and gentlemen, the grand prize", Howard announced. "One lucky person is about to win fifteen hundred dollars", he said, shaking up the box. Reaching into the box, the large crowd all seemed frozen as Howard pulled out a ticket. "And the winner of the 1990 Neighborhood Family Cookout grand prize of fifteen hundred dollars is ticket number... 67."

Everyone looked at their tickets. After a few moments, still no winner appeared. "Somebody has to have it", Howard yelled into the crowd.

Everyone double checked their tickets again and still no one claimed the prize money. "I lost", Alexis mumbled, looking at her ticket stub. "I had number 34. What's your number, Angel?" "What? I don't know. It's in my pocket", Angel said, eating on a hotdog.

Reaching into his pants pocket, Alexis pulled out his ticket stub. "It's number 67! You won, Angel! You're the winner!" she screamed. Dropping his hotdog on the ground, Angel snatched his ticket from Alexis' hand. "I won! I did!" he shouted out loud.

Everyone then looked at Angel as he waved his ticket in the air. "Angel, are you the winner?" Howard yelled from the stage. "Yes, I have ticket number 67", Angel answered. "Well, come up and get your prize then."

"I'll be right back, Alexis", Angel said, removing his apron and walking towards the stage.

Reaching the stage, the crowd all stared at Angel as Howard checked his ticket stub to confirm he was the winner.

"He's the winner!" Howard said happily. "What are you going to do with all of this money, lil man?" Howard asked, passing him fifteen crisp one-hundred dollar bills. Angel didn't respond immediately. His eyes roamed the large crowd. Finally finding who he was looking for, he suddenly grabbed the microphone from Howard's hand.

On Everything I Love

"Thank you, Howard, and I'm very glad I won. But ever since I was small, you and my mama would always tell me one thing", he said, looking at the hypnotized crowd. "Y'all would always say that giving is better than receiving. That God blesses those who give. And everyone is not as fortunate as us."

Looking up at her nephew, tears began to slowly fall down Vanessa's face. "I have everything I want because of you and Mama. So this prize money that I won, I'm giving it away." The whole crowd began to look stunned with amazement. "I'm going to give it to someone who can use it", Angel said as he dropped the microphone and walked off the stage. Walking through the astounded crowd, Angel stopped in front of three homeless people...two men and a woman. "Here, ya'll are the winners, he said, passing them each five one-hundred dollar bills a piece.

"Thank you, young man", the old homeless lady said with a flow of tears falling from her troubled eyes. The other two men expressed their gratitude, and after hugging each one of them, Angel walked back towards Alexis who couldn't believe her tearful eyes. At that moment, the whole crowd began to clap and whistle with excitement. Vanessa winked her eye at Angel, bringing a smile to his face. Howard just stood there knowing that Angel was like no other. Almost every female had a face full of tears, even some of the men. The crowd continued to cheer. Taking a seat next to Alexis, Angel could still feel all the eyes upon him.

"That was the nicest thing I ever saw", Alexis cried. "So you're not mad at me anymore?" Angel asked half confused. "No! How could I ever be mad at my boyfriend", Alexis said, kissing him on his cheek. Angel smiled, knowing now that Alexis was officially his; the girl that he had always wanted since the first time they met as little babies; and the only woman he would ever love. "So you're gonna stop being mad at me from now on? Angel asked, putting his arms around Alexis' shoulders. Making sure everyone saw them, including his young female admirers who all walked away with disappointed looks on their faces.

"Yup." Alexis smiled, looking into Angel's gorgeous green eyes.

"You promise me?"

"I promise you Angel."

"On everything you love, Alexis?"

"On everything I love", Alexis said, as she leaned over to kiss Angel on the cheek.

ELEVEN

Two days after the cookout, Howard, Kevin, and Joey sat inside of a Ford minivan. The time was eight o'clock and Howard was expecting Mitch and Anthony to show up soon. The sky was dark, with no stars or moon anywhere in sight. Howard told all the guys to meet him at a secret location in Fairmount Park.

"What's up, Howard? What's the emergency?" Joey asked, with no clue of what was going on.

"I needed to talk with you, Joey", Howard said.

"What's up? I came like you said at eight o'clock, and no one knows I'm here."

"Good. You sure no one knows?" Howard asked.

"I'm sure. I told my girl I was making a quick run", Joey smiled.

But Howard sat with the most intimidating expression on his face.

"What's wrong?" Joey asked.

"They told me what you did", Howard said, looking Joey in his eyes.

"What are you talking about?"

"Mitch and Anthony told me how you set me up, Joey."

"What! They're lying! They're fuckin' lying! I swear they're lying."

Pulling a black 9mm from under his shirt, Howard aimed it at Joey's head.

"Hold up, Howard. They're lying. They're trying to blame me for everything. Mitch was the one who set it all up. It was him and his cousin, Anthony. I swear", Joey begged. "They said it would be easy and no one would find out. All I did was wait inside the bathroom for you to drop the money off, and once you did, I got the money and walked out the side door. You didn't see me in the bathroom because I was sitting on one of the toilets with my pants down like I was taking a shit. When I saw the trashcan move, I knew it was you dropping off the money."

Howard and Kevin remained quiet as Joey nervously told the whole story.

"I'm sorry, Howard. Please, man. I still got most of my cut", Joey cried.

"How much did y'all take?" Howard asked, with the gun still aimed at Joey's head.

"The four of us got $125,000 a piece."

"Four! What do you mean four?" Howard yelled in a surprised tone.

"Somebody else was involved. I don't know who, but they knew a lot about your wife. Whoever it was knew Mitch and set it all up."

"What!" Howard screamed.

"I swear. That's the truth. Whoever it was told Mitch about your wife, then Mitch and Anthony put it all together, the mask, the stolen cars, the guns, they had it all mapped out. Please, Howard! Please don't kill me. I'll do anything, just don't kill me."

"Anything?" Howard asked.

"Anything! You name it."

"Follow me, Joey", Howard instructed, getting out of the minivan.

Scared and still nervous, Joey followed Howard. Standing just a few feet away from the minivan, Kevin could see them both talking. "Okay", Joey said, walking away and quickly disappearing into the park. Getting back into the minivan, Howard took a seat.

"Everything is going according to plan", Howard smiled.

"That nigga is scared to death", Kevin said.

"Yeah, and his scared ass is gonna do all of our dirty work."

85

On Everything I Love

Moments later, a dark grey Ford Taurus pulled up beside the minivan and parked. Mitch and Anthony both exited the car and climbed inside of the minivan.

"What's up, Howard? It's 8:30 like you asked", Mitch said.

"And we made sure nobody knew we were coming. Nobody!" Anthony added.

"That's good. Did y'all leave your guns like I told y'all?" Howard asked.

"Yeah, we left the hammers home", Mitch said, lifting up his shirt to show he was not carrying a gun.

"The connect came through?" Anthony asked. "Is that what you called us for?"

"Nope, not yet", Howard said.

"Then what's up?"

"Y'all two slimy motherfuckers", Kevin said, pulling out a Tec-9 from under his seat. Both men jumped back instantly, throwing their hands up in fear.

"Whoa! What's up? What's going on, Kev?" Mitch asked nervously.

"Y'all no-good motherfuckers", Kevin said, aiming the large gun at their heads.

"What did we do?" Anthony fearfully asked.

"Greed, ya'll two greedy motherfuckers set me up", Howard said as he pulled out a shiny chrome .380 handgun.

"What are you talking about, Howard?" Mitch asked, his hands still held high above his head.

"Don't play dumb, motherfucker. We know everything", Howard growled violently.

"Howard, you know I wouldn't do anything to cross you", Mitch cried out.

"Shut the fuck up, you snake!" Howard spat.

"I took care of you motherfuckers and look what you do", Kevin said upsettingly. "Go behind our backs and set Howard and his wife up. Y'all niggas ain't shift"

"It was Joey, man! He set it all up!" Mitch shouted.
Howard knew Mitch was lying to cover his own ass, knowing Joey was a follower and had always been a follower. But Mitch, on the other hand, was someone who always wanted control. Mitch was just like him, but worse. Howard earned everything he had. Mitch would rather take it and fake it.
"Stop lying, nigga! I know everything. How you set up everything, how you were the one calling all the shots", Howard said. "You always wanted to be the man."
"I told you don't trust that soft ass nigga", Anthony said, looking at Mitch.
"Shut up, nigga", Mitch yelled.
"Fuck that! I ain't dying for you! It was Mitch, Howard! He set it all up, him and that slut ass bitch!" Anthony yelled.
"You bitch ass nigga", Mitch angrily yelled back.
"Both of y'all motherfuckers shut up", Howard shouted. "Now, what is he talking about Mitch?"
Nervously shaken, Mitch remained quiet. Everyone's attention was now on Mitch.
"You have five seconds to open up your goddamn mouth or you'll be one dead ass nigga", Howard angrily said. "1... 2... 3... 4..."
"Tawanna! It was Tawanna who works at your wife's beauty salon", blurted. "Tawanna?" Howard asked in disbelief, trying to make sure he wasn't hearing things.
"Yeah, that bitch met me at an after-hour bar one night. As we were talking, we found out we had a lot in common. She told me about your wife and how she would leave the shop at all times of the night by herself. When I told her that I worked for you, she said that was even better because no one would suspect it to be one of your own guys. And no one would ever imagine Vanessa's #1 stylist having

anything to do with it. So I listened and fed into her little plan. I'm sorry, Howard. I still have most of the money. Please. Please, give me another chance", Mitch begged. "It was that bitch Tawanna who set it all up!"

"Tawanna!" Howard said, shaking his head in incredulity.

"Yeah, man, that bitch doesn't really like your wife. One night after Anthony and me both got her drunk and fucked her, she told us how she really felt about Vanessa. She's hated her since high school, she said. She felt that Vanessa always thought she was better than everyone else. And she even said she laughed when she found out your wife's mother and sister died, and how stupid your wife was to be raising a half breed. Tawanna even said she was going to quit after shit calmed down and open up her own shop with your money. That bitch is a snake!"

"That's enough!" Howard yelled. "Get out! Both of y'all get out now", Howard said, pointing his gun at Anthony's head.

After the men got out of the car, Howard told Mitch and Anthony to slowly walk in front of him and Kevin. "Please, Howard! Please!" Mitch begged. After walking about twenty feet, Howard told them both to turn around. "Please, Howard, don't kill me", Anthony pleaded, holding his hands up high. Pointing his gun at both men, Howard told them to get down on their knees. "Please! Please!" they begged. "Get the fuck on your knees!" Kevin ordered.

As they both dropped to their knees, Howard began to speak. "The two of y'all disappointed me. I'm sorry, but this has to be done", he said, putting his gun away.

Looking in amazement, the two quickly switched their eyes to Kevin who was still holding the Tec-9. Putting his gun down to his side, Kevin turned and started walking away, too. "What's going on?" Mitch asked, still on his knees. Howard then nodded his head. "Okay", he shouted.

Suddenly, walking from behind a large tree, Joey appeared holding Howard's loaded 9mm in his hand. Before either of them could get up and run, Joey stood behind them emptying every last bullet into the back of both men's heads, instantly killing them.

As the two bodies quickly slumped to the ground, both men died like Howard wanted them to - on their knees and begging for their lives. "I told you, Howard. I told you I would do it", an excited Joey said.

Walking from behind a tree, Kevin appeared holding his Tec-9 gripped with both hands. "H-Howard, you said y-you weren't going to kill m-me", Joey stuttered, slowly backing away. "You said that if I killed Mitch and Anthony, you would spare me my life. Please, Howard! Please, Kevin! Please don't kill me!"

Pointing the machine gun at Joey's head, the large gun jammed. Joey realized the only chance to save his own life was to run so he took advantage of the situation and quickly ran through the park. "Get that motherfucker!" Howard yelled as he took out his .380 handgun and started shooting. But just like that, Joey had managed to vanish into the safety of the trees.

As Kevin began to run behind Joey, Howard stopped him.

"Kev, let him go. He ain't no threat. That scared ass nigga just killed two people. We won't have to worry about him or those motherfuckers anymore."

"You sure, Howard? He can end up being a problem one day."

"I'm sure. He'll take that money and get as far away as he can. Let's get out of here", Howard said as the two of them began walking back to the minivan.
"I don't believe this fuckin' gun jammed again and that nigga is still alive. Damn!" Kevin shouted.
"Don't worry about Joey. He ain't nothing but a dead man walking", Howard said as they both got back into the minivan and quickly drove off. "Right now he's the scariest man in the world", Howard laughed.

~~~

Lying across his bed, Angel had just finished his homework when his phone rang.
"Hello", he answered, speaking into the phone.
"Hi, Angel, it's me."
"Hey, Alexis, what's up?"
"Nothing. I was just thinking about you."
"You were?" Angel said with a big smile displayed on his face.
"Yeah. Are you coming over this weekend?"
"Yeah. Howard's gonna drop me off. Why?"
"I was just making sure. How's little Chyna doing?"
"Being bad. That girl is always tearing up something."
"Just like you used to", Alexis laughed. "It must run in your family."
"I wasn't that bad", Angel laughed.
"Boy, don't even try it. You were one hundred times worse."
"Can I ask you something, Alexis?" Angel said in a serious tone.
"What Angel? What is it?"
"Why don't you ever tell me you love me?"
Pausing for a moment, Alexis thought about the question.
"Alexis, are you still there?"
"Yeah, I'm here."

"Well, answer the question. Why don't you ever tell me you love me?"

"Because", Alexis said.

"Because! Because what? That's all you can say is because?"

"Because love isn't to be told, Angel. It's to be shown. Everyday people are running around telling other people how much they love them, and they wind up being the person who hurts them most. The word love doesn't mean anything anymore. If a person loves me, then show me, because if I love them, I'll show them, and not with words but with actions. I just wanted to call you before I got ready for bed, Angel. I'll call you tomorrow."

"Okay, Alexis, I'll talk to you tomorrow", Angel said as they both hung up. Sitting up on his bed, Angel thought about what Alexis had just said, knowing that every word she had spoken was the truth.

TWELVE
The next morning...

Sitting inside his parked Acura Legend, Howard waited for Tawanna to show up for work. Vanessa decided to stay home, so on days like this it would be Tawanna who opened up the shop. Looking through his rearview Howard noticed as Tawanna pulled up behind him in her brand new Nissan Maxima. Not realizing it was Howard parked in front of her; Tawanna exited her car and began walking towards the shop. Removing her keys from her purse, Tawanna heard her name being called.

"Yo, Tawanna. Yo, Tawanna", Howard yelled, rolling down his window. Looking to see who it was calling her name, Tawanna spotted Howard and quickly walked over to his car. "Get in", Howard said before she could say a word.

Getting in the car, Tawanna smiled, wondering what could be so important that Howard would be waiting this early in the morning for her.

"Hey, Howard! What's up?" she smiled.

"I'm gonna get straight to the point", Howard said in an angry voice.

"What's wrong?" Tawanna asked, seeing the hard look on Howard's face.

"You, you slimy ass bitch!"

"What! What are you talking about?"

"Bitch, don't act dumb! You know what I'm talking about."

"I don't know what you're talking about Howard."

Starting his car, Howard pulled off and began driving fast down the street.

"Bitch, they told me you got me set up! I know everything, slut!"

"What! Who?"

"Mitch and Anthony told me. They told me everything."

"Howard, I don't know what you're talking about", Tawanna said as she began to shed tears.

"The tears ain't gonna help you. Tell me why you did it? And if you lie one more time, I swear, I'm gonna kill your ass with my bare hands."

"Please, Howard, they're lying on me. We can go get them now. They're lying", she cried.

"Too late. They're dead!" Howard said as he continued to drive.

"What? They're dead?"

"You heard me, bitch. Dead! D...E...A...D..."

"What happened?" she nervously asked.

Pulling over on a small street, Howard parked. Looking around, Tawanna noticed she was a few blocks away from the shop.

"It doesn't matter what happened. All that matters, you dirty whore, is who the fuck do you think you are", Howard spat, reaching over and grabbing her by her shirt.

"Please, Howard, please! I'm sorry. I'm sorry", Tawanna cried. "I still got $50,000 left. Please don't hurt me. I'll give it back and work the rest off."

"Bitch, keep the money. That ain't what I want from you."

"What is it that you want, Howard? Anything, just don't hurt me."

"I want you to take the money and leave town. Get the fuck out of the city."

"What!" a shocked Tawanna shouted.

"You heard me, bitch. Leave town. And I mean in twenty-four hours."

"But my family, my friends. Please Howard."

Reaching into his pocket, Howard pulled out a small piece of paper.

"Who do you know living at 1826 S. 23rd Street?"

"That's my mother's address. Why?"

"If you ain't out of the city in twenty-four hours, it will be your mother's former address."

"Please, Howard. I'm so sorry."

"Bitch, pack your shit and leave. That's all I got to say. I don't care where you go, just get the fuck out of Philadelphia."

Shaking nervously in her seat, Tawanna could see that Howard meant every word. If not for her being a female, she knew Howard would have definitely had her killed. Or killed her himself. Knowing that she was in a no-win situation, leaving town was her only option.

"Okay, Howard. I'll be gone tomorrow."

"Don't let me see you again, Tawanna, or next time I won't be so nice."

"Does Vanessa know?"

"No. I don't want to tell my wife that her no-good ass friend is the reason she was kidnapped. I don't want to hurt my wife. You ain't worth it."

"Thank you, Howard. Thank you for not telling her."

"Don't thank me. Thank God that you're a female. Now get the fuck out of my car."

With her head down and tears falling from her eyes, Tawanna got out of the car. Soon as she shut the door, Howard sped off, leaving her standing in the middle of the street. Knowing that her life had just been spared, Tawanna began her long walk back to her car. At that moment, so many thoughts ran through her confused mind, realizing she had only twenty-three hours and fifty-five minutes to leave town.

~~~

Later that night, sitting inside the living room, Vanessa and Howard were talking.

"I just don't understand. She quit", Vanessa said. "Just like that!"

"Maybe she found another job or something."

"She still could have given me some kind of notice."

"You know how she is anyway", Howard said.

"Yeah, but it's just really strange how she was acting on the phone when she called me."

"How was she acting?" Howard asked, flicking the channels of the T.V. with the remote.

"Scared! She was acting like she was terrified of something or somebody."

"You said she had a new boyfriend. Maybe that's it."

"I don't know, maybe so. All she said is she was moving to Atlanta."

"Stop worrying, honey. Maybe it's better."

"She was my top stylist, Howard. Now I have to hire somebody else."

"Just make sure you check out the person real good. Some people are cold blooded snakes."

"I will. Gloria's cousin does hair. I told her once I had an opening I would give her a job."

"Well, now you have an opening", Howard laughed.

"It's not funny, Howard. I'm gonna miss Tawanna."

"Tawanna doesn't care. If she did, she wouldn't just leave you like this. What kind of a friend is that?"

"Well, I hope she's still okay."

"She'll be fine. Now come here", Howard said, grabbing Vanessa in his arms and kissing her.

"Why are you so happy?"

"Today is a good day, that's why."

"Why is that?"

"Because I have you, my sweetie."

"Stop it", Vanessa said, blushing.

"I'm serious. Are the kids asleep?"

"Why?" Vanessa asked, smiling.

Pulling down his jeans, Howard smiled. "Yeah, it's 11:35. They're asleep", he answered himself, looking at his Rolex. "You horny lil devil", Vanessa giggled, noticing his full erection. Cutting the T.V. off with the remote control, the living room instantly became dark. "You couldn't wait till we went upstairs?" Vanessa asked while undressing. "Nope", Howard replied as he threw his jeans and boots to the side. "Lay back then", Vanessa said, clutching his dick in her palm as she got down on both knees.

Tightly gripping his hard erection, Vanessa began licking around the sensitive head. Suddenly, she began sucking every inch of him while all he could do was lay back with his eyes closed. Continuously, she stroked every part of him with her warm and wet mouth. After a few intense and wonderful moments of pure pleasure, Howard could stand no more as he released all that had been built up inside of him into her mouth. Without letting one drip hit the floor, Vanessa swallowed every drop. "This how you like it, Daddy?" she asked, wiping around her mouth with the back of her hand.

Still feeling the intensity of the orgasm, Howard remained speechless. "Never mind, you don't have to answer. Your body speaks for itself", she said, smiling. Pulling herself up, she then climbed on top of him, placing every inch of Howard inside of her soaking wet paradise. "Oooh", she moaned as she slowly began riding him nonstop, digging her long nails into chest. "Oooh, ahhh, oh, Howard, baby, it feels so good", she whispered. Unable to hold it any longer, she released a tremendous orgasm before slumping onto his hairy chest. As her body trembled uncontrollably, she melted into his loving arms and then peacefully closed her eyes. Howard smiled, knowing he had accomplished the two things that he set out to do. One, satisfy his loving and irresistible wife, and two, make her forget about Tawanna.

The next day, Tawanna left town, leaving in her new car with her last $50,000 in cash. Word on the street was Joey had also left the city and went to New York where he had some relatives living. The murders of Mitch and Anthony were never solved as police had no clues or witnesses. Howard and Kevin put together a new team of street workers, moving two street sergeants up in the ranks to take the place of Mitch and Anthony. Business remained very good for Howard and his young crew of hustlers. Now, on a daily basis, the crew was making over $700,000 a week, all from the illegal drug business.

Wisely investing his money, Howard opened up two more hair and beauty salons for Vanessa. He also opened up a pool hall and a Laundromat in his old neighborhood. But as Howard began to get more and more involved with his legal businesses, the thought of retiring from the drug game constantly entered his mind.

At thirty-two years old, Howard had accomplished everything he set out to do being a hustler in the drug game. He had also made all of his friends rich men, making sure neither them nor their families would ever need anything. He was still young, handsome, and very rich. In his heart, he knew it was time to quit and pass the torch. Over the years, he watched the game become more deadly than when he had first entered it over fourteen years ago. Now, every time he would read the paper or watch the news, someone in the game was murdered in the game or going to jail.

THIRTEEN
1997
Seven years later...

As the years quickly passed, Angel mastered everything Howard had shown him, though Howard tried his best to keep Angel straight and out of the cruel game. It was Angel who already had his mind set. Ever since he was seven years old, he knew what he wanted to be. A hustler, and no one could change his mind. Realizing this, Howard finally decided to slowly pass the torch to Angel, introducing him to people he needed to know and all the things he needed to understand. All Howard would do now is make sure his product would safely get into the city, with him mainly getting his drugs from Miami or New York. And every time he would have to go cop some drugs, only he and Kevin would go along with one of his trusted lieutenants. That was one factor of the business he would never involve Angel in, because he had always anticipated his two biggest fear. The fear of being killed while buying drugs or the fear of being locked away so long you'd never be able to adapt back to the ways of society.

Parked...

Inside his brand new 1997 Lexus coup, Angel waited out front of Central High School like he did everyday for Alexis to walk out the front door. Now standing an even six feet tall, Angel had grown and matured into a bright and very handsome young man. With his dark, curly fine hair and ocean green eyes, women could not resist his model-like looks and his lean 175 pounds that went with it. Angel had gone to another high school that was on the other side of town, but everyday he would make sure he was in front of Alexis' school when she was let out. Drawn to his gold Lexus, all the young girls couldn't help but stare at the young, handsome Angel, and at the same time, all the men couldn't prevent themselves from hating him. Though no one would try anything because everyone knew who he was and what he was about. Therefore, everyone gave him much respect, even those who disliked him. They all knew it was best to be Angel's friend rather than to be his enemy.

Seeing Alexis walk out the door with two of her girlfriends, Angel smiled. Alexis had grown into a very attractive and mature young woman. Standing 5'6" tall, she could easily pass for Janet Jackson's twin sister. Her smooth caramel complexion complemented her long black wavy hair that fell down past her shoulders. Her 34-24-34 figure was also a sight to see in Angel's green eyes. This was the love of his life. To him, no one was more beautiful than his Alexis.

"Hey, baby", Alexis said, getting into the car and kissing him on his cheek.

"What's up, baby? What took you so long?"

"My teacher had good news for me", Alexis excitedly said.

"What is it?" Angel asked as he slowly pulled off and drove down the street.

"I was accepted to Spelman College with a four-year scholarship."

"Spelman... Isn't that in Atlanta?"

"Yeah, but it's one of the best black colleges in the country."

"What's wrong with some of the city universities like Drexel or LaSalle or Temple?"

"Please, Angel, don't start this now. Please, not today."

On Everything I Love

"All I'm saying is Philly has some real good colleges. Why do you have to go all the way to Atlanta to get educated when we have good colleges right here?"

"Angel, you said you wouldn't pressure me and you'd support me on any decision that I made. Why are you being so insecure?"

"I'm not insecure. I'm just saying why do you have to go so far away to college?"

"I don't believe you, Angel", Alexis huffed, rolling her eyes and crossing her arms.

Seeing Alexis' expression sadden, Angel quickly changed the subject.

"Did you like your new outfit I bought you?"

"Yes, it's cute, just like all of the other ones."

"Well, I have a surprise for you. Here", Angel said, pulling out a small white box from in between his lap.

"You can wear this with it."

"What's this?" she asked.

"Open it and see", he smiled.

Opening the small white box, Alexis' eyes lit up. Seeing the 24-karat gold chain inside with a matching gold heart charm attached, her sad expression suddenly changed. "Oh, it's that gold heart I wanted! You went back and got it?"

"Thought I forgot, huh? Now we both have one", Angel said, pulling his out from underneath his white tee shirt. "Put it on."

Taking it from the box, Alexis put the gold chain around her neck.

"Promise me you won't ever take it off."

"I won't. I promise", Alexis said, a single tear dropping from her eye. "I won't ever take it off. Just like you never take your mother's heart off."

"Open it up and read what it says on the inside. Go ahead, it opens."

Opening up the small gold heart, Alexis read the words that were engraved inside.

*-From the cradle to the grave, you'll always be the
only woman I ever love. Your Angel.-*
As her dam filled with tears released, Alexis
reached over and kissed Angel on his cheek. "Thank
you, Angel", she sobbed, wiping her tears away with
her hand.

"I just want to make you happy, Sweetie."

"I know you do. I know."

"I apologize about the whole college thing. I'll be
open-minded. Nothing is more important to me than
your education."

"Thank you, baby", Alexis said, grabbing his hand.
"I just need you to be a little more patient with me,
Angel, just like you've been with sex. The time will
come, and the both of us can enjoy making love for
the first time together. I know it will be beautiful."

Pulling his Lexus in front of Alexis' house,
Angel smiled and agreeably shook his head. "We're
both seventeen and still have our whole life in front
of us. As long as we never cross each other and
never stop being friends first, we'll make it", she reassured him. Embracing in each other's arms, the
two began kissing. "I'll call you later, Angel. If you
aren't home, I'll call your cell phone", Alexis said,
now picking up her books from off the floor of the
car.

"I'll be in the house around 10 o'clock."

"Okay, Sweetie, I'll call you at ten", Alexis responded, getting out of the car and walking up her
steps. Pausing, Alexis turned around and blew Angel a goodbye kiss. Hitting the horn in response to
her kiss, Angel drove off down the street.

Alexis had no idea that Angel hadn't been a
virgin in two years. Since the age of fifteen, Angel
had been having sex with many different females.
Howard had even taken him out one special night
and had two women eagerly introduce him to man-

hood and happily take away his virginity. Even though he knew it was wrong to have Alexis believing he was still a virgin, Angel wanted to keep it that way. He knew it would break her heart if she found out he had given himself to another woman. Therefore, because of that and his love for Alexis, he would never let any other woman get close to his heart. Sex was sex and love was Alexis.

Driving with his windows rolled down and his music loudly playing, all eyes were on Angel as his good looks and expensive sports car was the center of attraction. Seeing his cell phone flashing, Angel picked it up and answered.

"Hello", he said, turning down the volume of the Wu Tang CD that was   playing.

"Hi, Angel, it's me, Sharita", a soft voice said, "What's up Pretty?"

"Why weren't you in class today? I was looking forward to seeing you."

"I figured since I passed English already, there isn't any need. So don't start with this school stuff, Sharita. What's up?"

"Tonight I'll be home by myself. Can you come by?"

"What time?"

"Around 9 o'clock."

"Nine is fine. I'll be there. And please, none of those school lectures."

"Alright, Mr. McDaniel, whatever you say."

"See you later, Sharita", Angel said, hanging up his cell phone.

Moments later, his cell phone rang again. "Hello."

"Are you on your way?" a voice asked.

"I'm on my way now. Give me half an hour. I had to drop my girl off.'

"Alright, 'cuz we've been waiting all day."

"I'm coming now", Angel said as he hung up his cell phone and turned his Wu-Tang CD back up.

"Cash... Rules... Everything... Around Me...Cream get the money", he rapped, saying the words to the popular Wu Tang song.

After filling up his tank at an Amoco gas station, Angel drove straight to his destination. Seeing the parked luxury cars outside of the Big Boy's Pool Hall on 33rd Street, Angel knew all of the guys were inside. Finding an empty spot, he parked his car. He retrieved a shopping bag from his trunk and he walked inside.

Inside, all six of the large pool tables were being used as Angel walked through the crowded pool hall. Video games and soda and candy machines were all lined up against the walls. A tall, light-skinned attractive woman was serving customers from behind a large counter. Noticing Angel had entered; she smiled and pointed to the stairs that were in the back of the pool hall. "Thanks, Tish", Angel said, walking toward the stairs.

The radio played as the smooth soulful sounds of Donny Hathaway flowed through its speakers. Walking by two old heads that were waiting their turn to get in a game of pool, Angel could hear them quoting every word of the late great one. "I been so many places in my life and times", one of the old men sang. Reaching the steps, Angel looked back over his shoulders and saw Tish still staring at him. Winking his eye, she began to smile, and then Angel proceeded up the stairs.

Reaching the top of the stairs, Angel slowly knocked five times on a thick door that was closed and locked. "What's the password?" a voice said from the other side. "Hustler!" Angel stated.

The door quickly opened, and Angel walked inside the room. Sitting at a large glass table filled with stacks of money, Kevin nodded and continued to count the cash. Duran, who was one of their best street lieutenants, quickly shut and locked the door. Sekou, who was another one of their street lieutenants, was also counting money at the table. Looking at the T.V. monitor on the wall, Angel could see everything that was going on downstairs in the pool hall. Inside the room, there was a smooth black carpet that lay on the floor. On another glass table, there were guns and ammunition...An AK-47, a .357 Magnum and two black 9mms.

"What's up, Kev?" Angel said, slapping him on the shoulder.

"You, Hustler", Kevin smiled.

"Where's Howard?"

"You know he isn't coming down here. His ass is home."

"But his Range Rover is out front."

"I'm driving it. My car is getting a new system in it. Plus, he hardly drives the Rover anyway", Kevin said as he laid a large stack of money into the counting machine.

"You need me to help count?" Angel asked, taking a seat.

"No, we're just about finished now", Kevin said.

"How much is it?"

"Its $660,000" Kevin answered...You ready, Angel?"

"Yeah, my car is parked right out front. Let me go change real quick."

With his shopping bag in his hand, Angel went inside a bathroom. While he was inside the bathroom changing his clothes, Sekou and Duran began to neatly straighten the bundles of money on the table. When Angel walked out of the bathroom he was dressed in tan Docker pants, a pair of black shoes and a button-up Nautica shirt. His hair was slicked back and he was wearing a pair of schoolboy frames.

"How do I look, fellas?" he smiled. "Man, you look whiter than the whitest motherfucka", Duran said as everyone burst out laughing. "Damn, dawg, you can fool the shit out of anybody", Sekou added. "Ain't no cop ever gonna stop you", Duran shouted. "How do I look, man?" Angel asked again, spinning around. "Like a fake ass Tom Cruise", Kevin said jokingly, causing the room to erupt into brash laughter. Even Angel had to laugh at himself because of how white he looked. "Do I have to hear this torture every week?" "Yup, Tom!" Kevin shouted, falling out of his chair in laughter. "Okay, okay, come on y'all. Put the money into the bag", Angel said. "Nigga, I know you hate it", Sekou said. "I know one thing. Howard is a smart motherfucka. Ever since he decided to use you as a decoy to take money back and forth across the city, shit's been so smooth", Kevin said.

"You got all of your paperwork?" Kevin asked.

"License, insurance, registration, everything", Angel named, passing the large shopping bag to Kevin.

"Do you need one of these?" Sekou asked, pointing at the guns on the table.

"No, I'm cool. I got my nine in the car."

After putting the money inside of the bag, Kevin passed it to Angel. "Okay, Angel, I'll call Howard and tell him you're on your way. Walk him outside, Duran", Kevin said as he took out his cell phone.

"Alright, Kev, I'll see you later", Angel said, walking out the door with Duran right behind him. Angel walked back downstairs through the crowd. No one paid him any mind because everyone knew who he was. They just never understood why sometimes he would be dressed so preppy.

"Bye, Angel", Tish called out, smiling once again.

"Bye, Tish."

"I'll call you later. I need to talk to you", she said as her eyes followed him to the door.

105

"Alright", Angel responded, walking out the door with Duran.

Once a week, Angel would go by the pool hall and pick up the weekly profits. This was his second most important job. The first was when Howard and Kevin would pick up the drugs. Realizing how important his role was to the squad, Angel played his position very well. Howard taught Angel how to use his white complexion to his advantage, and that was exactly what Angel did. Angel could be white one minute then black the next. White women were just as attracted to him as black women. Angel had the best of both worlds. After he would pick up the money, he would take it home, where he still lived with his Aunt Vanessa and Howard in Northeast Philadelphia.

His job wasn't too complicated-he had to check up on Howard's street lieutenants and to make sure that once a week he picked up the weekly profits.

Howard never wanted him involved when it came to purchasing drugs. He made sure Angel stayed as far away from drugs as possible. Howard had actually mapped out everything a few years ago, knowing that with Angel he could accomplish anything he desired. Howard knew that Angel would be the key to getting him into corporate white America; where the real hustlers are and the real money is being made. This is what Howard had been teaching and preparing him for the past ten years. How to cleanup dirty money and turn everything legal, and how to forget about Black Street and focus on Wall Street. Also the importance of investing and starting your own businesses and corporations. Teaching Angel how the ghetto had made many men very rich, so he should never turn his back on the ghetto. Howard's ultimate goal was to conquer white America to help black America. And Angel would help him do it. But it would not be as easy as he thought...

FOURTEEN
Later that night...

"Who is it?" Sharita shouted, hearing the knock at her door.

"It's me", a voice said.

"One minute, Angel. I'll be right there", she yelled. After putting on a robe, Sharita opened the door.

"What took you so long?" she asked.

"I had to take care of some business", Angel answered, sitting down on the sofa.

"Are you staying all night?"

"No, just for a little while", Angel said, kicking off his boots. "Where's your husband?"

"He's out of town again. He had to fly to Vegas. So he'll be gone a few days."

"I don't know how that crazy man leaves your pretty ass home all the time."

"Me neither", Sharita said, dimming the bright living room light. "So now, why weren't you in class today?"

"Don't start, Sharita! As long as I'm passing, that's all that matters."

"You're passing because of me. You haven't done any homework in five months."

"Why should I when I'm fucking the shit out of my English teacher", Angel smiled.

"Don't get big headed, Mr. McDaniels", Sharita said, sitting next to him on the sofa.

"I'm just playing", he laughed.

"If anyone ever finds out about this, Angel, you know I'll lose my job."

"Don't worry about that. Nobody knows", Angel reassured, taking off his jeans.

Married for six years and in her early 30s, Sharita was a tall, very attractive woman with hazel eyes and long black hair. A Black and Indian mix, she was every young male's favorite English teacher. She first met Angel as a cute 9th grader, though they've only been sexually involved for the last five months. She had always had a thing for the very handsome Angel who was now one of her favorite students. It all began when she helped him one day after school with his extra credit work. She reached under his desk and started playing with his dick. After introducing him to her wonderful blow job skills, the affair began and they enjoyed one another very much.

Standing up in front of Angel, Sharita removed her white robe. With nothing underneath, her nude pecan-complexioned body was now in full view. At 5'8" tall, Sharita's 34-25-36 figure was always a pleasure to see. Although one half of her would always feel guilty, the other half just couldn't resist the charm or looks of Angel. If she could, she would have given him all the love that her husband didn't deserve. But she knew this was nothing more than infatuation and lust. The thrill of a younger man making wild and aggressive love to her had turned her on, something that she was no longer getting from her busy and older husband. Therefore, every time he would leave town on one of his two or three-day trips, Sharita would call Angel over to satisfy her every need-something that Angel did very well and very often.

"I thought about you all day, Angel", Sharita said, dropping to both knees.

"You did?" Angel asked, now taking off his tee shirt.

"Yeah, you know I did. I thought you would be in class today. I still marked you present. I guess it doesn't matter now since you're graduating next month."

"That's enough school talk. Come here", Angel said, grabbing her by her hand.

"You don't want me to kiss it? You know I'm the best."

"No, I want you to ride it tonight", Angel expressed, adjusting himself in a more comfortable position.

"Okay, whatever you want, big boy."

Slowly getting on top of him, Sharita slid Angel's hard dick inside of her wet paradise. The pleasure was instant as she began to ride Angel nice and slow. Angel's dick was much larger than her husband's, so Sharita would always take her time when the two of them would have sex. Though Angel had only been sexually active for about two years, he had mastered his lovemaking skills far beyond the average young man his own age. Angel was always the more dominant partner of the two of them. His capabilities at his young age would constantly blow Sharita's mind. He did things that her husband hadn't done, and sexual positions that she never experienced until the two of them began their secret affair five months ago.

As Sharita continued to ride Angel nonstop under the dimmed living room light, the sound of his cell phone brought her to a sudden pause. "Oh. Not again. Why don't you leave your phone in the car she huffed with a face full of sweat falling down her beautiful face. "Just hold on a minute", Angel said, reaching for his jeans and taking out his cell phone. "I'll be one minute", he said, as he remained lying naked and dripping in sweat on the sofa.

"Hello."

"Hey, Angel, it's me", a voice said.

"What's up, baby?"

"I called your house. Howard said you weren't home, so I called your cell."

"What time is it?"

"It's 10 o'clock. I told you I was gonna call you at ten."

"Oh, I forgot."

"Where are you?"

"I'm over my buddy's crib. I had to come handle some important business."

"When will you be home?"

"In about an hour or so."

"Well, I'll be asleep. I'll see you tomorrow after school. I love you."

"I love you, too. Bye." Angel said, hanging up his cell phone.

"That was your girlfriend, Alexis?" Sharita asked.

"Yeah", Angel answered in a saddened tone.

"Well, don't get upset with me because your girlfriend is a virgin and you can't keep this thing in your pants."

"I'm not upset. I just don't want to hurt her", Angel responded, wiping sweat from his face.

"I told you when you're ready to stop this affair, I would be very upset, but that I would understand. I know how much you love that girl. Every time she calls when we are together, you feel so guilty afterwards because of what you've done and the lies you've told."

Raising up, Sharita sat down next to him and stared into his green eyes.

"You know what" she said, smiling.

"What?" Angel asked, reaching for his underwear.

"True love has a way of uniting souls. If she loves you the way that you love her, nothing or no one could ever come between that. One day you'll settle down and make some lucky woman a good husband. Maybe it will be her. But right now you're young and full of play. And doing the things you do, you're gonna feel guilty with yourself when you think of Alexis."

Now sitting up, Angel sat with his head hanging low to the floor.

On Everything I Love

"Angel, you're a good man and sometimes good men make bad mistakes. If it bothers you that much, you should stop and think about some of the decisions you make. Is it something about this girl that you're not telling me?"

"I just don't want to hurt her. I would rather die than cause her pain. And that's on everything I love", Angel said with sincerity.

"Those are some strong words."

"I mean them, too."

"I believe you. Your eyes don't lie. But love is in your heart and sex is in your pants. So until you truly understand them both, you'll continue feeling this way."

"Thanks, Sharita", Angel said, looking up at her.

"I understand. Believe me, I really do. There's nothing in this world more beautiful than love. And if someone loved or thought of me like you do Alexis, maybe we both wouldn't be here. I crave the love and affection of my husband, something we both shared so long ago, but people change and things change also. You're at a stage in your life when everything is all good. You're young, handsome, and very popular. Any man would love to be in your shoes, and every woman would love to be in your arms. I want you to remember something, Angel."

"What's that?"

"That life is what you make, and true love is hard to break."

Reaching over, Sharita gave Angel a friendly hug and kissed him on his cheek. This was one of the reasons why Angel enjoyed being with Sharita. She truly understood what he was going through and knew how to help him cope. Angel could confide in Sharita with some of his deepest and most personal problems. And often he did. She was indeed his teacher, but not just in school or during sex, but in love and in life more than anything else.

FIFTEEN

After dropping Alexis off at home from school, Angel and a few of his homeboys were all hanging around his Lexus watching some guys play basketball at a local playground. Pooda, a short, cocky dark-skinned man, and Rodney, a brown-skinned and much taller guy, were both close friends with Angel. They were waiting for another good friend of theirs to show up, and then the four of them would go joyriding and girl hunting like they always did.

"Where's that nigga at?" Angel asked. "He said he would be here at 4 o'clock", Pooda said, checking out a couple of females who were sitting on a bench admiring the group of young handsome men. "You know A.L. isn't ever on time for anything", Rodney said. "What has he been doing?" Angel asked, looking at his gold Movado watch. "I don't know, man. He's always been like that", Pooda answered, shaking his head. "Man, I'm ready to go. He just gotta get left behind", Angel said, opening his car door.

At that moment, A.L. walked from around the corner with a big smile on his face. "Yo fellas, what's up?" he yelled, rushing over to the car. "Man, why can't you ever be on time?" Angel said. With a dumb look on his face, A.L. didn't say a word. A.L. was a tall brown-skinned young man who was only 16 years old, but he looked much older than his age. He was the youngest of them all, and also the comedian of the crew.

"Your name really fits you, A.L., Always Late", Angel laughed. A.L. was always late no matter what the occasion. If somebody told him to be somewhere at 3 o'clock and that his life depended on it, he'd get there at 3:15. He was even born late, approximately two weeks after his mother's due date.'

On Everything I Love

"Shiz wrote me today", Angel smiled. "Oh yeah, what's up with his case?" Pooda asked. "He's going to trial soon. His lawyer thinks he can beat it", Angel said in a confident tone. "I miss him. It just ain't the same without that crazy ass nigga around."

Everyone nodded their heads in agreement. Shiz was the last member of Angel's wild young team, and considered the wildest of them all; while Angel was the leader and brains. Pooda was known for his fighting skills and Rodney for his slickness. But Shiz was the heart of the crew. For his homies he would do anything. After the four of them were all inside of the Lexus, Angel started his car and began blasting his CD;leaving a group of disappointed female bystanders watching the four of them joyfully drive away.

Upstairs inside the pool hall, Howard and Kevin were discussing business.

"Sekou can't drive to New York Friday", Kevin said.

"Why, what's wrong?"

"He broke his leg playing basketball earlier today."

"Well, what about Duran?"

"His license is suspended."

"Well, who's gonna bring back the product?"

"I was thinking maybe Tish could do it again."

"No. I don't want Tish traveling like that anymore. Last time was an emergency."

"That girl's a soldier. She doesn't care."

"I know she doesn't, but I do. Tisha is fine doing what she does, selling those birds from behind the counter. Is there anybody else?" Howard asked.

"Nope. There's nobody else left but lil Angel."

"No. I don't want Angel involved in transporting."

"We'll have to wait till Sekou's leg heals then."

"How long did they say?"

"About eight to ten weeks."

114

"Damn! That's too long. Shit! What are we going to do, Kev?"

"I think you should try Angel. I mean, he's ready now. This is the only thing he hasn't done. We can use him the same way we use him around the city."

"But this is different. This is dealing with the big boys. This is what I've kept him from."

"Well it's time for him to grow up. Everything will be okay. He can drive his own car. His license and paperwork are cool, and he's white. The New Jersey troopers and State Police will never pull him over."

After contemplating the idea of using Angel as a carrier and decoy, Howard said "I'll do it this one time and see how things go"; giving in. "Everything will be okay, Howard."

"I hope so. I'll tell him tonight when he comes home."

"Friday is only three days away", Kevin said.

"And that's the day he always takes his girlfriend out", Howard said as they both walked out the door and down the stairs. The thought of using Angel had still weighed heavy on Howard's mind, but Howard had always been a hardcore businessman, understanding that nothing came before business and making money.

Later that evening, after joyriding the whole day with his friends, Angel dropped each of them off at home. After stopping by Sharita's house for a dose of some good sex, he then went home. Walking inside his house, Vanessa was sitting on the couch doing Chyna's hair.

"What's up, Mama?" Angel said, kissing her on the cheek.

"Hey, Angel, Howard wanted to talk to you."

"Where is he?"

"He's downstairs in the basement."

"Did anybody call me, Mama?"

115

"Yeah. Alexis just called and Tisha called earlier."
"Thanks, Mama", Angel said, walking towards the basement door.
Walking down the stairs, Angel saw Howard sitting at a table with large stacks of money in front of him.
"Sit down. I've got to talk to you."
Angel sat in the seat beside him.
"I need you to do something very important Friday."
"What!" Angel asked confused.
"I need you to drive to New York behind me and Kev."
With a big smile now plastered on his face, Angel shouted "I'll do it!"
"This ain't no joke, Angel", Howard said seriously.
"I know, Howard. I'm just happy you're finally letting me be more involved."
"It's not that. You were my last option. If I had someone else you wouldn't be going"
"Well, I can handle driving to New York. That's light-duty."
"You'll be bringing back 50 keys with you...and that's not light."
"I understand, Howard. I drove around with a million dollars in my trunk before. I'm not afraid."
"This is different, Angel. This ain't no money, this is drugs!"
"Howard, stop worrying. I'm not scared. Plus, I was taught by the best", Angel said, trying to use reverse psychology on him.
"Friday night about eight o'clock we're leaving."
"Friday night!"
"Yeah, what's wrong?"
"I was supposed to take Alexis out to the movies and dinner. I'll just call her later and tell her something important came up, and we can go out on Saturday."

"Do what you gotta do. Just be ready Friday at eight."

"I'll be ready", Angel said, getting up from his chair.

Angel strutted up the stairs, grinning with each step. After talking to his Aunt Vanessa, Angel went to his room and called Alexis.

"Hello."

"What's up, baby?"

"Hey, Angel, thank you for the gold bracelet. My mom gave it to me when I came in. That was real cute, dropping it off to my mom."

"I just wanted to surprise you."

"And you did, like you always do."

"I have to tell you something."

"What?"

"Friday night I have to do something with Howard. Can we go out on Saturday?"

"Oh, I was really looking forward to being with you Friday."

"I know. I was, too."

"It's okay. Handle your business with Howard. I can wait another day."

"Thanks, baby."

"Just don't have any excuses on Saturday."

"I won't. I promise."

"Now, I have something to tell you."

"What?"

"I've decided to go to Spelman College. I hope you support me with my decision."

"If that's where you want to go, then I'm all for it."

"Thank you baby, thank you so much. I prayed that you wouldn't get upset."

"I'm not mad. I told you, your education is all that matters, whether it's in Atlanta or Philly."

"I was gonna tell you on Friday. Now we can celebrate on Saturday."

"I just want you to know that I'm very proud of you."

"Thanks, Angel. I love you so much."

"I love you, too, Alexis."

"It's getting late. I'll see you tomorrow after school and we'll talk some more."

"Okay. Goodnight, Alexis."

"Goodnight, Angel."

Alexis' decision to go to a college all the way in Atlanta did bother Angel, but he knew it's where Alexis really wanted to go. And as long as she was happy, Angel was happy.

After taking a shower, Angel laid across his bed and finally called Tish.

"Hello", she said, answering the phone half asleep.

"What's up, Tish?"

"What's up with you? I called you earlier."

"My aunt told me."

"I called you last night, too. You never answered your cell phone."

"I was busy."

"Why didn't you come by the pool hall today?"

"I was running around all day with some of my friends."

"You don't have to avoid me, Angel. What happened... happened! It was a big mistake for us to have had sex."

"I wish it never happened, Tish. I miss how we used to be."

"Me, too, but now that everything is taken care of, maybe we can become just friends again."

"I really would like that. You're not mad are you?"

"No! I wasn't ready to be a mother, just like you weren't ready to be a father. I'm twenty-one years old. I'm just not ready for a child in my life right now."

"Yeah, and I'm seventeen and still in high school."

"My uncle Howard loves you like a son. I don't ever want to be the one who comes between that. Inviting you into my bedroom the time I spent the night was a big mistake. You and I have been friends for almost nine years and that one night destroyed our friendship."

"No, it didn't. It just woke us both up. I'll always be your friend, Tisha."

"Sometimes I can't even look in Alexis' eyes when she comes around, knowing what happened and how she feels about you. That bothers me."

"Well, it's over now. Maybe things can get back to the way they used to be."

"Like I told you before, what's our business is between us. We both learned a lesson from what happened. Friends should never have sex. So now will you stop avoiding me?'"

"Yeah, Tish. I'll stop", Angel laughed.

"Then I'll see you tomorrow at the pool hall?"

"Yeah, I'll swing by to kick it with you like we used to do."

"Okay, Angel, then I'll see you tomorrow. Goodnight."

"Goodnight Tish ...oh, and thanks."

"You're welcome, Angel", she said as they both hung up.

Since meeting at Howard's family reunion eight years ago, Angel and Tisha had always considered each other cousins. Although Tisha was four years older than Angel, she was very much attracted to him. Being Howard's favorite niece, she would often spend nights or baby-sit Chyna when Howard and Vanessa would go out. Tisha was what you call a tomboy. Growing up, she would always wear jeans and sneakers, while other girls her age were wearing high heels and dresses. You would never catch Tisha in a skirt.

Born in the rough and rugged Richard Allen Projects of North Philadelphia, Tisha had grown up very hard though her outside appearance was extremely attractive. Being a tall, red-bone, with short wavy hair and sexy bedroom eyes, Tisha was not your average, sweet, little innocent home-girl. Tisha took no shit! If you pissed her off, you'd quickly see her transform into your worst nightmare. Howard called her his "secret weapon", because no one would ever suspect this tall, beautiful young woman to possess a cold-blooded killer attitude when she was called upon. Never without a loaded gun in her possession, she sent many men running like wild chickens with their heads cut off. And if she had to, she had no problem sending them to their graves. Everyone respected her, because respect is what she demanded. Much of Angel's street attitude came from being around Tisha. It was Tisha who taught him everything from fighting to shooting a gun. She would even take Angel down to her old neighborhood sometimes to show him how the less fortunate lived, reminding him how fortunate he was and to never take anything for granted.

Growing up on the tough ghetto streets of North Philly, Latisha Johnson feared no woman or man. This beautiful black female gangstress had only one weakness and his name was ... Angel.

SIXTEEN
The next day...

Sitting on the sofa, Vanessa was in total shock as she read the Philadelphia Daily News. The front headline read, "The Terrible Two", with a picture of a black man and a white man in handcuffs.

"Yesterday, Philadelphia homicide detectives arrested two men at the Mercy Mental Hospital located in West Philadelphia. After a four-month investigation, police finally received enough information and clues to help solve the rapes and murders of nine young women over an eighteen-year span. John Williams, 37, and Peter Smith, 40, were both arrested and charged with the murders of nine young teenage women in West Philadelphia, ranging in ages from 12 to 19. Each woman had been raped and brutally murdered, all no less than four blocks away from Mercy Hospital, where both of these men had been patients for over twenty years. Philadelphia medical examiners said that the sperm cells found in each of these young women did indeed match both suspects. A few months ago, an employee at Mercy caught both men sneaking outside through a small window inside a supply closet. After both men were locked down, Peter Smith, with a noticeably large scar across his neck, admitted his participation in all nine murders. After congratulating the staff member for catching them, John Williams said in his own words, 'We would have kept killing those girls if not for you.' After the man notified police, a four-month undercover investigation was done at Mercy, where samples were taken of the men's blood, fingerprints, hair, and sperm. After the completion of the tests, it was confirmed that both men were responsible for the murders of all nine women. When police asked the two men about any other victims they had murdered, each man denied there were any more. However, both men did tell detectives about one lucky girl who they had both raped and decided to spare her life, admitting that it was their second rape victim at the time which occurred sometime in the winter of '79. Police have no information to confirm their story. No victims ever came forward. When asked why they decided to spare the young girl's life, John Williams' response was, "Because we had to hurry up and go watch our favorite T.V. show." When police asked what show it was that saved the young woman's life, both men eagerly shouted, "Good Times", a T.V. show they would never miss. Both men are currently being held at the Curran Fromhold Correctional Facility on State Road."

Throwing the paper on the floor, Vanessa could do nothing but cry and think about Penny and all the pain and fear her younger sister had to endure on that tragic day. As she sat back and wiped her tears, the telephone rang.

"Hello", Vanessa uttered.

"Mama, is Howard there?"

"No, Angel, he's out with Kevin somewhere", she said tearfully.

"Is everything okay?" he asked, hearing the sadness in her voice.

"Yes, baby. Everything is fine."

"You sure? You sound like you've been crying."

"I'm fine. I'll be okay."

"Mama, what's wrong? Do you want me to come home?"

"No, Angel. I'm okay. I just read some very upsetting news, that's all."

"What?"

"Something in the paper today."

"What could be that bad?"

"Did you see the newspaper today?"

"Yeah, Tisha has one right here on the counter. I saw those two crazy dudes on the cover, but I haven't read the story."

"Read it! Read it and you'll see why I'm crying."

"Mama, are you okay? I'll come home if you want me to."

"No, Angel, I just want to be alone right now. Those two lunatics have spoiled my day."

"Who?"

"The two men on the front page. I hope they both pay for what they did to my sister", she shouted out angrily.

"What!"

"Angel, I'll see you later, baby. I really don't feel too well. Just read it and you'll know exactly what I'm talking about."

"Okay, Mama. I love you."

"I love you, too, Angel. Bye, bye", Vanessa said, before hanging up the phone.

Angel knew whatever his aunt read definitely affected her a lot. And nothing bothered him more than seeing his mama upset and crying.

"Tish, pass me the newspaper."

Walking down to the end of the counter, Tisha got the newspaper and gave it to Angel.

"Is everything okay with Aunt Vanessa?"

"No. Something she read made her cry", Angel said, staring at the front page.

"Cry? Not Aunt V."

"I'm telling you, she's very upset about something."

"What could it be?"

"I don't know, but I'm gonna find out right now", Angel said, turning to page one of the Daily News to read the story about the two men who were arrested.

As Tisha went to help a waiting customer at the other end of the counter, Angel began reading the emotional and personal story. After reading the entire story, Angel understood now what had made his aunt so very upset. She was going through a very serious and personal time and looking at these two insane individuals, Angel could not block out the fact that one of these men was in fact his father. A man he had hated since he was told the story of his existence. Ripping the newspaper in half, Angel called Tisha. Noticing Angel's watery eyes, Tisha knew that whatever it was, had to be serious.

"What's wrong?" Tisha asked concerned.

"I'll tell you on the way. Come on", Angel said, breathing heavy.

"Come on where?"

"To C.F.C.F.. Lock up the pool hall. Visits are over at nine o'clock."

"Why are you going down to the jail tonight?"

"I gotta go visit a friend. It's very important. Just come on."

"Everybody, we're closing early tonight", Tisha shouted at the few customers who were hanging around talking and shooting pool.

"Aw, man!" an old man shouted out.

"Mr. Smitty, don't start", Tisha calmly said, giving him an intense look.

"Okay pretty, but you owe me a dollar. I just put one in that pool table."

"Here's your dollar back", Tisha said, passing the old man a dollar bill.

"Thank you he said, walking out the door.

After everyone left, Tisha noticed the distant look on Angel's face.

"Are you sure you're okay?" she asked.

"I'm fine. Do you have any money here?"

"Yeah, why?"

"I need two thousand dollars. I'll give it back tomorrow."

"Yeah, it's in the safe. I'll get it. Hold on", she said, walking into the small back room.

Moments later, Tisha walked back out with a large stack of money in her hands.

"Here, its two thousand", she said, handing it over to Angel. "Why do you need two thousand dollars?"

"I need it for somebody's books in jail."

"Two thousand dollars! What are you paying for, his bail or something?"

"No, he ain't getting out of jail any time soon."

"What's he in for?"

"Attempted murder. You remember my homeboy, Shiz, right?"

"Oh yeah, your friend who shot the cop. That boy's crazy!"

"Yeah him. He's waiting to go to trial."

"Didn't you help pay for his lawyer?"

"Yeah, and now I have to see him."

After turning off the lights, Tisha set the alarm, and she and Angel walked outside. After locking the door, they got into his Lexus, drove off and headed toward C.F.C.F., a city detention center that housed some of Philadelphia's worst convicts. Since knowing Angel, had never seen him this upset. This look was set in his green eyes, and even she wasn't going to ask what was wrong. She could tell that whatever it was, it was tearing him to pieces inside because he could not hide it on the outside. So Tisha sat back and didn't say a word as Angel headed towards the expressway that would take him to State Road.

Walking inside of the house, Howard noticed his tearful wife sitting on the couch. Dropping the dozen roses he had in his hand, he quickly ran to her side.

"What's wrong, honey? Is everything okay?"

"I'm fine, baby. I'll get over it."

"Get over what? Why are you crying?"

"Remember when I told you the story about my younger sister, Penny?"

"Yeah, you said she was raped by two men and one of them was Angel's father. Why?"

"Because they finally caught these two crazy bastards, see!" she said, pointing at the front page of the paper that was lying on the coffee table.

"I read that earlier. Those two crazy motherfuckers are the ones who raped your little sister?" Howard said angrily.

"Yeah, it's them. I'm sure it's them. They even admitted it."

"I read about them saying they let one of the victims live. That was your sister?"

"Yup, that was Penny they were talking about. She said all she could remember was a scar across one of their throats", she said, pointing at the white man on the cover of the paper.

"Is that..."

"Yup, he's Angel's father", she tearfully interrupted.

"Does Angel know?"

"Yeah, I told him earlier today. I hope he doesn't get into any trouble. He hates his father."

"I know. He told me before he hoped he was dead. And if he wasn't, he would kill him if ever met him."

"Well, he's locked up now. I feel so bad for all of those young girls them two crazy bastards killed."

"Everything will be okay, baby", Howard said, placing his arms around his lovely wife.

"I feel sad for Angel. If he could, I know he would kill those two guys. Luckily, they are in jail."

"I just can't believe after all of these years they are just being caught. Don't worry, though. They'll get what's coming to them, baby. God will punish them for what they've done."

Nestled in Howard's protective arms, Vanessa continued to cry. Knowing the pain his wife was going through, Howard would be there to love and comfort her to the very end. At that same time, Angel was already at C.F.C.F. with other plans in mind.

SEVENTEEN
One hour later...

The Philly night was chilly and windy as Angel walked out of C.F.C.F and into the parking lot where Tisha had been waiting in the car. Opening the door, Angel got inside and sat down with a smile on his face.

"Did you handle your business?" Tisha asked, turning down the radio.

"Yup. I saw Shiz, and I put the money on his books."

"So will everything be taken care of?"

"Well he said it shouldn't take no longer than a week."

"Why so long?"

"Because he has to pay a few other people to help him."

"Oh, that's what the money was for?"

"Yup, one thousand dollars."

"What happened to the other thousand?"

"Oh, that went to Mark."

"Who's Mark?"

"He's a C.O. that's going to make sure everything goes smoothly", Angel smiled as he turned on his car and drove out of the parking lot.

"He's working on the floor where they're all being held."

"You sure you can trust him? A cop is a cop!"

"I'm positive", Angel assured as he continued to smile.

"Why are you so positive and sure?"

"Because he hates rapists."

"Everybody hates a rapist, so what!"

"Yeah, but you hate them even more when one of the girls that was raped was your niece", Angel said, looking at Tisha's face.

"Oh, shit!" Tisha laughed, shaking her head in disbelief.

"Yeah, that's what I said when Shiz told me the C.O.'s niece was one of the nine victims."

"This is a small world", Tisha said, turning the radio back up.

"You're right about that, Tish. You're right about that!" Angel said, getting on the expressway.

~~~

While Vanessa was upstairs getting Chyna ready for bed and school in the morning, Howard was down in the basement calling his New York connect on his private cell phone.

"Hello", a deep voice said.

"Yo, it's me, Philly."

"What's going on, Philly? Is everything okay?"

"Yeah, everything is fine, New York. Just making sure everything is still cool for tomorrow."

"Ain't nothing changed in New York. How's the weather in Philly?"

"It's been real nice. I even saw about fifty whole birds in the sky today."

"When you get to New York, the cab will be waiting for you again."

"Your cabs are so expensive. Do the rates ever change?"

"For you, Philly, the cab driver will charge you just eighteen dollars a mile."

"Okay, I can deal with that. It makes this trip worthwhile."

"Two of my most loyal cabbies will be there to take care of you."

"The same two from before?"

"No, two different ones."

"Okay, New York. I'll see you tomorrow around eight o'clock."

"Perfect, I don't have to miss my Yankees game", he said, laughing.

"Bye, New York."

"Bye, Philly. Take care", he said, hanging up the phone.

Howard hung up his cell phone and opened his safe. He removed large piles of money, putting each stack on a table. After counting out all the money he would need, he put it inside a black brief-case and locked up his safe. Howard went into a small closet and walked out with a bulletproof vest and a 9mm handgun. After putting everything on the table, he walked up the stairs and turned out the lights. Everything was all ready for his trip to New York.

As Howard was coming up from the base-ment, Angel was walking into the house.

"What's up, Angel? I wanted to talk to you."

"What's the deal, Howard?"

"How are you feeling?"

"About tomorrow?" Angel asked, taking a seat on the sofa.

"No! About the news today. The two guys who were caught."

"Oh, I'm fine. I'm cool. I ain't stressing it."

"I'm surprised! Are you okay?"

"Howard, I'm cool. They'll get what's coming to them", Angel smiled.

"Yes. God will take care of them."

"Yeah, or he might send one of his angels to do it."

"Is there something you're not telling me?" Howard asked, sensing his sarcasm.

"No, Howard. I'm just saying what goes around comes around."

"Well, I'm glad you're taking this well. I was really worried about you."

"Why? I ain't trippin'."

"Because I know you, and you might fool your aunt or your friends, but you can't fool me. It wouldn't surprise me if you tried to get those guys touched in jail."

"Howard, I'm fine, and I'll be ready for tomorrow. Is that it?"

"That's it. Six o'clock, meet me and Kev down at the pool hall."

"Okay. I'm tired. I got a big day tomorrow", Angel said as he got up off the sofa and ran upstairs.

Entering his bedroom, Angel shut his door. Lying across his bed, he picked up the phone and called Alexis.

"Hello."

"Hey, baby, what's up?"

"Hey, Angel, I was just about to call you."

"Miss me?"

"To death!"

"Stop that."

"I'm serious. It seems like it's been days since I've seen you."

"I picked you up from school today."

"So what! A minute away from you is like an hour."

"I miss you, too", Angel smiled.

"I can't wait to be with you Saturday."

"I can't wait either."

"Did you read the Daily News today?"

"Yeah, I read it", Angel said.

"Those two guys are crazy. Thank God they got caught. That mental hospital isn't too far from my house. It scares me every time I see it."

"Don't worry. They won't ever hurt anybody again."

"I hope not. There are so many crazy people out there."

"Well, thank God, that's two more off the streets."

"I prayed for all of those girls. I even cried when I read the article."

131

"I was pretty sad myself. It felt so personal."

"Let's not talk about them. It gives me the creeps", Alexis said.

"How do you feel about graduating in a few weeks?" Angel asked, changing the subject.

"I still can't believe it. No more school. How about you?"

"I'm just happy it's over. Finally! Twelve long years!"

"This summer we'll have so much fun. Just like last summer."

"What do you want for your birthday?"

"It's not for another few weeks. I haven't thought about it too much. Do you have something in mind?"

"Yup", Angel said.

"Don't say it. Just surprise me."

"Okay, can I at least give you a hint?"

"Nope! I'll wait."

"I'm about to jump in the shower. Do you want me to call you back?"

"No, you don't have to. I'm sleepy. I'll just see you tomorrow after school."

"I love you, Alexis."

"I love you, too, Angel. Bye bye", she said, hanging up the phone.

EIGHTEEN
New York City
Friday night, 7:50 p.m...

On a small dark street in lower Manhattan, Howard and Kevin both calmly sat inside Howard's sky blue Range Rover. Parked just a few feet behind them inside his gold Lexus Coupe, Angel patiently waited for the cab to arrive; a cab that would be containing fifty kilos of cocaine at $18,000 apiece. This dark Friday night, the New York traffic was non-stop as the crowded city streets were full of moving automobiles, coming and going in all directions.

A few yellow cabs had passed the waiting men and kept driving, so Howard knew if it was the cab he had been waiting for they would have stopped.

With their bulletproof vests under their dark black tee shirts, Howard and Kevin remained silent as they both kept an eye on the moving traffic and their hands tightly gripped around their black 9mm handguns with attached silencers. Howard and Kevin knew the game very well, knowing that when you're dealing with drugs, it's best to bring the least attention to yourself as possible and never get caught sleeping.

Slowly driving up the small dark street, a yellow cab with two men inside slightly paused as it drove by Howard's Range Rover.

"Oh, shit! Keep going!" the passenger inside the cab told the driver before he parked.

"Why? That's them. They're our buyers."

"I know them. Just drop me off around the corner and you come back and take care of this one by yourself", the man said in a frightened voice.

"You know the boss don't like us doing this alone, Joey."

"This is very important, man. Just do it and hurry up. I'll tell you what's going on when you come back."

"Is everything okay?"

"Everything is fine. Couldn't be better", Joey smiled. "Couldn't be better."

After dropping Joey off a few blocks away, the driver headed back to where Howard and Kevin were parked. The time was 8:15 and this was the first time the person that they would meet was ever late. Howard did not like this at all. A few minutes later, the cab entered the street. "This has to be the one", Howard said, looking through his rearview mirror.

In an empty space in front of Howard's Range Rover, the cab pulled in and parked. Noticing it was only one man inside, Howard sat and waited till the man got out of the cab. Emerging from the cab, a tall dark-complexioned man with dark glasses on and a head full of long dreads walked up to Howard's driver's side.

With his hand gripped tightly around his gun, Howard rolled down his lightly-treated window. "Philly, plus fifty", the man said, whispering the code only the right man would know.

"Yeah, but it was supposed to be two of y'all. Where's the other guy?"

"I had to come alone this trip. My partner had a sudden emergency", he said smiling.

"Did you drive by a few minutes ago?" Howard asked.

"No, this is my first time. Are you ready? I have more pickups to make."

"Yeah, you can get it and put it inside of the Lexus that's parked behind me. The trunk should be already open", Howard said, never taking his eyes off the man and never taking his hand off his gun.

Walking back to his cab, the man opened up the trunk and pulled out a large green duffle bag. Making sure that the coast was clear, he quickly walked to the back of Angel's Lexus. Upon lifting up the unlocked trunk, he noticed that the only item inside was a black briefcase. After placing the large duffle bag neatly inside the trunk, he opened the black briefcase. Stacked neatly inside was $900,000 in brand new one hundred dollar bills. Closing the briefcase, he nodded his head at Angel who was watching his every move. Angel got out of the car and walked back to where the man stood and opened the duffle bag and looked inside. After verifying that all fifty were there and everything was okay, Angel handed the briefcase to the man and shut his trunk. Then, Angel went and sat back inside his car and waited for Howard. Walking past Howard and Kevin, holding the briefcase in his hand, the man never looked back as he got inside his cab and quickly drove off. Moments later, Howard pulled off and Angel followed right behind him as they all headed back to Philly.

Getting back inside the cab, Joe shook his head. He still couldn't believe his luck of running into Howard and Kevin, the two men who had introduced him to this game of deceit, desire, and decisions. They were also the same two men who had tried to kill him seven years ago in Philadelphia.

"Now, tell me what's going on, Joey!"

"Guz, you wouldn't believe it!"

"Believe what! Stop talking in code and tell me what's going on."

"Remember when I told you about my problem I had in Philadelphia?"

On Everything I Love

"Yeah, you told me that somebody had robbed you and tried to kill you. That's why you came to New York to stay with me."

"Those were the guys. The two men inside the Range Rover."

"What! You sure?"

"It's them. I could never forget those faces. Never!" Joey sternly said.

"But they're one of the boss's biggest buyers. He dealt with them when he was down Miami."

"Now they are, but seven years ago they were two cold-blooded killers. How do you think they got so much money? By robbing niggas like me, them no-good bastards."

"Well what do you want to do?"

"How often do they come to New York?"

"Every few weeks. They always meet at the same spot."

"Well, next time, we're going to set them up."

"And rob them!" Guz shouted.

"Yeah, and kill 'em! Fuck them cowards. They ruined my life. I have to sneak back and forth to Philly to see my mom. I'm tired of living like that."

"So what's the plan?"

"The next time they come to New York, I'll be waiting for them."

"We'll need somebody else."

"Why?" Joey asked.

"Because they know the boss sends two of us all the time."

"Oh, that's right. Then we'll get on this."

"Yeah, RaRa is crazy. He'll do anything for a few dollars."

"A few! We're talking about $900,000 in cash. We can split it three ways."

"What about the cocaine?"

"We'll just take it back to the boss and say they never showed up."

"Do you think it will work?"

"I'm positive. Me, you, and RaRa will be 900,000 bucks richer."

"You sound like you did this before", Guz said, smiling.

"I have a little experience in this field", Joey smiled back.

"Okay, then it's on. The next time they show up will be their last time."

"Yup! And I can't wait! What goes around comes around" Joey smiled, as he sat back in his seat.

Opening up the black briefcase, Joey looked at all the money inside. "Next time, this will be all ours", he said as Guz shook his head and continued to drive through the rough New York City traffic.

~~~

Later that night, upstairs inside the pool hall, Howard, Kevin, and Angel all sat around the fifty kilos of cocaine that were lying on top of the table. "Put twenty-five of those up for Tisha", Howard instructed Angel. Opening a closet door, Angel began laying them neatly inside on the floor.

"Kevin, call Cheeze from West and tell him we're ready."

"What did he want?"

"His usual, eight. Tell 'em they're going for twenty-six."

"He's gonna be pissed..."

"Yeah, but he'll still get 'em. Dudes is thirsty and twenty-six thousand is still the best deal around."

"Okay, I'll call him and tell 'em what's up", Kevin said, pulling out his cell phone.

"I'm finished", Angel said, shutting the closet door and walking up to Howard. "Do you need me to do anything else, Howard?"

"No, Angel, we're fine now. Thank you, lil buddy. I might even use you again", Howard jokingly said as he put his arm around Angel's shoulder.

"Whatever you need me to do, Howard."

"I know, Angel. I know I can always count on you."

"Always!" Angel said sincerely.

"When you go downstairs, tell Tisha to call Sekou and Duran and tell them to come to the pool hall."

"Okay. Anything else?"

"Oh yeah, tell her she's back in business, and I'll see you later when get home."

"Okay", Angel said, giving Howard a warm hug and walking out the door.

"Cheeze said he's on his way", Kevin said, hanging up his cell phone.

"I told you he would get 'em", Howard smiled.

"What do you think of Angel?" Kevin asked.

"He handled the job very well. Better than I thought for it being his first time."

"I don't think that boy fears anything", Kevin commented.

"He doesn't. And once he realizes it, he's gonna be a problem."

"What do you mean?"

"Angel has never known fear because he's never had to face it. All of his life he's been fortunate, the looks, the money, all a young man desires. All he's ever known was happiness and love. Everything was handed to him on a silver platter. Our reality is all just a game to him. The seriousness of this business is not his concern. He doesn't fear prison or death, or any man."

"Every man fears something."

"Maybe so, but as long as I've known Angel, I can honestly say he's like no other. To be seventeen, he is very mature. I guess time will tell. Life gets more difficult as you get older. The obstacles become harder."

"True indeed, Howard. True indeed", Kevin said, shaking his head.

~~~

After leaving the pool hall, Angel called Alexis on his cell phone to hear her lovely voice before she went to bed. After saying goodnight and hanging up, he quickly made a U-turn and drove over to Sharita's house, where he would find her all alone once again.

NINETEEN
Saturday Night...

After leaving the Franklin Mills Shopping Mall in Northeast Philadelphia, Angel and Alexis sat inside of his Lexus that was parked on the large mall's parking lot. The sky was full of stars and very dark on this mild Saturday night. All morning the two of them had been together since Angel had picked Alexis up from her house. After a wonderful buttermilk pancake breakfast at IHOP, Angel had taken Alexis by one of his Aunt Vanessa's beauty salons where she had gotten her hair and nails done. Once Alexis was all set, they went and had lunch at a small cozy soul food restaurant on South Street. Then, they went to Tower Records and bought a few new CDs of their favorite R&B and Rap artists. Everyone could see how deeply in love these two were. You could see it in their eyes and also in their actions; as they held hands, kissed, hugged, and did all the things people do when they're young and crazy about each other.

After leaving South Street, they went and saw an afternoon movie at the Riverview Movie Theater on Delaware Avenue. When the movie was over, Angel decided to take Alexis shopping, although he had already filled her closet to capacity. He was always looking for new and different things to make his girlfriend happy. Seeing Alexis smile always brought comfort and pleasure to Angel's heart. For Angel and Alexis, no one or nothing was more important than each other's love.

"I enjoyed my day with you baby", Alexis said, kissing him on the cheek. "I enjoyed mine, too, Boo", Angel replied, starting up his car. "Are you ready to go home now?" Angel asked, driving out of the parking lot.

"No, it's still early. Are you trying to get rid of me already?"

"No, Boo. It's just that I know you have to get yourself ready for church in the morning."

"You think you know me, huh?" Alexis smiled.

"Yup! I know I know you", Angel smirked.

"Wrong! I'm not going to church tomorrow morning."

"You're not!" Angel said surprised.

"Nope, smarty."

"But you always go to church."

"I know, but I already told my parents I would be out with you all night and probably stay over your house."

"You did?"

"Yup, I did."

"I'll call home and tell my aunt you're staying the night over", Angel said, taking out his cell phone.

"No, no", Alexis said, snatching his cell phone from his hand.

"What's wrong?"

"Nothing. We're not going to your house, stupid."

"We're not?"

"No."

"Well, where are we going then?" a confused Angel asked.

Sitting back with a big smile on her face, Alexis whispered "A hotel", in her sexiest tone.

"Hotel!" Angel blurted out, looking at Alexis, not believing what he had just heard. "Yeah, I'm ready. I want you, and I know how much you have always wanted me."

"You sure? I can wait."

"I'm positive. I'm one hundred percent positive", Alexis said, reaching over and grabbing Angel's rock hard dick.

"I'm still gonna call my aunt and let her know I'm with you and we're fine."

"Okay", Alexis said as she continued to rub Angel's dick while he drove.

After dialing the number, Alexis passed Angel the cell phone.

"Hello."

"Hey, Mama, it's me."

"Hey, Angel", she said sounding a bit down.

"Are you alright, Mama?"

"Yeah, I'm fine. I just got finished looking at some old pictures, thinking about my sister."

"Don't worry, Mama. Everything will be okay."

"I'm fine but...I still can't get over what happened to her and that horrible news the other day. But I'll manage."

"I promise, Mama, everything will be okay."

"Anyway, how are you doing?" Vanessa asked.

"I'm okay. I'm out with Alexis."

"Are y'all two having fun?"

"Yes. I just wanted to let you know we'll be out pretty late tonight."

"Okay, y'all two be safe."

"We will Mama, and Mama?"

"What, Angel?"

"Please cheer up. Everything will be okay."

"I'll try, Angel. Love you."

"Love you, Mama. Bye, bye", he said, hanging up his cell phone.

"Is everything alright with Aunt V?"

"Yeah, but she's been a little down lately."

"I know. My mother told me she's been feeling depressed. What's wrong?"

"She just got some bad news a few days ago."

"What news?"

"Some old family problems, but things will be alright."

"I hope so."

"They will", Angel smiled as he continued to drive.

Looking over into Alexis' eyes, Angel smiled as he took his hand and slid it under Alexis' skirt. As Angel began playing with Alexis' hairy pussy, she closed her eyes and let the wonderful and enjoyable feeling take her away.

Many times the two of them came close to having sex, but Alexis would always back out. But tonight was different from all of the other days because Alexis was ready to finally give herself to Angel, the man she had always loved and always knew would be her first.

For fifteen years, this was the day both of them had been waiting for. A night both would always remember and neither would ever forget.

That night...

Inside the pool hall, Tisha was helping a customer when two men entered. Holding a backpack, the dark-skinned man stayed by the door while the short, husky brown-skinned man approached Tisha at the counter.

"What's up, Tish", he joyfully said.

"When did you get out, Lucky?" Tisha said, half smiling.

"The other day, pretty", Lucky smiled, taking a seat at the counter.

"What's up, Lucky? It's real busy tonight?"

"Damn! That's how you talk to your former man?"

"Boyfriend! You don't know shit about being a man."

"Aw, baby, you know I love you girl. And you know you love me."

"Lucky, stop with all the bullshit! Now what's up?" Tisha said, looking him straight in his eyes.

"I came to get something. I need some shit", he said discreetly.

"What! You're a stick-up boy, not a drug dealer."

"Tish, can I get something or not? My money's not good?"

"I don't know, Lucky. You just popped up out of no-where wanting to buy shit..."

"Never mind, Tish, I'll go get it down 7th and Lehigh", Lucky huffed, getting up from his seat.

"Yeah, well go down there then and cop yourself an ounce", Tisha said sarcastically.

"An ounce!" Lucky smiled. "Tish, I wanted to buy two keez", Lucky whispered in her ear.

"What! Yeah right."

"June, come here", Lucky said, calling to the guy near the door.

Walking over to the counter, June took a seat. "Give it to her. Hand her the backpack", Lucky said. After passing Tisha a black backpack, she walked in a small room that was behind the counter. Fifteen minutes later she emerged with the backpack in her hand and passed it to Lucky.

"You're straight, Lucky. Bye", she said, walking down to the opposite end of the counter to help a waiting customer. "Alright, Tish. I'll call you", Lucky said, smiling as he began walking out the door. "Don't bother. I got my number changed", Tisha hollered. "Well, this is my new cell phone number. Call me", Lucky said, laying a piece of paper on the counter then rushing out the door.

Tisha and Lucky had broken up right before he had caught his last bid eight months ago. The two of them had an on and off relationship for about four years. They met at a summer basketball game down 17th Street where Lucky was the point guard for his team. Still, Lucky was nothing more than a two-bit petty hustler who would rather take money than make money. Known for his bad attitude and good looks, Lucky and Tisha instantly hit it off. He earned the name Lucky from being shot five times on three different occasions, hit by a car, stabbed nine times and still lived to talk about it. Standing 5'9" and 190 pounds, Lucky was also well known around North and West Philly as a stick up boy and a snake! Many times Howard warned Tisha about Lucky, saying he was nothing but trouble. But realizing his words fell on deaf ears, he left the situation alone. Tisha had finally got fed up with Lucky's bullshit of going in and out of jail, and left him alone for good.

Angel, too, disliked Lucky. After seeing Alexis downtown one day, Lucky insisted she take his number, knowing damn well whose girl she was. Even though she threw it away, Alexis still told Angel, who had been bitter ever since and felt very disrespected. Angel never told Tisha about the situation because he didn't want to break her heart over this no-good boyfriend whom she had acquired feelings for.

Standing behind the counter, Tisha thought about the sale she had just made and knew she had made a big mistake by selling Lucky the two kilos of cocaine. But when she saw the $52,000 neatly stacked in hundred and fifty dollar bills she lost focus and sold it to him anyway. Deep down, Tisha still had feelings for Lucky, and he knew it. He always had a way of convincing her to do what he wanted, and she hated that. This time, however, the situation would be more than Tisha would ever expect or ever imagine. The man that she once loved and would do anything for would soon hurt her in the worst way.

Lucky had no idea that June, whom he had met only a few weeks earlier inside the joint, was actually a paid government informant who was working with the F.B.I. The informant had overheard Lucky talking about Howard and Kevin's street empire and their million-dollar-a-day drug operation. After befriending Lucky, the smooth talking June told Lucky he'd be getting out soon, and that he had money to buy two kilos. Lucky took the bait and from there, June easily reeled him in. He used Lucky to get to Tisha, with hopes that she would bring the F.B.I. one of their most wanted drug kingpins, her uncle...Howard 'Da Hustla' Johnson.

TWENTY
Inside Suite 610

In the Holiday Inn Hotel on City Line Avenue in West Philly, Angel and Alexis were laying on the bed kissing. As they both lay totally undressed, a loud bump on the wall made them suddenly jump up.

"What's that?!" Alexis said, looking around the large room. "That's next door. I heard them earlier when we came in." "What are they doing over there?" Alexis smiled. "Handling their business", Angel answered, smiling back. "Well, they need to keep it down over there." "It's probably some newlyweds or something and they're celebrating."

Putting his ear to the wall, Angel tried to listen to what was going on in the next room. "Oh, shit! I heard somebody say spank me", he laughed. "Boy, stop being so nosy and come here", Alexis giggled, grabbing his arm. "Hold up! They said it again. They're on some freaky shit over there." "Don't make me call you again, Angel", Alexis said, crossing her arms like a spoiled brat. Seeing the sexy look on Alexis' gorgeous face, Angel crawled over and began kissing her softly on the neck. "Mmmm, that feels good, baby", she moaned.

As he began to kiss her breasts, a knock at the door interrupted them. "Who's that?" Alexis asked as she quickly got under the covers. "Probably room service", Angel said as he put on his jeans and walked over to the door. Looking out the peephole, he said "Yeah, it's them" before opening the door.

"What's up, buddy?" Angel said, standing there in only his jeans. "Here's the bowl of strawberries you ordered", the skinny white man said. "And your chocolate fudge cake."

"Oh, I forgot", Angel replied, reaching into his pockets, pulling out a hundred dollar bill and giving it to the man. "Will that cover it?"

"Yes, thank you, sir. Thank you very much. Please, enjoy your stay", he said appreciatively as he walked away.

"Yo, hold up a minute", Angel said, stepping into the hallway.

"What is it, sir?" the man asked.

"The people next door in suite 609. Did they just get married or something?"

With a big smile on his face, the man started laughing out loud.

"What's so funny?" Angel asked.

"I'm sorry. It's just funny you asked about them."

"What? Tell me what's so funny."

"It's not a couple. It's three of them", he whispered.

"Oh shit! A ménage a toi"

"Yeah, I guess that's what you call it, but the three people next to ya'll are all men", he laughed out loud.

"Dudes! They're faggots!" Angel said.

"Yup, and they're here faithfully every weekend", he laughed.

"Damn!" Angel said, scratching his head in disbelief.

"It's two black men and a white guy. The staff calls them the three stooges. Homo, Mary, and Shirley", he laughed while walking away.

"Thanks, my man", Angel said, rolling the food tray into the room and shutting the door.

"What took you so long?" Alexis asked.

"I was talking to the room service guy."

"About what?"

"About the three faggots next door", he laughed.

"Faggots! They're men over there making all that noise?"

"Yeah, three of them. He said they're here every weekend and they call them the three stooges, Homo, Mary, and Shirley", Angel said as they both burst out laughing.

After calming his laughter, Angel said, "Here are your strawberries", taking one from the bowl and feeding it to Alexis. "What's that?" Alexis said, pointing. "That's dessert! Chocolate fudge cake", Angel smiled. "Then what am I?" Alexis purred in a sexy voice. "You're dinner!" Angel said, laying her down on her back and throwing the cover to the floor.

Looking at Alexis' beautiful cocoa brown body instantly turned him on. Seeing her hairy pussy and plump erect nipples had made his dick rock hard. Quickly sliding off his jeans, Angel began to kiss on her soft breasts. Licking down her stomach, Angel continued till he came across her hairy and very wet pussy. Gripping both her legs with his arms, Angel slowly began to suck Alexis' sensitive clitoris.

"Ohhhh, mmmm, ahhhh!" she screamed out in pure pleasure. "Ohh, Angel", she moaned. With both her legs still lightly gripped in his arms, Angel continued to suck every part of Alexis' wet and inviting pussy, and she could do nothing but dig her nails into the sheets and enjoy the feeling. Reaching over and grabbing a strawberry from the bowl, Angel placed it in his mouth and started eating it slowly around Alexis' soft pink pussy lips. The feeling was so good that tears of joy began falling from her brown eyes as she watched everything he was doing from the ceiling mirrors above the bed.

"Ohhhh, God! Ohhhhhh, ahhhhh", she screamed as she exploded with a devastating orgasm. This was her first time experiencing this wonderful feeling her body began to shake uncontrollably as she dug her acrylic nails so far into the bed that three of them broke. Lifting her legs up higher, Angel began licking around her asshole.

"Ohhhh", she screamed out. "I can't take it! Put it in me!" she begged him. While her body continued to shake and the tears continued to fall, Angel slowly climbed on top of Alexis. Placing both her legs on his broad shoulders, he slowly inserted every inch of himself into her wet and tight pussy. "Ohhhh, ahhhh", she screamed as he slowly stroked, in and out with perfect motion. "Ahhhhh!" she yelled as she began to dig her remaining nails into his strong back. Grabbing her hair, Angel started kissing her as he continued to stroke her nonstop. With her legs still strapped around his shoulders, she released another wonderful and intense orgasm. Screaming, crying, and shaking, she continued to hold on and enjoy this painful but wonderful feeling that she had never experienced before. Seeing the trails of blood all over the white sheets turned Angel on even more, and he turned Alexis around and began fucking her from behind.

"Ohhh, baby, it feels so good!" Angel grunted. "I love you!" she screamed out. "I love you, Angel!" she said. "I love you, too, Alexis", Angel said as he pulled on her long black hair and stroked her until they both climaxed together.

Lying back on the bed, Alexis began crying. "What's wrong, Boo?" Angel said, putting his arm around her.

"It felt so good", she said, still shaken from the after effects.

"How did it feel to you?" she asked.

"It felt good", Angel said, kissing her on the cheek.

"It hurt a little, but the pleasure was better than the pain", she said.

"We're not virgins anymore", she smiled.

"Nope. No more, baby", Angel said, smiling back. "Alexis, can I always count on you to be there for me?"

"You know you can, Angel. On everything I love baby, you can always count on me." Alexis replied as she laid her head on Angel's chest.

This night was a night of first and one they would never forget. After knowing each other for fifteen years, the two had come to a point where they could express their love on one of the highest physical levels. And although it wasn't the first time Angel had sex, it was his first time making love.

Later that night...

Inside of June's small apartment on 54th Street in West Philadelphia, Lucky and June were talking.

"Do you think we can get more when we sell this?" June asked.

"Man, we can get however much we need. I got Tisha wrapped around my fingers. She'll do anything I ask her to do", Lucky said, breaking down one kilo into ounces.

"She's fine as hell", June said. "Damn, she's fine!"

"Oh, you like her, huh? Well, partner, I could even hook that up", Lucky smiled.

"She's still a little mad at me, but she always comes around. I remember once I even had her stealing her uncle's guns and giving them to me", Lucky bragged.

"The guy Howard that you told me about?"

"Yup!" Lucky said, putting the ounces into empty Ziploc bags. "Like I said, she'll call me. She knows I'm home now."

"So what about me, you, and her?"

On Everything I Love

"No problem, partner. Give it about a week or so and I'll have her back where she belongs. Eating out of Lucky's hand", he laughed.

Sitting back and weighing the ounces on a small scale, June listened to Lucky as he told him everything he needed to hear. And the more Lucky talked about how good the sex was with Tisha, the more June wanted to find out on his own. While Lucky continued to blurt out everything he knew about Tisha, Howard, and Kevin, he had no idea that June was recording the entire conversation. June knew the system very well and if the government needed him to, he was going to testify against Tisha to get to Howard. And if Lucky didn't cooperate and testify against Tisha, he would spend the rest of his life in prison. Something that he knew Lucky would not want to do.

Lucky had no idea that June was building up a case with him to eventually take down Howard. Lucky believed that he was a king in this game of ghetto street chess, while the whole time he was just a pawn slowly being set up for the checkmate.

~~~

Early the next morning, Angel and Alexis were leaving the room where the two of them had been making love all night. While they waited for the elevator to come, the three men from the room next door walked out. As they waited for the elevator also, Angel recognized one of the men immediately. Although the man had no idea who Angel was, Angel had seen his pictures many times on the walls of his own house. It was Mr. Jerome Taylor, Sharita's husband. He had been lying to her about business trips and meetings out of town while she stayed at home waiting for him, just wanting him to love her. After six long years of marriage, Sharita had no knowledge that her 6'3", 245-pound husband was an undercover homosexual who was fucking her over mentally while he was literally getting fucked.

They all entered the elevator and Angel could not help but stare at the large muscular man, as he thought about Sharita. Knowing this man had a very beautiful and caring wife at home, but he'd rather be out with two men getting fucked, made Angel sick. Thinking about Sharita brought Angel a sudden sadness. She was his friend, someone he really cared for. And now the reason why she was lonely, sad, and always crying was standing just a few feet away. After returning their room keys in the lobby, Angel and Alexis left the hotel. Once they were inside his car, Angel drove off.

Looking over at Alexis who had her eyes closed, Angel smiled. *'Nothing will ever come between us';* he thought to himself as he drove down City Line Avenue early that Sunday morning. Opening her eyes, Alexis caught Angel staring at her. "Just don't stop!" she said as she smiled and closed her eyes again.

"Stop what?" Angel asked.

"Loving me", Alexis said.

With a big smile on his face, Angel thought about how much he did love Alexis.

TWENTY-1
That Evening...

Angel and Sharita were inside his Lexus, that was parked a block away from Sharita's house.

"What's the news?" Sharita asked. "What's so important?"

"Where's your husband?" Angel asked.

"Why? What's wrong? He just called and said he was on his way home soon."

"I saw your husband today", Angel said.

"How? He's been in Vegas all weekend. Did you go to Las Vegas?"

"No! And he didn't either. I saw him at the Holiday Inn Hotel on City Line Avenue earlier today."

"What! Are you sure it was him?"

"Sharita, I know who your husband is. He doesn't remember me, but I remember him very well."

"The Holiday Inn!" she said, confused.

"Yup, and the man who works there told me he's there almost every weekend, him and his friends."

"Friends! That no good ass cheating bastard. I knew he was having an affair with that slutty secretary of his, but he insisted and swore on the Bible he didn't find her attractive. But I can't imagine who the other woman could be!"

"They weren't women!" Angel said, looking into Sharita's watery eyes.

"What! What do you mean they weren't women?"

"They were men! Your husband was in a hotel room all night with two men."

"Men! Are you telling me that..."

"Yup! Your husband is gay! He's an undercover faggot. I'm sorry, Sharita, but it's true."

"I don't believe this shit! That motherfucker! Now I know why he doesn't like to have sex with me. And all this time I thought it was me. My fault!"

Sitting back in her seat, Sharita burst into tears.

"I'm sorry, Sharita, but it's the truth. If you don't believe me, he'll be there next week. You can go see for yourself."

"I don't believe that no good ass bastard. All these years I have been faithful to him and he was out cheating on me with men. That faggot ass mother-fucker! Damn him! His ass might even get AIDS. I hope he had the decency to use condoms!" Sharita shouted.

"Calm down, baby! Everything will be okay", Angel said, grabbing her hand.

"Angel, you don't understand! That man ruined my whole life. I gave him everything. Eight years! Eight fuckin' years! How could he do this to me?!"

"Please, Sharita, calm down before you have a heart attack or something."

"My life is fucked up! I don't have anything! No man, no kids, nothing!"

"You got me", Angel said, wiping away the tears on Sharita's face.

"Angel, you have your own life ahead of you."

"Sharita, you are a part of my life."

"But just a part. We both know we could never be together or have anything serious."

Angel knew the words Sharita spoke were true. Still, she had become a very good friend of his; someone that Angel truly cared for and couldn't stand to see in pain.

"I don't know what to do now! I'm so confused. I just feel like dying!"

"What! Sharita, don't talk like that. He ain't worth it!"

"I'm serious, Angel. You can't imagine how much this shit hurts! Imagine your girlfriend one day deciding to leave you for another woman."

Sitting back in his seat, Angel thought about it. "Damn!" he responded, shaking his head.

"That's how I feel! That's what I'm living with! I hate his ass!"

"I'm sorry, Sharita. I really am."

"Thank you, Angel. I know you're just trying to help, but this pain will never heal."

"Do you need me to do anything?"

"No, I'm okay. I'll handle it."

"Please don't do anything stupid, Sharita."

Reaching over to Angel, Sharita kissed him on his cheek. "Thank you so much, Angel. I love you", she said as she got out of the car.

Watching Sharita walk down the street, Angel couldn't help but feel sad and sorry for his friend. All that night he thought about Sharita and what she was going through. He prayed that everything would turn out right and Sharita could turn her life around.

~~~

The next day, inside the halls of North East High School, everyone was talking about the tragic news. Walking down the hallway, Angel stopped a male student who he knew.

"Ricky, what's going on?" he asked.

"Didn't you hear? You don't know what happened?"

"Hear what?" Angel said.

"About Mrs. Taylor."

"What about Sharita...I mean Mrs. Taylor?" a confused and anxious Angel asked.

"Mrs. Taylor died last night!"

"What! What are you talking about?"

"You didn't see the news or the paper?"

"No! I didn't see anything", Angel said in disbelief.

"She overdosed on sleeping pills inside the bathroom of her house."

"No! No! No! Oh my God, No!" Angel shouted.

"Are you okay?" Ricky asked, seeing the devastated look on Angel's face and noticing how hard he was taking the news.

"She was my favorite teacher."

"She said that in the suicide note."

"What! What suicide note?"

"The one she wrote before she died. They read it on the news."

"What did it say?"

"It said she couldn't take living anymore and she loved working at the school where she had many good friends and students. Then she said she was sorry and how everything was now in God's hands, and that she would miss Mrs. Nelson, the science teacher, Mrs. Smith, the gym teacher, and Angel McDaniel, her favorite student and close friend. We are all gonna miss her. The whole school is hurting today."

"Thanks, Ricky", Angel said, walking away as he tried his best to hide the tears that fell from his face.

'Damn, Sharita! Why go out like that...You didn't have to take life', he thought to himself. It was a day of sadness for Angel. He had truly lost a good friend.

That afternoon...

On the corner of 30th and Lehigh Avenue, Howard and Kevin were sitting inside his Range Rover. A few moments later, a grey Chevy Caprice pulled up in back of them. A tall dark-skinned, heavy-built man with dark shades on his face and a briefcase in his hand suddenly got out of the car and quickly got in the back of Howard's Range Rover. "Drive off!" he ordered.

Turning the truck on, Kevin immediately pulled off.

"What's the important news, Rasheed?" Howard asked, looking at his good friend.

"I came to warn you, Howard."

"Warn me about what?" Howard asked.

"About the F.B.I. that's been investigating you and your crew."

"What! The Feds!"

"Yeah. They've been asking a lot of questions about you and Kevin. Last week they took photos of your pool hall, Laundromat, and all of your cars."

"What!"

"They are working out of our office, getting all the information on you they can get. Evidently, someone told them about you and they've been on you ever since, my friend."

"Damn! Who could it be?" Howard wondered, shaking his head.

"Do you know a guy named June?"

"Who?"

"June! Here's a picture of him from our files", Rasheed said, opening up the briefcase and taking out the photo of June, and giving it to Howard.

"I don't know him. Never saw him a day in my life."

"You sure, because he knows a lot about you."

"I don't know how. Do you know him, Kev?" Howard asked, passing the picture to Kevin as he pulled behind a car and parked.

"Nope. Never saw him", Kevin said, passing the picture back to Rasheed.

"Well, June is an F.B.I. informant who's planning on taking y'all down."

"I don't see how he could do that. We're real cautious about who we deal with", Howard said.

"He has help. He's not alone. There's another young man who doesn't know he's working with an informant."

"One of my guys?"

"Here", Rasheed said, passing Howard another photo. "Do you know Leroy Conners?"

"Oh, shit! That's Lucky."

"You know him?"

"Yeah. He used to date my niece. He's locked up."

"He was locked up! He's been out for a while now. Seems Mr. Conners met June in prison and ran off his mouth to him about you and your crew. The whole time he never knew June was a working F.B.I. informant. To this day, he still doesn't know."

"That stupid motherfucker! I never liked his ass", Howard said, clenching his teeth.

"That's not all", Rasheed said.

"What else is it?" Howard asked, wondering how the news could get any worse.

"A few days ago, June and Lucky purchased two kilos of cocaine from your pool hall."

"What! Oh shit! "Howard and Kevin both shouted at the same time.

"I don't believe Tisha. She knows not to sell that nigga shit", Howard said.

"Well, she did. She sold it to Lucky who got the money from June who got the money from the Feds. The Feds are building up a strong case against you, my friend. They are trying to get everything they can on you and take you down. June is their informant and Lucky is helping them to bring you in without even knowing it."

"What can we do, Rasheed?"

"The Feds are planning on using June to testify against you if you take it to trial. Lucky will probably turn against you too, because with his track record he will definitely be facing life himself. Right now, June and Lucky are all the Feds have to take you and your crew down. They are the strongest pieces of evidence and the Feds are really interested in seeing you spend the rest of your life behind bars. I'm sorry, Howard, but there's not much I can do. The Feds are watching everything. They are keeping this case very confidential. If I wasn't a captain, I wouldn't have known any of this."

"Did you hear anything else?" Kevin asked.

"I'm pretty sure that an indictment will be coming soon. Once the Feds have gotten all the evidence they need to take to a grand jury, they'll move swiftly to get the case over with."

"What can we do?" Howard asked.

"I don't think I need to tell you that, Howard. Only these two men can take you down. If they suddenly disappear, the Feds will have no case. Nothing! Not even the drugs they bought would matter. The case will be over. A failure! They need people to testify. They need June and Lucky!"

"Thank you, my friend. Thank you very much, Rasheed. I mean, Captain Rasheed Brown." Howard said, shaking his hand. "This will be taken care of very soon, I promise you."

"Do what you gotta do and do it fast. The sooner they're dealt with the better."

Agreeably shaking his head, Howard turned around in his seat and looked at Kevin who couldn't believe what was going on. Both men knew what to do now, and that was to get both June and Lucky a new place to live; six feet underground where neither one would be able to testify on them. Starting the Range Rover up, Kevin slowly pulled off, and took Rasheed back to his car.

For the rest of the ride back, neither man said a word.

TWENTY-2
That evening...

Laying on top of his bed and watching reruns of his favorite T.V. show, *Good Times,* Angel was startled when the phone rang. Turning the volume down on his 52-inch Sony color T.V., Angel answered.

"Hello", he said.

"Yo, what's up, dawg? You alright?" a voice asked.

"Yeah, I'm cool, Pooda. I'm just chillin' today."

"I heard what happened today, about your teacher. It's all over the news."

"Yeah, I saw it, too."

"Don't sweat it, dawg. You know life must go on."

"For us it does!"

"You should get out. Get some fresh air, clear your mind."

"Naw, I'm cool today. Maybe tomorrow."

"C'mon, man, me and Rodney are down here at the arcade. We're waiting for Al. You know his ass is always late", Pooda said, laughing.

"It sounds good, Pooda, but I'm really not in the mood tonight."

"You sure, dawg?"

"I'm positive. I got a lot of shit on my mind."

"What's up? Can we help?"

"No, homeboy, I got to handle this one alone."

"What are you talking about, Angel?"

"Nothing!" Angel quickly said.

"I know you. You're up to something, nigga."

"I'm cool, just a little sad, that's all."

"Well, dawg, I hope you cheer up. If you do decide to come out later, we'll be here at the arcade on 12th Street. Peace out."

"If I change my mind, I'll see y'all. Peace out, dawg", Angel said, hanging up the phone and laying back across his bed. Turning up the volume of his T.V., Angel finished watching *Good Times,* the same show that his mother watched seventeen years earlier.

~~~

"What the hell were you thinking about, Tisha!" Howard yelled in an angry voice. Shutting the door behind him, Kevin took a seat. The three of them were all inside the room upstairs inside the pool hall.

"Girl, are you fuckin' crazy?"

"I'm sorry, Uncle Howard", Tisha cried.

"I told you about that fucking nigga! I warned you he was nothing but trouble."

"I'm so sorry."

"Tisha, I taught you better than this. Why do you keep letting this nigga get you in trouble?"

"I just wasn't thinkin'. I was just so surprised to see him again."

"That nigga doesn't care about you! He's using your ass to get to me. To bring us all down! Can't you see that? You're nothing to him but a piece of pussy and a five-minute conversation. Two fucking kilos! Damn, girl!"

"I'm sorry. I'm so sorry."

"You know what this means, right? Lucky and his friend have to go. I already have somebody on the job."

Looking into Howard's eyes with a stream of tears falling down her face, Tisha said, "I'll do it!"

"What?"

"Please, Uncle Howard, let me do it. I'll take care of everything. I promise."

"I don't know, Tisha."

"Please. I fucked things up, so let me fix them. I did it before."

Looking at Kevin, they both shook their heads, agreeing with the idea.

"Okay, you got two days to take care of this. Two fucking days. Not a minute longer. When I get back, I expect this whole mess to be taken care of", Howard said, standing up.

"Where are you going?" Tisha asked.

"Me and Kevin are taking the ladies to Miami for a couple of days. Since the Feds are watching my every move, I don't want to be anywhere in sight when those two bastards' checkout. Your aunt is packing now. I'm counting on you, Tisha", Howard said, walking out the door and down the steps.

Standing up, Kevin walked over to Tisha and put his arms around her. "Are you okay, Tisha?" he asked in a concerned voice.

"I'm fine" she said, putting her head down in disgust.

"I know you have feelings for Lucky, but he brought this all on himself."

"I understand, Kev. That's why I'd rather handle this than someone else."

"Duran will bring you whatever you need. Silencers, guns, vest..."

"I'm okay. I have all that."

"The hardest part is taking out someone you once loved."

"I still do love him, but its business, and business is never personal. Isn't that what you and my uncle taught me?"

Seeing the sad look on Tisha's face, Kevin gave her a hug and walked out of the room, leaving Tisha standing alone to cry her tears of regret.

~~~

After telling Angel they would be out of town for a few days, Howard and Vanessa dropped Chyna off at Alexis' house where her mother would watch her until they returned. Later that night, Howard,

Kevin, and both of their wives boarded a flight to Miami.

~~~

    That night, inside her plush apartment, Tisha called Lucky on his cell phone.

"Hello" Lucky said, answering his phone.

"What's up, Lucky? It's me."

"What took you so long?"

"I just couldn't run back to you like I was sweating you", Tisha said.

"You miss me?" Lucky asked.

"You know I do. You know I can't stand being away from your ass."

"How much did you miss me?"

"Too much! You couldn't imagine how much."

"Would you prove how much?"

"I'll do anything! You name it!"

"Anything?" Lucky smiled.

"Anything you want, daddy! Don't I always?"

Clearing his throat, Lucky began.

"Well, I have this friend of mine."

"Male or female?" Tisha interrupted.

"It's a guy this time, the dude you saw me with the other day."

"Oh, I remember him."

"Well, how about me, you, and him get together later at his house?"

"Not tonight. Tomorrow's better. I have something to do tonight."

"Tomorrow is fine, then. Write this address down.

"Okay, go ahead. I have a pen."

"It's 5426 Chancier Street."

"Okay, what time tomorrow?" Tisha asked.

"Nine o'clock, be there at nine."

"Okay, Boo, I'll be there. Y'all just be ready. I have a big surprise for y'all."

"Just like before, Tish?" Lucky laughed.

"No, better! Tomorrow will be like never before."
"Oh, shit! That's what I'm talking about, girl. Give it all to me."
"I will, Lucky. Every single bit."
"I'll let my friend know. Don't be late, Tish."
"Oh, don't worry, Lucky. I wouldn't miss this if my life depended on it."
"Girl, what's got into you?"
"You daddy. I miss that big black dick of yours. I'm gonna fuck you to death."
"To death!" Lucky smiled.
"To death, daddy, like a bullet through your forehead."
"Oh shit! My dick is getting hard!"
"Nine o'clock, Lucky. I'll be there. Bye", Tisha said, hanging up the phone.

Taking out a picture of her and Lucky from a few years ago, Tisha couldn't help but sit back and start crying as she reminisced on the good times they used to have together. But then she remembered a line her uncle often said, *"It's the ones you love who hurt you most."*

TWENTY-3

The bright sun was beaming down hard on this Tuesday afternoon. Standing next to her 1997 silver convertible Saab, Tisha watched a bunch of little kids playing as she waited for Angel to arrive. Dressed in a white Dolce & Gabbana spring dress and a pair of soft-soled matching designer shoes, her light tinted Armani frames hid the lonely tear that fell down her beautiful face. All night she couldn't sleep.

When she saw Angel drive up in his gold Lexus coup, she quickly wiped away her tears so he wouldn't see her crying; that was a side of her Angel had never seen before and a side she would keep away from him as long as she could. Getting out of his car, Angel walked over to Tisha who was now sitting on the hood of her Saab.

"Everything is all set, Tish", Angel said. "I drove by the house already. I even saw Lucky and the other guy with him. They were leaving."

"Thanks, Angel."

Seeing the sad look on Tisha's face, Angel said, "It's alright to cry, Tish. Crying is the beginning of healing."

"I'm okay. He brought it on himself", she said.

"Remember, you're gonna do that favor for me that I need."

"I told you I would. You don't have to remind me."

"Well, I got to hurry up and go get Alexis before she gets out of school. I'll be there at 9:15 on the dot."

"Don't forget, Angel, 9:15, not a minute later."

"Don't worry. I can't wait", Angel said, kissing Tisha on her cheek and walking back to his car. As they both got into their luxury vehicles, they sped off in opposite directions.

Turning up her CD player, the sounds of Toni Braxton smoothly flowed from her speakers. Driving down 29th Street, her tears started to fall again; reminding her that nine o'clock was not far away.

~~~

After picking up Alexis from school, Angel dropped her off at home, and then headed down the neighborhood to hang with his friends. Inside his home, Mr. Taylor sat on the side of his bed holding a picture of Sharita in his hand and talking to one of his close male friends.

"What are you gonna do now?" the man asked.

"I'm not sure. Everything happened so fast."

"What do you think happened?"

"I covered it up as best as I could. I don't know how she could have found out."

"Well, at least you didn't have to do it yourself, or pay those thugs you hired to do it for you. You saved yourself $25,000 dollars", the man smiled.

"Yeah, but now I'm not entitled to the insurance money."

"Why not?"

"Because our insurance didn't cover suicides. One million dollars down the drain!"

"Well, at least she's gone and out of our hair", the man said as he reached over and started sucking on Mr. Taylor's neck.

"Not here, Charlie! Her family will be coming by soon to pick up some of   her stuff."

"I'm tired of keeping our relationship a secret, Jerome."

"Once everything is over, we can go on with our lives honey, and soon move to San Francisco like we planned. Me, you, and Leon."

"Did you ever love Sharita?"

"I cared a great deal for her, and sometimes I tried to love her, but I just couldn't. She was nothing more than someone who kept my image secure."

Looking into Charlie's eyes, he said, "I love you! From the moment she introduced us, I've been in love with you."

"So we'll just continue meeting at the hotel. Once I sell the house and car, we can get as far away from Philadelphia as we can."

After French kissing each other, Charlie stood up and walked to the door.

"I'll be home if you need me. Call me later."

"Okay, and don't forget to tell Leon that Saturday night we'll see him as planned."

"I won't, honey", Charlie said, closing the door behind him.

~~~

Noticing the time was now eight o'clock Angel dropped each of his friends off at home and quickly headed to his house to change his clothes. After he put on a pair of black jeans and a dark grey tee shirt, Angel called Tisha on her cell phone.

"Hello", Tisha answered.

"It's me", Angel said, tucking his black 9mm handgun in his jeans. "Are you ready?"

"Yeah. I called Lucky a few minutes ago and told him that I was on my way soon."

"Are you okay?"

"I'm fine. I'm just ready to get it over with."

"Okay, Tish, 9:15. I'll be there, not a minute later. See you in a few."

"Bye", Tisha said, hanging up the phone.

Dressed in a sexy red Versace dress and a pair of black patent leather high-heeled Prada sandals, Tisha grabbed her matching red purse and walked out the door. Looking like a top model that just finished a photo-shoot for VIBE Magazine, this gorgeous girl was indeed sexy and dressed to kill. The diamonds that were in her Rolex watch and matching necklace sparkled bright as the stars. Her shiny, long black hair laid straight down her back and her fingernails were freshly manicured with glossy clear polish. No man in his right mind could resist this beautiful and very appealing young woman. That's why Howard called her his "secret weapon", because no one would ever expect this sexy ass woman to be the heartless gangstress that she was.

Climbing inside her Saab, Tisha started the car, then cut her music on and drove off. Looking at the time, Tisha noticed it was now 8:25. She lit a Virginia Slims cigarette, turned up her music and headed toward West Philly.

~~~

Walking out the door, Angel heard the phone ring and ran back to answer it.

"Hello", Angel answered.

"Hey, boo, it's me."

"Alexis! What's up, baby?"

"Nothing. Just wanted to call and talk to you. Chyna just fell asleep".

"She did?"

"Yup. Now I have time to talk to you."

"I was on my way out the door, boo."

"Where are you going?"

"I have to do a big favor for somebody."

"It's almost nine o'clock. Why so late?"

"I'll be back home soon" Angel said, avoiding her question.

"Call me when you get back in, if it isn't too late."

"I will boo. Love you."

"I love you, too. Bye, bye" Alexis said, and hung up the phone.

On Everything I Love

After Angel hung up the phone, he quickly ran out of the house, locked the door, got into his Lexus and drove off.

~~~

Hearing the hard knock, Lucky quickly jumped up from the couch and ran to the door. When he looked through the small peephole, a large smile came to his face as he saw the beautiful Tisha standing there waiting. Opening the door, Tisha walked inside.

"What's up, baby", Lucky said, giving her a warm hug. "You daddy, I thought about you all day", Tisha smiled. "I thought about you, too", Lucky said, rubbing her on her soft round ass. June walked in from another room and took a seat. "This is my man, June, I was telling you about", Lucky said, smiling.

"How you doing, June?"

"Fine now", he laughed. "Never felt better."

"What's up, fellas? Are you ready or not?"

"Damn, girl, what's the rush?" Lucky asked.

"I'm just ready to have you, daddy, that's all", Tisha whispered in a seductive voice.

"Where's the bedroom?"

"Back there", June said, pointing to a back room.

"Well, come on, I'm ready", Tisha said as she began walking towards the room.

"Damn! She is finer than a motherfucker", June whispered.

"Didn't I tell you, man? Didn't I tell you she would do anything I want?" Lucky smiled.

After turning off the living room lights, both men walked back into the bedroom where Tisha was now laying across the bed with her shoes off.

"I turned on the music. I hope y'all don't mind", she smiled. "No, it's cool", June said, taking off his white tee shirt. "My neighbors don't care."

"Are you okay? You need anything?" Lucky asked. "We got some weed and beer."

"Just you, daddy. Just you", Tisha said as she began taking off her dress.

"Oh shit! I forgot my purse. I left it on the table in the living room."

"I'll get it", June said, staring at her beautiful body.

"No! No! I have a surprise for y'all. I'll get it. Y'all just get undressed. I'll be right back", Tisha said, walking out of the room wearing only her thong.

Walking into the living room, Tisha grabbed her purse from the table. She then walked to the front door and made sure it was unlocked. As both men sat there undressed, Tisha walked back into the bedroom holding a loaded, silver 9mm with an attached silencer. Both men quickly jumped back.

"Whoa! Whoa, baby, what's up?" June said. "Tisha, what the fuck is going on?" Lucky shouted loudly over the music that was playing. "Put your fucking hands up, motherfuckers!" Tisha yelled, pointing the gun at Lucky's head. Both men quickly put their hands up in the air.

"Baby, what's going on? Why are you doing this?" Lucky asked, standing there undressed, private parts fully exposed, with his hands up in the air.

"Do you know this motherfucker, Lucky?"

"Yeah, he's my man. Why do you ask?"

"Because your man is an informant working for the Feds."

"What!" Lucky shouted, looking at June.

"She's lying!" June said.

"This motherfucker is a snitch, trying to take down my Uncle Howard!"

"Tish, are you sure?"

"Positive! The money he has is from the Feds. We know all about him."

171

"That's why you kept asking me so many questions about her uncle", Lucky angrily said, turning towards June.

"Man this bitch is out of her mind!" June shouted.

"No, motherfucker, you're out of your mind!" Angel said, walking into the bedroom holding his black 9mm in his hand.

Without any hesitation, Angel squeezed the trigger, unloading four quick and life-ending bullets into June's head. As June's body fell to the floor, Angel stood over him and dumped four more into his bare chest.

"Angel, look, man, I didn't know he was working with the Feds, I swear!" Lucky said as he stepped away from June's mangled and bloody body and into an empty corner. "Fuck you, Lucky", Angel said, pointing his gun at his head.

"Tish, Tish, don't let him do this, baby. Don't let him kill me like this. I love you, baby. You know I love you", Lucky begged. "You don't love me. You love to manipulate me. You never did love me."

"Tish, please! Please, sweetie!" Lucky pleaded, falling to his knees.

While looking into Lucky's scared eyes, tears began to drop from Tisha's eyes.

"Please, baby! Please!"

"I'm sorry, Lucky, but your luck has finally run out!" Tisha said, squeezing her silver 9mm and emptying six silent bullets into Lucky's chest.

As his dead body slumped to the floor, Tisha quickly grabbed her shoes and dress and walked out of the room. As Lucky and June's bodies both laid slumped on the floor, Angel began going through all of the drawers, throwing clothes all around the room to make it look like a robbery had taken place.

Opening up a closet door, Angel threw everything on the floor. Noticing a black backpack on top of a shelf, he grabbed it and opened it. "Bingo!" he shouted, seeing all of the bagged up ounces of cocaine inside. Walking back into the room, now fully dressed, Tisha couldn't help but look at Lucky's corpse that was lying in a pool of blood. "Tish, it's done. Let it go", Angel said. "He got what he deserved. It was him or us."

"I know, Angel, but why did it have to happen like this?" Tish said as the tears came once again.

"Only God knows the answer."

"What's that?" Tisha asked, noticing the backpack in Angel's hand.

"You wouldn't believe what I found."

"What?"

"The drugs they bought from you."

"What!?" Tisha half smiled.

"Yup, they didn't even get a chance to give it to the Feds", Angel grinned, then paused. "Is everything cool, Tish? You make sure everything is straight?"

"Yeah, no fingerprints, and I opened the living room window."

"Okay, let's get out of here. Where did you park? I didn't see your car anywhere."

"I parked around the corner on 53rd Street", Tisha said.

"I'm on Locust Street. I'll walk you to your car. Come on."

Looking at Lucky's body one last time, Tisha walked out of the room. "Bye, bye Lucky", she whispered under her breath. No one was outside on the chilly spring night as Tisha and Angel walked down the dark street. Upon reaching Tisha's car, they both got inside and quickly drove off. After taking Angel to his car, they both headed off in different directions. That night both young adults experienced something life changing. For Tisha, it was the guilt of killing a person she still loved. For Angel, it was

173

the excitement of killing a man for the very first time.

TWENTY-4
Two days later...

It was Thursday morning and almost the entire school was at Sharita's funeral on that rainy spring day. The faculty and student body packed the inside the Glory Baptist Church located in Upper Darby, PA, a suburb of Philadelphia, to say their final farewell.

Mr. Taylor sat in the front row next to Sharita's parents, crying like a lost man, and Charlie and Leon sat a few feet behind them pretending to cry on each other's shoulders. In an all-white casket, Sharita's body laid surrounded by hundreds of different colored flowers. As the procession of individuals slowly walked behind each other for their final viewing of Sharita's body, Angel made sure he was the last person in line. As he approached Sharita's casket, the sight of her caused a lonely tear to fall from his watery green eyes. Standing over her casket, Angel leaned down and kissed her cold lips. Walking by Mr. Taylor, Angel couldn't conceal the cruel look that was on his hardened face, knowing that he was the reason Sharita had killed herself. Seeing the cold stare in Angel's eyes, Mr. Taylor turned away and continued to cry along with Sharita's family. After everyone returned to their seats, Angel walked out of the church where Alexis had been holding an umbrella and waiting for him.

"I'm sorry, baby. I know she meant a lot to you", Alexis said, grabbing his hand.

"I'm going to miss her" Angel said.

"She was such a beautiful woman", Alexis said as they began walking towards Angel's car.

"Yes, inside and out. She was one of a kind."

"What makes a person like her do what she did?"

"Dying is easy, but living is hard! And only one thing can drive a person to do something like that" Angel sadly said.

"What's that?"

"Love!" Angel said, opening the passenger's door so Alexis could get into the car.

After they were both inside Angel's Lexus, he reached over and kissed Alexis on her cheek.

"What's that for?" she smiled, but still thinking about the deep comment he had just made.

"I love you, that's why."

"I love you, too."

"And you better not ever leave this world without me", Angel said, driving off.

"I don't know what I would do without you in my life, Alexis."

"And I don't think I could live without you either, Angel. I really don't."

Alexis responded, "Dying is easy, but living is hard' still roaming in her head."

That evening...

Inside their suite in the Delano Hotel in Miami, Florida, Howard and Vanessa had just returned to their room after leaving the mall. As they both relaxed inside the Jacuzzi, Howard reached for his ringing cell phone.

"Hello", he answered as Vanessa lay between his legs and his free hand played with her soft breast.

"Hi, Unc, it's me", a voice said on the other end.

"Is everything okay back home?"

"Everything is fine. I just called to let you know business is straight again."

"I knew I could count on you", Howard smiled. "That's the best news of the day. I'm proud of you."

"Thank you for letting me show you I could be responsible."

"I never doubted you. I always knew your potential. Your aunt and I will be home tomorrow afternoon, so I'll see you then."

"Okay, Unc. Bye, bye."

After he set down his cell phone, Vanessa turned around and got on top of Howard. "Was that Angel?" she asked as she slid his rock hard dick inside of her. "No, it was Tish letting me know she did what I asked her to", Howard smiled. "Well, whatever it was must have been very important to you. This is the first time you've smiled this whole trip" Vanessa said, as she began slowly riding him up and down.

"It was very important. Now, let's not talk about that. We only have this last night to enjoy wonderful Miami, Florida", Howard said, smiling. They moved their lovemaking into the Jacuzzi, and once they had enough fun in the steamy waters they moved onto the king size bed. There they explored each other's body until the late hours of the night.

Later that night...

Inside his one-man cell, Peter Smith never had a chance to protect himself as three large men quickly threw a pillowcase over his head and began stabbing him repeatedly with handmade knives. His mutilated body lay surrounded in a pool of his own blood, after the men punctured his body over twenty-five times. He had been brutally stabbed and left to die, and then a broomstick was shoved up his anus as a sign of disrespect to all inmates who raped women.

Then, after quickly leaving Peter's bloody cell, they entered the cell of John Williams that was just down the hall. As he lay snuggled under the warm sheets, he, too, was caught off guard by the three men. In unison they gripped him up and savagely began stabbing him in his face and chest. When John tried to scream for his life, one of the men took his 6-inch blade and sliced it across his throat. His large body fell to the cold prison floor, and each man began stabbing John over and over again until his mangled body showed no signs of life. After the bloody massacre had taken place, he, too, shared the fate of a broomstick being shoved up his anus.

In less than fifteen minutes, both men had been brutally murdered. Just like their nine victims, these men had been taken advantage of and left to die with no respect at all. There were no witnesses as the three inmates committed these savage and brutal murders. Even the two C.O.'s who had just returned from a smoke break didn't have a clue that the two men were now dead inside their cells, just a few feet away from their post. All appeared normal and one of the C.O.'s took out a deck of cards and the two officers sat down to play spades. Neither one of them would know that just steps away two corpse lay hardening, with broomsticks up their asses until the next count-which was still hours away.

TWENTY-5
Friday afternoon...

Vanessa was stunned as she sat quietly inside Howard's Range Rover looking at the front page of the Philadelphia *Daily News*. After eighteen years, her prayers had finally been answered. The two men who had raped her younger sister, and were the cause of her losing her life, had been viciously murdered inside a Philadelphia prison-in the same manner in which they had killed nine young female victims. Feeling delighted because of their demise, yet saddened over her sister's death, tears slowly fell from her beautiful brown eyes. But these tears were cleansing because after living with this pain for eighteen long years, knowing her sister's killers finally met justice now freed her up to begin healing.

"The Terrible Two Murdered" the headline said, as Vanessa began reading the tragic story.

"Last night, in C.F.C.F. located on State Road in Northeast Philadelphia, the two men known as "The Terrible Two" were violently stabbed inside their cells while they slept in the late hours of the night. Correction officers found both men with numerous stab wounds to the face and body. Both apparently bled to death and each was found lying in pools of his own blood. John Williams, 37, and Peter Smith, 40, had been arrested and charged with the murders of nine young girls from West Philadelphia just one week ago. Prison authorities told police that the murders had to occur sometime between shift changes or when the C.O.'s took their breaks. Warden Timothy Brooks promised a thorough and immediate investigation. The F.B.I. will also help assist in solving this strange and bizarre case of the double murder. Special Agent Stan Reynolds said he believed there was cooperation from the inside that led to these two men's tragic deaths, and he would do all he could to solve this case. There were no witnesses or evidence found. Homicide Detective Bruce Carter said, 'It was the perfect double murder. No witnesses and no weapons. And the first time in over five years that two inmates had been killed on the same day in a Philadelphia prison."

After reading the story, Vanessa folded the newspaper and sat back in her seat and smiled.

"What goes around comes around, huh?" Howard said as he continued driving home. "Did you have anything to do with that?" Vanessa asked, looking at Howard. "Nope! Somebody beat me to the punch", Howard smiled.

~~~

Inside the pool hall, Angel and Tisha were talking.

"Did you see the news today?" Angel asked with a huge smile plastered on his face.

"I sure did. Those two crazy motherfuckers got what they deserved."

"Yes, they did! Yes, they did!"

"The Feds are picking up the case, I heard", Tisha said.

"So! Fuck the Feds!"

"Yeah, but they always find a way to make somebody talk. They're worse than criminals."

"I'm not worried about anybody doing any talking. The Feds don't have anything."

"That's what I heard on the radio today, that there weren't any witnesses or weapons found."

"See! They've got nothing."

"Still, remember what Uncle Howard always told us. 'Sometimes even the dead can talk from their graves. So make sure no one or nothing can come back and haunt you.' Do you trust Shiz?"

"With my life! He'll never flip, never!"

"Okay, Angel, maybe you're right."

"I'm 100 positive", Angel said.

"Do you still need me to do that favor for you?" Tisha asked, changing the subject.

"Nothing has changed", Angel said.

"I'll be ready Sunday morning, and make it fast. I have to go to church', Tisha smiled.

"Girl, you're a trip!"

"I know" Tisha said, opening a can of Pepsi and taking a sip.

"Did you get rid of all the stuff?" Angel asked.

"Yup, I took everything out of here like Uncle Howard told me to."

"Oh, shit! I'm supposed to meet them at home", Angel said, rushing out the door.

"Tish, I'll call you later", he hollered back.

Getting inside his Lexus, Angel quickly headed home.

F.B.I. headquarters, Downtown Philadelphia...

"Those two men were set up and I'm going to get to the bottom of this!" Agent Stan Reynolds said to his partner, Mitch Sanders. Stan Reynolds was a tall, slim white man with a full dark beard and a bad attitude. Mitch Sanders was a short, cocky version of Stan. The two had been partners for six years and both came from the Philadelphia Homicide Unit before joining the F.B.I.

"It just doesn't add up", Stan said angrily. "Calm down, Stan. We'll get to the bottom of this", Mitch said, patting his friend on the back. "That's four unsolved murders this week, Mitch! Four! The boss is still pissed off about June and Lucky. That whole case is fucked up. Now this shit! The D.A. wants some answers. He's wondering how a F.B.I. informant can get murdered right under our noses. What's going on? We leave June alone for two days and the son of a bitch ends up with four bullets in his head", Stan vented. "He was robbed", Mitch said, sipping on his black coffee.

"Somebody robbed him."

"Robbed my ass! I believe somebody found out he was working with us and got to him."

"But who? No one knew he was an informant but us and a few officers on the police force."

"I don't know, Mitch. I just don't understand", Stan said, rubbing his head. "That was going to be our biggest drug case in years. And the Terrible Two was an open and shut case as well. Now, instead of finishing up two of our major cases, we're back to square one looking for the sons of bitches that killed all four of them."

"And we'll get them, Stan. Something will come up soon", Mitch reassured him.

"I *hope* so. I can't take another one of these."

"We still have a lot of interviews to do on the Terrible Two case. Hopefully we'll find something", Mitch said, looking out the window at downtown Philadelphia.

"How can two C.O.'s go on a smoke break at the same time and leave an entire prison block unsupervised? Something just isn't right with that story."

"I believe one of them left those men's cells open on purpose...the victims' and the murderers'. That's the only way those two men could have been killed, Mitch."

"They said they checked all of the cells before they took their break."

"I don't care what they said. Somebody's lying, and I'm going to find out who", Stan said, grabbing his jacket from off of the back of a chair and furiously walking out of the room.

~~~

Back inside the pool hall, Tisha was helping a customer out when the shock of her life walked through the door. Nervous, scared, and confused, Tisha approached the older woman who was standing at the counter.

"Tisha, Tisha, I missed you so much", the woman said, giving her a big, warm hug. "I missed you, too, Mrs. Conners", Tisha said sadly. "I just wanted to come by and give you something", the woman said, reaching into her purse. Pulling out a gold chain with a small photo attached, the woman handed it to Tisha. "Lucky wanted me to give this to you. Remember when I took that picture of y'all at Great Adventure a few years ago?"

"Yes, I remember", Tisha said as the tears slowly began to fall down her face. "He told me, 'Mom, if anything ever happens to me, tell Tisha that even though at times I didn't show her, she is the only woman I ever loved', and to give you this gold chain."

"I can't take it, Mrs. Conners", Tisha said, wiping her tears with her hand. "Please, Tisha, it was his final wish. I'm sorry he had to die the way he did, but we both know Lucky led a wild life. Hopefully, they'll find the man who killed my son and he'll be punished. As for my son, I pray that God has mercy on his soul."

"I'm so sorry, Mrs. Conners", Tisha said, hugging the woman tightly in her arms. "I'm so sorry." "It's okay Tish. It was just his time to go. We all have a time, some just sooner than others. Will you

183

be at his funeral?" Mrs. Conners asked as she began to tear up...

"I can't, Mrs. Conners. I just can't take it", Tisha said. "I understand. That's the same way I felt about his father and brother. When they leave us, they do not understand how much pain they leave behind."

"When is his funeral?" Tisha asked.

"It's Monday at the Mt. Zion Baptist Church in North Philly. If you can't make it, I understand", she said, walking towards the door. "I have to go, Tisha. I have a meeting with the funeral director in a half hour."

"Bye, Mrs. Conners", Tisha tearfully said.

As Mrs. Conners was about to walk out the door, she paused and turned around. "You were always my favorite, Tisha. Maybe if you were still in his life, this wouldn't have happened. God knows this world could use more good women like you." Waving, Mrs. Conners walked out the door. Looking at the picture of her and Lucky, all Tisha could do was cry.

~~~

Inside the basement of their house, Howard and Angel were both sitting down talking.

"How was your trip?' a smiling Angel asked.

"It was okay. Your aunt and I definitely needed one.

"I'm glad. She seems so happy now. The trip did wonders."

"It wasn't the trip that did it alone", Howard said.

"What else was it?"

"Don't play stupid, Angel. I told you it isn't cool."

"What are you talking about Howard?"

"You know damn well those two crazy motherfuckers were killed."

"That's what they get. Now, Mama doesn't have to suffer anymore."

"Angel, don't lie to me. Did you have anything to do with that shit?"

"No! I didn't have anything to do with it. I swear I didn't."

"I hope not. I saw the news earlier and the Feds are determined to find out who did that shit."

"It wasn't me" Angel said, with a straight face.

"I talked to Tisha today. She told me you drove the other night."

"Yeah, I waited for her to come outside."

"She knows I didn't want you involved in anything like that."

"All I did was wait outside for her. She did all the work", Angel said.

"I know it hurt Tisha to kill Lucky, but we had no choice."

"She understood. It was you who told us, Hustlers hustle and get that *doe*. Pimps pimp and control they *hoe*. Gangsters kill and let they pistols *go,* but a hustler is smarter than them *all* because he only controls that money and kills when his back is against the *wall.*"

"You're right, and don't you ever forget that. There isn't anything cool about killing."

"I won't forget Howard."

"I'm proud of you, Angel. You know you're the son I never had", Howard said, smiling.

"And you're the father I never had", Angel smiled back, as they begin laughing.

TWENTY-6

"Do you think we could use him again?" Howard asked Kevin as the two were sitting inside Kevin's white Mercedes 500 SL early Saturday morning.

"Why not? Sekou is still hurt, and it went smooth the last time."

"I don't know, Kevin. I still don't like the idea of using Angel as a driver."

"Howard, he's our best chance. Stop fooling yourself."

"Why, 'cuz he dropped off a little bit of money here and there for us around the city?"

"No, 'cuz he's white! And you know just as well as me that the chances of him getting pulled over on some Jersey highway are very slim."

"I told you, Kevin, I don't like using him for that."

"What is it with you, Howard? Why do you get so defensive when we talk about Angel? You know that boy is our smartest and most dedicated soldier. Anything you ask him to do he does it and does it well. Everything Angel learned in this game, he learned from you. He isn't anything but a younger version of you...only he's white!" Kevin said, looking at Howard.

"It's just...it's just..."

"What? What is it? That boy has *been* ready! Why are you limiting him?"

"It's because of Vanessa", Howard finally blurted out.

"Your wife?!"

"Yeah, that's why I haven't been using Angel like I should or overdoing it."

"What are you talking about? What does Vanessa have to do with any of this?"

"Everything, Kevin! That's her only other living blood relative. Her mother, father and sister are all deceased. If anything ever happened to Angel, she would just die. He's all she's got in this world. She loves Angel more than you could ever imagine. Sure, I know he's ready and very much capable of running things for us, but I don't want to be the cause of anything ever happening to him. That's why I act that way about him, because of my wife. And I think he knows it."

"All I'm saying, Howard, is just this last time. It's our biggest load. We have to be as safe as possible. Bringing a hundred kilos from New York to Philadelphia is risky."

"Bringing one kilo is risky."

"Yeah, but when you add ninety-nine more, there's no need in letting our pride get in the way and taking unnecessary risks. Isn't it you who's always shouting, 'B.C.F.', Business Comes First?"

"Okay, one last time, Kevin, and that's it! One last time. After Friday, I'm not using Angel to go to New York no more, so don't ask."

"B.C.F., right, Howard?" Kevin smiled, patting Howard on his back.

"Yeah, B.C.F.,'Beggin' Close Friends", Howard said, laughing.

At that very moment, a brand new red Jaguar XK8 pulled up behind Kevin's car. "About time", Howard said, looking at the passenger side door mirror. Opening Kevin's back door, the man got inside.

"Did I take long, fellas?"

"No, just an hour, Rasheed", Howard smiled.

"What's the word?" Kevin asked.

"The case is closed for now. No witnesses, no drugs, no fingerprints, no case", Rasheed smiled. "I see you don't waste any time, huh?"

"Time is money", Howard interrupted.

"So we straight now?" Kevin asked.

"Should be. I don't see why not. The Feds' two witnesses are dead. They have to start from square one again. Plus, the two agents who were working on your case got a much bigger problem on their hands."

"What's that?" Howard asked.

"You know those two psychos who were killed the other night?"

"The two crazy motherfuckers in jail?" Kevin asked.

"Yeah. Well, they been assigned to that case. It's been the talk of the town...and City Hall."

"What does City Hall have to do with it?" Howard asked.

"The mayor wants some answers. And it doesn't look good with his re-election coming up soon. It's all some political bullshit to show the people that he's tough on crime."

"What are they saying about the case? I heard it was the perfect double homicide", Howard said, smiling.

"So far it was, but the Feds will try and find some answers. You know them."

"Yeah, the devils themselves", Kevin commented.

"Okay, fellas, I have to get back to wifey and the kids. It's my day off. Time to spend quality time with the family", Rasheed said.

"How did Ann let you get away?" Howard smiled.

"I told her I was getting a tune up on the car."

"She went for that?" Howard asked.

"No, but she said hurry up and be back in an hour", Rasheed laughed.

Reaching under his chair, Howard pulled out a Nike sneaker bag.

"Here you go, Rasheed. I'll see you next month", he said, handing over the bag.

"Twenty-five thousand. Don't spend it all up in one day", Kevin smiled.

"Twenty-five! Oh, I got a five thousand dollar raise", Rasheed boasted with a broad smile.

"You earned it this month", Howard said. "Just be ready next Friday around ten o'clock."

"Howard, ain't I always ready when you come back from New York? Isn't me or one of my men waiting to make sure you are never fucked with?"

"Just makin' sure, that's all."

"Just let me know the car and who's driving. We'll do the rest."

"It's gonna be Angel again. And I'm renting a car. I'll let you know the make and color."

"I don't believe lil' Angel has grown up so fast", Rasheed said, shaking his head.

"Too fast", Howard added.

"Well, I'll be ready, Howard. Ten o'clock Friday. You can count on me. Oh, and thanks for giving to the Philadelphia Police Fund", Rasheed said, laughing as he got out of the car holding his Nike bag full of money.

Entering his Jaguar, Rasheed quickly pulled off and drove down the street and made a U-turn. Kevin and Howard also drove off.

Early Sunday morning...

After Jerome, Charlie, and Leon left their Holiday Inn suite from a weekend filled with sex and drugs, the three of them were talking as they walked through the underground parking lot. As they approached Jerome's black Lexus LS400, no one noticed the masked man who was quietly easing from behind another parked car and holding a black glock with an attached silencer.

189

"Oh shit!" Jerome shouted, lifting up his hands immediately upon spotting the man. "He has a gun!" Leon shouted. "Please, don't shoot. Just take the car", Jerome said, throwing his keys at the masked man's feet. As the three men stood there in fear, all they could see was the evil green eyes under the face-mask that stared at each of them.

"I don't want your car, you fuckin faggots!"

"Please, take whatever you want. Just don't kill us", Charlie pleaded with his feminine voice.

"Here, we have money", Leon said, taking out a large stack of hundred dollar bills from his shoulder bag.

"I don't want your money either. I didn't come for that!"

"Well, what is it that you want?" Charlie asked, as fearful tears fell down his face.

"Me! He came for me", Jerome said, looking into the masked man's eyes.

Jerome realized who it was. From that day at his wife's funeral, he never forgot those scary green eyes or the person to whom they belonged.

"Isn't that right? Is..."

Before he could finish his sentence, three silent and life-ending bullets entered his head. His lifeless body slumped to the ground, then the masked man stood over him and shot him two more times in the chest, then ran away.

"Jerome! Jerome!" Charlie screamed out as he leaned down on one knee at his side. But it was too late. The five bullets that had entered his head and chest had quickly done their job. And just like his troubled wife, he, too, was now another statistic.

Quickly running through the parking lot, the masked man disappeared between the parked cars. "Somebody please help us!" Leon shouted. "Help! Help!"

"Jerome, I'm here, baby", Charlie said, kissing him as the flow of blood ran from his forehead. "Oh my God! No! No! No!" Charlie screamed as Jerome's eyes finally closed.

~~~

Jumping inside the silver convertible Saab that was waiting for him around the corner, Angel removed his mask. "It's over", he said, breathing heavy from running through the parking lot. "You sure?" Tisha asked, starting up her car and driving down the street, watching as the speeding police cars passed by. "I'm sure! He's dead. Just like his wife", Angel said, taking off the black tee shirt that he wore over top of a white one.

"He almost said my name."

"You're lucky", Tisha said, turning onto the expressway.

"I don't believe in luck" Angel snapped.

"Well, Angel, he's dead now. How do you feel?" Tisha asked, turning on her radio.

"Dying is a part of living. It's something we all have to face one day. Sharita, her husband, you and even me", Angel said, sitting back and closing his eyes.

TWENTY-7
Sunday afternoon...

Sometimes a man will cry and no one ever sees his **tears.**
When only love can cure his struggles and help heal his deepest **fears.**
In this life that we do not know, we could never **understand**
The wrath of the ghetto we live in and how it constantly breaks a **man.**
How can riches be given to others, but many stay poor and in **need.**
And for us to achieve that same wealth, we must cause a man to **bleed.**
Why do we live with pain and sleep with death in all of our hurting **years?**
Create an ocean of a million sins from all of our falling **tears.**
Though we scream and shout love, we mostly do it in **shame.**
Why in order to experience true love, we must first experience **pain?**
If this place ain't hell, then what is it? An introduction to its **class?**
Is there somebody up there mad at us, just waiting for this world to **pass?**
And when you come, will you come with a rage, so no one can ever **forget you?**
And for all of the evil we've done in this world, would you still take us **with you?**

"It's called '*Artificial Love*'. It's by a poet named Jimmy DaSaint', Alexis recited to Angel as they sat on her step. "Man, I like that", Angel said, looking at the white piece of paper Alexis was reading from. "He's telling the world to love and stop hating. He's saying those who do not love will not be loved. Who do you love?" Alexis asked with a big smile on her face.

"You! More than you could ever know. I feel like you're my soul mate, Alexis. Like I was meant to be with you. Like God gave us each other. You're my strength."

"And I feel the same way, but like I told you a thousand times, not by my mouth, but by my actions, I will prove it to you. And one day you'll understand. Now what was so important you had to show me?" Alexis asked, smiling.

"Walk me to my car", Angel said, standing up.

"What is it, Angel?" Alexis said, following behind him.

"You'll see." Angel smiled, as they both reached the car and got inside.

"Close your eyes."

"Here we go again", Alexis said, as she tightly closed her eyes.

Going into his pocket, Angel pulled out a small white box. "Okay, you can open them now." Opening her eyes, Alexis noticed the small box that Angel held in his hand. "What's this?" she asked nervously as he passed her the small box. "Open it and see."

Alexis pulled out the small piece of paper that was inside.

"Read it!" Angel said.

"What are you up to, boy?"

"Just read it."

Unfolding the small piece of paper, Alexis began reading aloud.

-You're the reason why I smile, and my heart feels no sorrow. It's because I have you today that I look forward to tomorrow.-

"Oh, Angel, that is so sweet" Alexis said, as tears of joy danced down her face. Looking up at Angel, Alexis then noticed the gold, diamond ring that Angel had in his hand.

"What's that?"

"It's yours. Here", Angel said, passing the precious shiny stone to Alexis.

"Oh Angel! Oh, my God! It's beautiful."

"Read the inside."

Looking at the small engraved words on the inside of the band, Alexis begin to read the inscription.

"Diamonds may last forever, but not as long as my love for you...Angel & Alexis."

"Oh, Angel, I don't know what to say...", Alexis chocked up.

"Just tell me yes."

"Yes to what?!" Alexis nervously asked.

"That once you graduate college you're going to be my wife."

"Yes! Yes! Yes! I would love to be your wife", Alexis said, without hesitation as she began to hug her new fiancé.

After placing the ring on her left ring finger, they kissed zealously.

"I love you, Angel! I love you so much", Alexis cried.

"Even though my birthday isn't until next week", Alexis laughed, while wiping her tears of joy from her eyes.

"I know, but I couldn't wait any longer", Angel smiled.

"You are full of many surprises, aren't you?"

"Yup, and just wait till Thursday when we both graduate."

"Angel, you don't have to. You've already done too much."

"There's never enough for you."

"So do you think you can make it in time for my graduation?" Alexis asked.

"I'll try. It'll be hard since both our graduations are at the same time."

"Well, I'll get it videotaped for you."

"And Mama said she was videotaping mines."

"I'll give it to you at our graduation party at your house."

"Okay, 'cuz that's when you'll get your other surprise."

"What are you up to, boy?"

"You'll see", Angel smiled as he started up his car.

"Where are we going?" Alexis said, staring at her diamond ring.

"To celebrate. You and I are going to celebrate."

"Where?"

"A nice cozy restaurant I know downtown", Angel smiled as he drove off.

"I have a better idea", Alexis said, grabbing his hand.

"What?" Angel asked, stopping at the light.

"How about a nice cozy hotel I know that's also downtown?" Alexis smiled.

"Sounds good to me", Angel said, pulling off as the light turned green.

Monday afternoon...

Inside the Mt. Zion Baptist Church, the small crowd of family and friends all came to see Leroy "Lucky" Conners' final farewell. The large church was a Philadelphia landmark, built over one hundred years ago by former slaves who had escaped the racism and agony of the south to start a new life in Philadelphia. But today, it would become the last place that anyone would ever see Lucky's face.

On Everything I Love

After the choir finished singing, the short grey-haired preacher approached the microphone. "Thank you. You may all be seated now", he said to the men and women who were all standing. "Is there anyone who would like to say a final prayer or a few words about this young man?" There were stares but no responses as everyone looked around. "If there is something that anyone would like to say, please step forward and say it now. After today there will be no more chances", the preacher said, looking down at the small crowd.

"Okay, then..."

"Wait, I have something I would like to say, Reverend", a voice yelled out from the back of the church. "Will you please stand up?" the Reverend asked.

In a black Versace dress with a pair of matching dark shades, Tisha stood up and walked toward the front of the church. With her long black hair falling past her shoulders and down her back, the tearful Tisha whispered in the preacher's ear. "Sure, you can read a poem", he smiled. After passing the microphone down to Tisha, the Reverend took a seat.

Staring into the crowd, Tisha noticed Mrs. Conners sitting in the front pew. After waving a hello to Mrs. Conners, Tisha pulled out a white piece of paper. The small crowd immediately grew silent as everyone waited on Tisha to begin.

"This is a poem that I wrote for my dear friend, Lucky. It's called *'If I Could Have Back Yesterday'* ..."

If I could have back yesterday, I would love you the **same.**
I would be your light in this dark world, protecting you from the **rain.**

*If I could have back yesterday, I wouldn't change you at **all**.*

*And before you took your final steps, I would catch you before you **fall**.*

*If I could have back yesterday, I would show you how much I **cared**.*

*How I love you so much, your sweet gentle touch, and no one could **compare**.*

*If I could have back yesterday, I wouldn't be feeling this **agony**,*

*For turning my back on a loved one now, I know that God is **mad at me**.*

*If I could have back yesterday, my tears would not be **shown**.*

*Maybe we would be wrapped in each other's arms, or just talking on the **phone**.*

*If I could have back yesterday, it would be you that I'd still **adore**.*

*It would take away this pain that I self-inflicted, just to see you smile once **more**.*

*If I could have back yesterday, maybe I wouldn't feel like **dying**.*

*If I could have back yesterday, today I wouldn't be **crying**.*

After saying the poem she had written, Tisha passed the Reverend the microphone and tearfully walked over and kissed Mrs. Conners on her cheek. After both women emotionally embraced each other, Tisha walked past the tearful crowd and straight out the door, never turning back. Outside the church, she got into her convertible Saab and drove away.

TWENTY-8
Tuesday afternoon...

Inside the basement of his house, Howard had just made a call to his connect in New York.

"Hello" a voice said.

"What's up? It's me, Philly", Howard said.

"Philly! What's going on?"

"Same ol' thing."

"How's the weather in the City of Brotherly Love?"

"It's pretty nice today. I saw about one hundred pigeons in the sky."

"Oh, yeah? So, when are you coming to the Big Apple to check out Broadway?"

"Friday, same time, same place."

"I look forward to seeing you then, Philly."

"Are those crazy cabs up there still expensive?"

"Same as usual, about eighteen dollars a mile."

"That isn't bad. I'll see you Friday. Peace out", Howard said, hanging up the phone.

"What did he say?" Kevin asked, counting large stacks of cash with the money machine.

"He said eighteen thousand a key, same as before. How much is that on the table?"

"Four million", Kevin said, placing the stacks of money back inside the large safe.

"How much is in the safe?"

"Total, its eleven million and some change", Kevin said as he closed and locked the safe. "Are you ready to go by the dealership now?"

"Yeah, I'm ready", Howard said as they both walked back upstairs.

Inside the kitchen, Vanessa and Chyna were sitting at the table eating.

"Honey, I'll be right back", Howard said, kissing Vanessa on her cheek.

"I thought you were staying home today", Vanessa said.

"I got to go by the car dealership, remember?"

"Oh, that's right. Don't forget, Angel said blue."

"I won't", Howard said, walking away with Kevin.

"Bye, Daddy!" Chyna shouted out.

"Bye, sweetie, I'll be right back", Howard said as he and Kevin walked out of the front door.

An hour later...

"There are two types of niggas", Angel said while he and his friends were hanging outside at the playground.

"What's the two?" Pooda asked, smiling.

"The nigga who lies down and the nigga who lays 'em down", Angel said.

"Well, which one are you?" Rodney asked.

"All I'm gonna say is that I don't like to get my clothes dirty", Angel answered.

"Where's A.L.?" Rodney asked.

"I told that nigga to meet us here at two-thirty. It's now three o'clock."

"He better hurry up. I have to be somewhere at four o'clock", Angel said, looking at his watch.

Just then, pulling up in a black Toyota 4-runner with three attractive women, A.L. parked and got out.

"Yo, what's up, fellas?" A.L. smiled as he greeted everybody with a hand slap. "Who are the honeys?" Pooda asked, looking in the Jeep. "Lisa, Monica, and Kelly", A.L. said. "Well, what's up, nigga?!" Rodney asked.

"I brought them over to meet y'all. They wanted to hang out, and the one named Kelly wanted to meet Angel."

"What!" Angel said, smiling and looking into the Jeep.

"Yeah, the girl Kelly said she's been trying to see you for the longest."

"Where did you meet these chicks, A.L.?"

"I met them at Spiro's Deli Shop, but they all go to Central High School."

"That's Alexis' school!"

"That's where she said she saw you, parked in your Lexus a few times."

"Yeah, well, I'm cool. I ain't doing nothing", Angel said, walking toward his car.

"Man, are you crazy? That bitch is fine as hell", A.L. said.

"So what! I ain't fucking nobody who knows my girl. And I'm pretty sure they all know Alexis."

"Them bitches don't care!"

"Well, I do. I'm chilling for awhile. I'm cool, dawg. Y'all three go have some fun."

"Angel, I'm telling you, you don't know what you're missing. The girl has a bachelor's degree in dick sucking from Swallow University-in Deep Throat, Michigan", A.L. said as everybody burst out laughing.

Getting inside his car, Angel started it up, and then leaned out of his window. "Well, when she gets her masters, tell her to come see me", he said, driving off.

"What's up, A.L.? Why did Angel leave?" Kelly yelled out the Jeep window. "Oh, he had something important to do at four", A.L. said, walking back to the Jeep. "It's okay. I'll see him again. He doesn't know it yet, but I'm going to have that gorgeous motherfucker", Kelly said, licking her lips. "Well, you know he has a girl", Pooda said. "So? That never stopped me before from getting what I want."

Looking at Kelly's thick-figure and beautiful pecan brown complexion, with her long straight black hair laying down her back, the guys all knew this attractive female could probably have anyone she desired. But unlike most men who had drooled over Kelly and sweated her constantly, Angel-whom she had always had a secret crush on ever since she saw him outside her school one day picking up Alexis- had never even noticed her or paid her any mind.

~~~

Driving down 29th Street with his music blasting, Angel never noticed the stop sign and continued to drive. Hearing the loud sounds of a police siren behind him, Angel realized his mistake and pulled over to the side of the road. Turning down his radio, Angel quickly changed the rap station to another station that played the top 40 pop hits. Through his rearview mirror, Angel could see the two white officers checking his license plate. Calmly, Angel waited in his seat while one of the officers got out of the patrol car and walked up to his window.

"You didn't see that stop sign back there?" the officer asked, surprised to see it was a young white man driving a Lexus and not the stereotypical drug dealer who was usually black.

"No, officer, I honestly didn't see it, sir" Angel replied, using his best all American white-boy impersonation.

"This is a bad neighborhood. What are you doing around here?"

"Oh, I help out at the local community center. I help the poor black kids with their math."

"Them little bastards need all the help they can get" the officer said, and both him and Angel began laughing. "Do you have your license and registration?"

On Everything I Love

"Yes, sir, I have it right here", Angel said, opening up the glove compartment.

"Don't worry about it. Just watch yourself out on these streets. And try not to drive through any more stop signs."

"Thank you, officer", Angel said, starting his car back up.

"You're welcome. And I hope you can do some of those little niggers some good", he said, smiling.

"I'll try my best. You know them people need a lot of work", Angel replied back.

"Well, the ones you can't help, we always have a place for them", he said sternly.

"I'm sure you do", Angel responded as the officer walked away. "I'm sure you do."

After getting back inside their patrol car, the officers pulled off. Once they were gone, Angel changed back to his rap station and drove away. Reaching under the passenger seat, Angel grabbed a black plastic bag that was filled with $150,000 in cash. "Suckers! Just like Howard said, my complexion will always get me over", Angel thought to himself.

Looking at his watch, he noticed it was 3:45 and Howard was waiting for him to drop off the money. As he was getting on the expressway headed home, his cell phone rang.

"Hello", Angel said.

"Where are you?" Howard asked in a concerned voice.

"I'm on my way home right now. I got pulled over by some cops."

"Is everything alright?"

"Yeah, I'm cool. They let me go again", Angel laughed.

"Well, I took care of that for you. I just got back a few minutes ago."

"Is it blue?"

"Sky blue, just like you asked."

"Thanks, Howard. She's gonna love it", Angel smiled.

"You're welcome. Now try and make it home without getting pulled over again", Howard laughed.

"I'll be there in twenty minutes", Angel said, hanging up the phone.

TWENTY-9
Thursday afternoon...

Inside the large living room, family and close friends were gathered for Angel and Alexis' high school graduation party hosted by Vanessa and Howard.

Sitting on the large soft leather sofa, Kevin and his wife were talking to Alexis, congratulating her on her big day while Angel stood just a few feet away talking to Alexis' parents.

"We're so proud of you, Angel."

"Thank you, Mr. Richy", Angel said, shaking his hand. "We wanted to talk to you about that ring", Sandy said, smiling. "I know, Mrs. Sandy. We're both too young to be thinking about marriage and it's a big step and people change. Is that what you're gonna tell me?"

"No! We wanted to tell you good luck and you have our best wishes", she smiled.

"What!" a shocked Angel replied.

"Yeah, we talked with Alexis and she's positive there is no other man in this world for her. You two have been this way ever since y'all were kids. We knew this day would soon come", Mr. Richy said, patting Angel on his back.

"What we are saying, Angel, is that we would never come between y'alls love for one another. Alexis means the world to us and you mean the world to her."

"Thank you, Mrs. Sandy."

"Twenty years ago we knew two young people who also were very much in love and knew they were both meant to be together", Sandy smiled.

"Who?"

"Us!" Mr. Richy answered, putting his arm around his wife. "We were young at the time when my wife decided to leave South Carolina and move to Philadelphia with me and raise our family. But our love for each other was genuine. That's why we understand."

"Thank y'all so much. And one day, I'm gonna make Alexis the happiest wife in the world. I promise."

"We know you will, Angel, cause she's happy now", Sandy said.

On the couch, the conversation between Alexis and Kevin and his wife picked up.

"So you're going to Spelman College in Atlanta, huh?" Kevin said.

"Yes."

"What are you going to major in?" Kevin's wife asked.

"Criminal Law. I want to be a lawyer one day", Alexis smiled.

"A lawyer. Now that's what we need more of. Black female lawyers", Kevin beamed.

"I'm sure you'll be good at whatever you choose, Alexis", Kevin's wife added.

"Oh, we almost forgot", Kevin said, reaching into the inside pocket of his suit and pulling out a white envelope. "Here, Alexis, congratulations, sweetheart. This should help you with your books." Kevin smiled as he passed the envelope to Alexis.

"What's this?"

"A gift from us" Kevin's wife said, smiling.

Opening up the envelope, Alexis pulled out the check that was inside.

"Ten thousand dollars!" she shouted. "Thank y'all so much!" Alexis said, hugging them both.

"You're welcome, and if you need anything else, you let us know", Kevin said.

"This is more than enough. Thank you, thank you so much."

Turning down the music on the stereo system, Howard asked for everyone's attention. "Alexis, can you come here, sweetie, for a second." Standing up, Alexis walked over to him. "Yes, Howard?" she said. "Let Vanessa cover your eyes?" He smiled as Vanessa walked into the living room holding a black blindfold. "What's going on?" Alexis smiled. "Angel... Mom... Daddy, what's on'?"

"I don't know", Angel said with a dumb look on his face.

"Okay, let's get this over with", Alexis said, closing her eyes and allowing Vanessa to wrap the blindfold around her eyes.

"Everybody, follow me", Howard ordered.

Holding Alexis' hand, Angel guided her behind everyone. Walking through the house, everyone followed Howard to the garage. "Okay, you can take off your blindfold", Howard said. Once the blindfold was removed, Alexis looked around and noticed that the garage was empty. "What is it? What's going on everybody", she smiled.

At that moment, Tisha pulled up in a brand new 1997 sky blue BMW 3281 convertible with all white leather interior, and the words "Congratulations Alexis" written across the windshield.

"Congratulations!" everyone shouted out in unison. "Oh, my God!" Alexis nervously shouted as she began crying. "It's my favorite color, too", she stated, hugging Angel.

"Do you like it, baby?" Angel asked.

"I love it. Thank you, Angel", Alexis said gratefully. "It's your gift from us, me, Mama and Howard", Angel smiled.

After getting out of the car, Tisha passed Alexis her new set of car keys. "Get inside and check it out, Alexis. There's another surprise", Tisha smiled. "What?" Alexis asked curiously, looking around at everybody's smiling faces.

Alexis nervously sat inside of her new car as Angel walked around to the passenger side and got in. Opening up the glove compartment, Angel passed Alexis the car's title and owner's manual. "Here, it's all yours, baby", he smiled.

"Thank you, Angel. Thank you all so much", Alexis cried.

Reaching back into the glove compartment, Angel pulled out a white envelope.

"What's this, Angel?"

"Another gift from all of us, everybody here", he smiled, passing it to Alexis.

Taking a deep breath, Alexis slowly opened up the envelope and noticed a check inside, just like the one Kevin and his wife had given her only moments ago. Everyone gathered around the car. Taking another long deep breath, Alexis finally looked to see how much the check was made out for. When she spotted the words "fifty thousand dollars" written out across the amount line, Alexis almost fainted.

"Fifty thousand dollars!" she shouted.

"You never know how much your books will cost" Angel said, and everyone one started laughing.

As the flow of tears traveled down her face, Alexis reached over and hugged Angel.

"I don't know what to say", she cried. "I love all of you. Thank y'all for making this day so special."

"And we all love you, Alexis" Vanessa said, as she too could not help but cry along with all the other females.

"I have a special surprise for you, also, Angel", Alexis whispered in his ear.

"What is it? I told you not to buy me anything."

"I had to get this", she smiled.

"What? What are you smiling for?" Angel asked.

"I'll show you later...after the party when we're alone tonight. The day is hardly over yet", Alexis said, smiling deviously and getting out of the car.

"Girl, what are you up to?" Angel asked as he also exited the car.

After everyone walked back inside, Alexis grabbed Angel's hand. "You'll see later. Now come on and let's go enjoy our graduation party."

Following everyone back inside, Angel wondered what the surprise was that Alexis had for him, but for the rest of the evening, everyone just enjoyed themselves by eating and talking amongst one another. Angel and Alexis were meant to be together is what everyone thought. Even Tisha who had always had a very deep love for Angel couldn't deny the love connection between these two young adults. Love was in their eyes and everybody could see it. Knowing that Angel was someone she would never have, Tisha sat down and thought about Lucky, wishing he was still alive so the two of them could make things work out. As tears of sadness ran down her pretty face, she knew Lucky was dead and gone forever, and she couldn't escape the fact that she was the one who put him in his grave.

Later that night...

After everyone had finally gone home and Vanessa and Howard had cleaned up and went upstairs to bed, Angel and Alexis remained.

"Are you ready for your surprise?" Alexis asked, smiling.

"I've been waiting all night", Angel said.

"Well, we have to go somewhere private so I can show you, baby."

"My car or yours?" Angel smiled.

"My car. I'll drive you", Alexis said, grabbing his hand and pulling him out the door.

Forty-five minutes later, inside the Four Season's Hotel in Center City, Philadelphia, Angel lay undressed across the large bed while Alexis was inside the bathroom getting herself ready.

"Are you ready, baby?" Alexis yelled out.

"Been ready", Angel answered.

As Alexis emerged from the bathroom, Angel's rock hard dick got even harder from seeing his beautiful woman in a sexy red lingerie set, with a pair of matching red high-heeled shoes. Her long black hair laid down her back as she walked back and forth across the room, showing off her perfect figure. Angel couldn't take anymore of the sexual teasing, so he grabbed Alexis by her hand and overpoweringly threw her on the bed.

"Hold up. I have something to show you", she said, taking off her bra.

"Surprise!" Alexis said, showing Angel the small tattoo of an angel over her heart and the words "Forever yours" written under it.

"God, when did you get that done?" Angel smiled.

"Yesterday. Do you like it?" she asked, kicking off her shoes.

"I love it", Angel said, feeling it with his hand.

"Now I'll always have you near my heart", Alexis smiled. "I love you, Angel. And I told you my love for you is and will always be real. Now, can you come tame this kitten that's been waiting for you all day long?" she smiled as she took off her thong and lay across the large bed.

Getting on top of her, Angel put both of her legs on his broad shoulders and slowly entered Alexis' wet and tight pussy. As the wonderful feeling instantly ran through both these young lovers, Alexis whispered in Angel's ear. "Now my day is complete", she said as Angel smiled and continued to slowly and deeply stroke her warm and wet paradise. After dimming the bright light, the two of them continued to enjoy each other's affection as they made love all night long.

THIRTY
Friday evening...

"What is it, baby?" Howard said, rushing towards the door holding a black briefcase in his hand with almost two million dollars in cash inside. Kevin and Angel are outside waiting for me", he said as they both stood in the doorway. "I just wanted to tell you Chyna was very upset", Vanessa smiled.

"Why? What is it now, her Barbie doll broke or something?" Howard laughed. "Baby, I gotta go", he said, kissing Vanessa on her cheek and walking away. "No! She's upset because she's not going to be the only child any more", Vanessa shouted.

Suddenly stopping in his tracks and quickly turning around, Howard walked back to Vanessa. "What did you say!?" he asked, making sure he had actually heard her correctly the first time. "You're gonna be a daddy again", Vanessa smiled, looking into Howard's stunned face. "When did you find out?" Howard asked, hugging Vanessa tightly in his arms. "A few days ago. The doctor said I'm six weeks. Now maybe we'll have that boy you've always wanted", Vanessa smiled. "A baby boy..." Howard smiled, not knowing what else to say. "Just hurry back home. I know this caught you off guard, so we'll talk when you get back in tonight", Vanessa said.

After planting another kiss on her lips, Howard smiled and started walking towards the parked cars where Kevin and Angel were both waiting. "I love you", Howard yelled as he opened the door to the rented green Ford Taurus that Kevin was waiting in. "I love you, too, baby", Vanessa said, rubbing her stomach with both hands. "I'll be back before you know it", Howard shouted as he got into the car and shut the door.

211

On Everything I Love

Standing in the doorway, Vanessa watched as Kevin pulled off with Angel following right behind them in a rented blue Ford Taurus. Seeing his beautiful wife in the doorway, Howard waved and blew her a big kiss. Blowing back a kiss, tears began slowly falling down Vanessa's face as she watched the cars pull onto the road. Going back inside the house, Vanessa sat down on the couch and continued to cry. Maybe it was her woman's intuition that brought on these sudden tears. Whatever it was, for some strange reason, she could feel that something was wrong.

New York City,
A few hours later...

On a small dark street, Howard and Kevin waited patiently for the yellow cab to arrive. Parked on the opposite side of the street this time, Angel sat inside his rental car, also waiting. He could barely see what was going on because his car was parked behind a large white bread truck. The traffic was moving swiftly up and down the street on this dark Friday night. The sky was pitch black with only a few shining stars showing and a few people walking. Sitting in the passenger seat, Howard tightly held the black briefcase in his hand while clutching his 9mm in his palm under the briefcase. With his Glock 17 tucked in his jeans, Kevin waited, too, as he continued to look through the driver's side window waiting for the cab to arrive.

At that moment, a yellow cab entered the small dark street. Seeing the empty parking space in front of the Ford Taurus, the cab quickly parked. Looking through the cab's back windows, Howard could see there were two men this time inside of the cab. After the cab pulled into the space, Howard watched as a man got out and walked over to Kevin's side of the car.

"What's going on, fellas?" the man said. It was the same man who had brought the fifty kilos on the last trip. "Do you have it?" Kevin asked, staying strictly business. "One hundred of 'em!" he smiled. A short dark-skinned stocky man suddenly got out of the car and walked to the back of the trunk. "They're inside the trunk", the man said to Kevin. "I'll go check it out", Kevin told Howard as he opened the door and got out of the car.

Walking up to the back of the cab's trunk, Kevin waited for the man to open it up so he could check and make sure the product was okay. As the man began opening the trunk, Howard patiently waited with the money and gun inside of the car.

As the trunk slowly opened, Joey quickly sat up catching Kevin off guard. With a loaded .357 Magnum gripped in his hand, he fired two deadly shots into Kevin's unprotected chest before he could react. Death was instant, taking him before his lifeless body slumped to the hard ground. Immediately opening his door, Howard began firing his loaded 9mm. At the same time, RaRa and Guz each pulled out their weapons and began exchanging gunfire with Howard. The few people who were walking outside quickly ran for cover as gunshots and screams filled the air.

As RaRa tried to run behind the cab, Howard shot him once in the back and once in the head. RaRa's body fell to the ground and his blood immediately began covering the sidewalk. Now sitting up in the cab's trunk, Joey began firing into the rented Ford Taurus. Then Guz ran swiftly behind the side of the cab and began unloading his chrome.380. The barrage of gunfire immediately hit Howard twice in the chest and legs. Howard fell to the ground, but not before he fired his final two bullets, hitting Guz in his head. Jumping out of the trunk, Joey approached Howard with his .357 pointed at his head. Looking up at the man who was standing in front of him, Howard realized it was Joey, a ghost from the past.

"Remember me?" Joey said with a vengeful look on his face. "Ready to die, motherfucker?" "Fuck you!" Howard said, holding his bloody chest as he laid breathing heavily in a pool of blood. Before Joey pulled the trigger, three fatal bullets from Angel's 9mm quickly entered the back of Joey's head. Watching Joey's body fall to the ground, Angel quickly ran to Howard's side.

"Howard, are you okay?" Angel shouted. Barely conscious, Howard managed to speak. "I'm not gonna make it, lil man", he said in a low shaky voice. "No! Don't say that." Angel said, grabbing Howard by his arm. "Angel, get out of here", Howard said. "No! Not without you", Angel cried, hearing the sounds of approaching police sirens.

Angel fretfully continued to pull Howard from the ground. "Get out of here, Angel! I'm not gonna make it, but you can", Howard said as he began coughing loudly. "Get the money and leave. Get out of here. Your aunt needs you. I'm counting on you." "Please, Howard! Please! Don't do this!" Angel cried. "I can't leave you like this", he continued. "Get out of here before the cops come. Don't be a fool. I taught you better than that," Howard managed to say, though he felt his life escaping his body.

Looking up at Angel's confused face, Howard could see the fear staring back at him from Angel's watery green eyes. A fear that he had never seen before. "I'll be alright, lil man", he said with a smile on his face. "Six feet under isn't that far down", Howard mumbled as he finally closed both his eyes and died in Angel's arms. "Howard! Howard!" Angel yelled out. "No! No!" he screamed into the New York night.

After laying Howard down, Angel got up off the ground and ran over to the bullet-ridden car. Grabbing the briefcase full of money, Angel looked around at all of the corpses scattered about, each covered in its own blood. Shoving his gun down in his jeans, Angel paused and looked at Kevin's dead body. For a moment, Angel thought he was dreaming, but the loud sirens snapped him out of it and he continued on.

Angel looked inside the cab's trunk, and noticed the two large green duffle bags packed on the trunk sides. Opening up one of the bags to check its contents, he snatched up one of the large duffle bags with his empty hand and dragged it to his car. After placing the briefcase and the duffle bag inside the car, Angel ran back to look at Howard's body one last time. Angel couldn't believe that his mentor was now gone. With tears still falling from his eyes, he pulled his 9mm from the waistband of his jeans, walked over to Joey's corpse and began firing the remainder of his bullets into Joey's face. Then he grabbed the last duffle bag and dragged it to his car and placed it inside with the other one. He quickly got inside the car and started it up. Looking out his window, Angel couldn't believe his tearful eyes as the five dead bodies laid scattered in the street.

When he pulled off all Angel could think about was Howard. The man who taught him everything he knew about life and the game. Angel had finally gotten his wish. He was now the man. However, this was never the way he planned to inherit the throne. He believed Howard would always be there, but someone much higher had other plans.

On Everything I Love

With almost two million dollars in cash, and a hundred kilos of cocaine inside his car, Angel thought about Howard's final words..."Six feet under isn't all that far down". That was the Howard he had always known. A man like no other, a man who stood above all the rest, and a man who accepted the reality of his approaching death-and showed no fear in his final minutes of life. Now the torch was being passed, and Angel was its newest recipient. A torch that Angel had always wanted, but even with Howard's help, he never fully understood it. A million thoughts ran through Angel's head. But his biggest concern now was how could he look into his aunt's eyes and tell her that her husband was dead.

THIRTY-1

After Howard and Kevin's tragic death, Vanessa decided to leave Philadelphia and all of its bad memories far behind. For her, the City of Brotherly Love had never shown her anything but pain and heartache; taking every person she had ever loved to an early grave. After moving to Virginia Beach, seven months later, Vanessa gave birth to a 6-pound, 4-ounce baby boy. She named him Howard Johnson, Jr. after his beloved and never forgotten father.

Vanessa sold the house and Angel moved into a plush center city condominium and he now in charge of Howard's legal and illegal businesses. Howard's two loyal workers, Duran and Sekou, both decided to exit the game after Howard and Kevin's tragic deaths; each taking their money and moving far away from Philly to begin their new lives. Angel quickly recruited a new crew, Pooda, Rodney, and A.L., all of his childhood friends. Alexis was now finishing up her freshman year at Spelman College in Atlanta, Georgia, where she was majoring in Criminal Justice and Pre-Law.

New York City police were still baffled by the brutal shootout that left five young black men gunned down on a Manhattan street. No drugs or money were found, only bodies and guns. And the only clue that police had was from witnesses who said they saw a white man driving away from the scene in a blue Ford Taurus.

A month later, Shiz was convicted by a jury for the attempted murder of a Philadelphia police officer and was sentenced to thirty-eight years in a Pennsylvania maximum security state prison. Angel made sure his friend would never need a dime and had also paid for one of Philadelphia's best attorneys to represent Shiz on his appeal.

Never really getting over Lucky's death, Tisha still remained by Angel's side, helping him and his new crew of hustlers maintain and run her uncle's legacy. While Angel and his young crew were living the life of ghetto superstars, buying cars, jewelry, clothes and everything else that drug money could get them, F.B.I. Special Agent Stan Reynolds was keeping a very sharp eye on Angel and his friends. He was slowly unraveling bizarre clues about the mysterious life of Angel McDaniel.

THIRTY-2
Summer 1998...

Inside her apartment, which was just a few blocks away from Spelman, Alexis and a friend were talking.

"I'm so glad you came down from Philly to visit me, Kelly", Alexis said as she opened up a drawer and pulled out a few old pictures she had. "I missed you, girl, and plus, I needed to get away", Kelly said, lighting a cigarette. "Well, since I don't have to work today, what do you want to do?" Alexis asked, passing Kelly the pictures. "For three days you've been spoiling me. It doesn't really matter", Kelly smiled. "What are these?" she said, looking at the small stack of pictures. "They are more pictures of Angel and me. I still don't believe you don't know him. Everybody knows Angel", Alexis said, smiling at the thought of how popular her man was.

"Like I said, I would always see you getting into a gold Lexus, but I never paid attention to who was driving."

"Well, that's my Boo! And one day he'll be my husband", Alexis said, showing off her diamond engagement ring.

Staring at the photos, Kelly couldn't help but get caught up in Angel's handsome face and dreamy green eyes, but still she played it off.

"Nope, I never saw him before", she said, passing the pictures back to Alexis.

"He's coming here tomorrow. I'll be at work when he gets in town."

"Is he coming by here?" Kelly quickly asked.

"Yeah, he's going to wait here until I get off. He's a nice guy. Wait till you meet him."

"I can't wait", Kelly said, smiling. "Y'all two make a cute couple."

"Thank you, Kelly. He doesn't like me having a job", Alexis said.

"Why not? What's wrong with working?"

"He's just always trying to spoil me, but it will be so boring on this summer vacation if I didn't have a job. Plus, I like working in the laboratory."

"No man really wants his girl to work. I wouldn't if I didn't have to", Kelly smiled.

"I like working. My bosses are real cool, and I'm learning so much about different types of drugs and chemicals that companies use to make things with. My boss, Ronald, said if I wasn't going to be a lawyer, I would be a helluva scientist", Alexis smiled. "I know he's only messing with my head though. He's the only other black person who works there besides me. He's single. Maybe I'll introduce y'all two."

"What does he look like?"

"He's cute. Tall, dark, and okay", Alexis smiled.

"That's okay! I'm working on someone else that I'm very much interested in."

"I wish you luck, girl. Good men are so hard to find."

"I'm not looking for a good one. I'm looking for a bad boy", Kelly smiled.

"You go, girl!" Alexis said, as they both burst out laughing.

"So, do you think you'll get this man you want?"

"When the right time comes, I will", Kelly smiled again.

"Well, you never had a problem with the guys back in high school. Why is this one such a problem?"

"He's not. It's just somebody's in the way, that's all."

"I wish you luck", Alexis said, walking into her bedroom. "Just don't hurt anybody else to get him. It isn't worth it", she hollered out.

"It is to me", Kelly whispered to herself. "It is to me", she repeated as she finished smoking her cigarette and turned on the large T.V. in front of her. Lying across the plush sofa, Kelly continued to think about Angel. Alexis had no idea that her girlfriend from back home had only befriended her for one reason. And that was to do whatever she had to do to get Angel.

Philadelphia, PA...

Driving down 43rd Street in his brand new white 1998 Mercedes Benz 500SL, Angel noticed a strange car had been following him for quite some time. Pooda sat in the passenger's seat listening to music and Rodney, in the back seat, was also enjoying the sounds. Angel made a sudden turn down 42nd and Westminster Avenue, pulling into an empty parking space. Moments later, the tinted black Ford Taurus that had been following Angel drove down the street and turned at the corner. Once the car had turned off the street, Angel quickly pulled out of the space and continued driving down the street. Seeing the car waiting at a traffic light, Angel made a right turn and drove in the opposite direction.

"What wrong?" Pooda asked, noticing the serious expression suddenly appearing on Angel's face. "That black Ford Taurus was the Feds!" Angel said as he continued to drive faster. "The Feds!" Rodney said, as he looked through the back window. "Y'all heard me. The motherfucking Feds were following us!" Angel yelled. "Oh shit! How long do you think they've been tailing us?" Pooda asked. "For a while. And now that I think about it, I remember seeing that same car a few other times, too."
"You sure it was the Feds, Angel?" Rodney asked.

"Man, there are two things that I'm sure of. One, that every man will one day die, and two, those were the motherfucking Feds! Howard told me a long time ago that once you become too big for the local cops, you become first priority for the Feds. Their specialty is convicting men who are untouchable. Niggaz like me."

"Well, if it's them, what should we do?" Pooda asked.

"We're gonna chill for awhile. If they had something, they would have been arrested somebody."

"But you know the Feds could have shit on you, then come snatch you up when you least expect it", Rodney said, shaking his head in disbelief.

"All we can do is wait. I'll call Tisha and tell her to lay low. I'm going to Atlanta tomorrow to see my girl. I'll be gone a few days."

"I'll let everybody know we're on chill status for a while", Rodney said, taking out his cell phone.

"I wonder where they went", Pooda said nervously.

"I don't know, Pooda. With the Feds it can be anything. They were on my Uncle Howard before he was murdered. They wanted him bad."

"Do you think they're on you now?"

"Maybe, but I don't know what for. I've been running a tight operation."

Hanging up his cell phone, Rodney leaned up in the back seat.

"I just got off the phone with A.L."

"Why wasn't he at the pool hall when I picked y'all up?" Angel asked.

"He said he was late. When he got there, Tisha told him we had just left. I told him everything is shut down for now and to let everybody else know."

"What's wrong with that boy? He'll probably be late for his own funeral", Pooda said, as everyone started laughing.

"I want everybody to watch what they say on these phones. From now on, if you have something to say, say it in person."

Pulling into his private parking space outside his condominium complex, everyone got out of the car. Standing in the half empty parking lot, Angel cautiously looked around. Noticing two men inside a telephone company van, Angel walked over to the van and tapped on the window.

"What's up?" the skinny white man who was behind the wheel asked.

"Are y'all gonna lock me up?" Angel said, staring at both men.

"Excuse me, sir!" the black man in the passenger seat said.

"I know y'all are cops. I'm not stupid. Who are y'all, the F.B.I. or DEA?"

"What are you talking about, mister?" the black man asked, with a strange look on his face.

"If y'all aren't cops, then y'all are two lazy mother-fuckers, 'cuz I've been seeing this same telephone van for three days and there isn't anybody in the building whose phone is being worked on yet."

"Mister, we don't know what you're talking about. We're just on our lunch break", the white man said.

Looking at his platinum Rolex watch, he said disbelievingly, "Lunch break, huh, at 4:30 in the afternoon? If y'all aren't the cops, I apologize." Angel started to walk away but paused. "But if y'all are, fuck y'all", he said, turning away and walking towards his friends. Stepping inside his condominium complex with Pooda and Rodney, Angel looked back through the glass door and watched as the telephone van quickly drove off.

"Who was that?" Pooda asked.

223

"They look like cops", Angel said. "I think they're the Feds."

"Man, you just trippin' now", Rodney said. "They're just the telephone company fixing somebody's phone."

"Maybe, maybe not. But if they are the Feds, they know I know now."

Seeing the apartment manager walking down the hall, Angel approached the middle-aged short white man.

"Mr. Stein, do you have a minute?" Angel asked, before he walked into his office.

"Sure, Mr. McDaniel, what is it?"

"Did the telephone company ever come out and fix the problems with the phones?"

"What problem? No one here complained about any telephone problems. Not that I'm aware of."

"Are you sure? I thought I overheard somebody saying the phone service was acting up."

"I would have been notified first. And the telephone company can't get into anyone's apartment unless I give them a key. And I haven't given anybody any keys."

"Thank you, Mr. Stein."

"Is everything okay, Mr. McDaniel?"

"Yes, everything is fine now."

"Oh, you know what, Mr. McDaniel? Someone did call my office and ask if you lived here about a week ago."

"They did?" Angel said, looking confused but very curious.

"Yes, but I told them I wasn't allowed to give out that kind of information to anyone."

"Did they leave a name?"

"No! They just hung up and my caller I.D. said the number was not listed."

"Thanks, Mr. Stein", Angel said, walking down the hall with his friends.

"Like I said, they were the fuckin' cops", Angel added, looking at both his friends.

Unlocking his apartment door, everyone entered the large plush apartment and took a seat on the long, black soft sofa.

"They're on our shit", Rodney nervously said.

"They don't want y'all. They want me! They're watching me. I know they are", Angel said, with a distant look on his face.

Getting up off the sofa, Angel walked over to a closet and took out a large empty suitcase.

"I don't want y'all to tell anybody where I'm going", Angel said.

"How long will you stay down in Atlanta?" Pooda asked.

"I'm not sure, but I want to get out of sight for awhile."

"Well, we're gonna just chill till you get back to Philly then", Pooda said.

"Remember; don't say anything over those phones."

"We won't", Rodney said, standing up to look out the window.

"What do you want us to do in the meantime?" Pooda asked.

"Nothing! Nothing at all! Don't spend any money on anything. Just chill till I get back. I'll see Tisha before I leave for Atlanta and tell her what's happening. Shit is too hot right now. We have to let things cool off."

Looking at Pooda and Rodney's faces, Angel could see the fear in their eyes. "Don't worry, y'all, everything will be okay. Just do as I say." Hearing Angel's positive words, both men's expressions changed. And although they tried not to show fear, both of them were scared as hell; even though they had been forewarned about this side of the game.

On Everything I Love

When Angel walked into his bedroom, he laid the suitcase on his bed and started packing for his trip. He knew he would soon find out the reason that the Feds were watching him so closely.

THIRTY-3
1:15 p.m.
The next day...

Seeing the cab pull up outside Alexis' apartment, Kelly watched as Angel got out of the car holding his large suitcase in his hand. After Angel paid the cab driver, Kelly quickly ran to open the front door. Standing in the doorway in a half cut white tee shirt and a pair of men's boxers, Kelly's seductive body frame quickly grabbed Angel's attention. Her long black hair was still wet from just getting out of the shower, and her fully plumped nipples were on full display, poking through her tee shirt. For a second, Angel thought he was at the wrong apartment until Kelly called his name in her sexiest voice.

"Are you Angel?" she asked, eyeing him up and down.
"Yes. You must be Kelly", Angel said, walking into the apartment.
Closing the door behind him, Angel sat his suitcase down and took a seat on the couch.
"Are you thirsty?" Kelly asked as she strolled in front of Angel with her sexiest walk.
"Yeah, can you get me a glass of cold water, please?"
"As you wish", Kelly said, walking into the kitchen.
"What time does Alexis get off work?" Angel yelled.
"Four o'clock. She gets home around five", Kelly yelled back.
Walking back into the living room, Kelly passed Angel a large glass of cold water and sat down next to him.
"Don't I know you from somewhere? You look so familiar", Angel said, drinking from his glass.

"No! I don't think so", Kelly quickly answered.

"Alexis said you're from Philly", Angel said, grabbing the remote control and turning on the T.V.

"I am. I'm from West Philly."

"Maybe that's where I've seen you. I'm always in West Philly."

"Maybe so, but I stay in the house. I'm not really into the streets like that", Kelly smiled.

"I can't place it, but I know you from somewhere", Angel said, looking into her eyes while trying his hardest not to lust over her gorgeous body.

"Maybe you saw me at school. I went to school with Alexis."

"That's probably it. She told me that y'all went to high school together."

"You go to Spelman, too?"

"No, I go to Community College in Philly. I'm just on summer vacation now. And since I don't have anything to do this summer, I came down to Atlanta to see my homegirl."

"I can't believe you can't find anything to do. Guys should be knocking down your door", Angel smiled.

"They do until they find out that I'm a virgin!"

"What! You a virgin?" Angel said shocked.

"Why do you sound so surprised? Can't a girl be a virgin?" Kelly asked.

"Yeah, I just..."

"Just what, can't believe it? Well, I've never been touched before. I'm waiting for Mr. Right", Kelly smiled.

"Damn!" Angel said, shaking his head in disbelief. "You're gonna make someone a very happy man, Kelly."

"I hope so. I can't wait", Kelly said, getting up off the couch and walking back into the kitchen.

Standing up, Angel walked to the front door.

"I saw this park down the street. I'm going for a walk", Angel yelled.

"Do you want me to walk down there with you?" Kelly said, walking back into the living room with a pint of Haagen-Daz butter pecan ice cream in her hands.

"No, I'm okay. I need to clear my head for a minute."

"If Alexis calls, I'll tell her you're here and that you went for a walk."

"Thank you, Kelly", Angel said, walking out the door.

As Angel walked down the street, Kelly's eyes followed him the entire way. She knew her plan to entice Angel was working. But she also knew that it would take some time.

Walking down the street, Angel couldn't help but think of Kelly's gorgeous body and sex appeal. If she wasn't Alexis' girlfriend, he would have bent her over and started fucking her right in her fat juicy ass. But he would never disrespect his woman, no matter how good her girlfriend looked or made claims of being a virgin. That's why he got up and walked away, because a man will be a man; and sometimes another woman can make even the most loyal man a cheating motherfucker.

Three days later...

Lying in bed next to Alexis, Angel was talking to Tisha on the phone. "What's up, Tish?"

"Nothing. Everything is cool."

"Is everybody chilling?"

"Yup, just laying low, enjoying the nice weather."

"I just wanted to make sure everything is okay. I'll call you back tomorrow."

"Okay. Tell Alexis I said what's up?"

"I will."

"Hold up, I almost forgot. You got some mail yesterday."

229

On Everything I Love

"From who?"

"Your friend, Shiz. He wrote you."

"Do you have it there with you?"

"Yeah, I have it right here."

"Open it up and read it for me."

"One minute", Tisha said, grabbing the letter from off her dresser.

"Hello."

"I'm still here. Go ahead and read it."

After taking the letter out of the envelope, Tisha began reading...

"What's up, dawg? I got that money you sent me. Thanks, nigga. You were always one who kept his word. I'm writing to let you know I'm being transferred soon. I don't know where to, but my counselor told me last week I would be leaving here. Something isn't right, Angel. My counselor asked me if I was still in some type of trouble. I'm telling you, dawg, shit is crazy. Yesterday the Feds came to talk to me. Two motherfuckers in tight ass black suits. All they asked me were questions about you. How long did I know you? Are we related? All types of crazy questions. They got these niggaz on the block thinking I'm a snitch or something. I didn't know these motherfuckers were coming here. Now they're moving me to another joint. Shit is crazy Angel. Anyway, I told them I didn't know shit. Fuck 'em! Them motherfuckers gave me thirty something years. They can kiss my black ass! Look here, dawg, your secrets are safe with me. I'd rather hang than sing, so it ain't nothing. When I get to where I'm going, I'll write you. I don't want to call because I just don't trust these people. They control too much as it is. This is one black man's mind that they won't manipulate.

230

Love, Shizz
"P.S. Death B-4 Dishonor..."

"Hello, Angel, you still there?"
"Yeah, Tish. I heard every word. Thanks. I'll call you tomorrow. Bye."

Hanging up the phone, Angel sat back and thought about all that was going on, realizing sooner or later everything would be out of the dark and into the light.

THIRTY-4
The next day...

While Alexis was at work, Angel was peacefully asleep in the bedroom. A soft knock at the door
quickly woke him up.

"Who is it?" Angel yelled out.

"It's me, Kelly."

"What's up, Kelly?"

"Do you have a minute?"

"Yeah, one second, I'll be right out", Angel said,
pulling on his shorts and tee shirt. After putting on
his sneakers, he walked out of the bedroom. Standing there in a long white men's tee shirt with no underwear underneath, Kelly half smiled.

"Oh, were you still asleep? I'm sorry I woke you."

"It's okay. What's wrong?"

"I need you to help me move the T.V. set in the living room. Alexis said I could redecorate the living
room for her."

Walking into the living room, Angel noticed
how everything had been moved around. "Damn,
you did all of this by yourself?"

"Yup, but the T.V. was just too heavy for me", she
smiled.

Walking over to the T.V., Angel picked it up
with both hands.

"Where do you want it?"

"Over there", Kelly said, pointing at a corner.

Walking over to the corner, Angel sat the T.V.
on top of a wooden stand.

"Thank you, Angel."

"You're welcome. Anything else?" Angel said, noticing she had nothing under her shirt.

"Nope, that's all. I'm alright now. Alexis is so lucky
to have a strong handsome young man like you
around."

"I hope so", Angel smiled, shaking his head.
"You two are a very nice looking couple. It's cool that you don't mind her working around all of those guys at her job."
"All what guys?" Angel asked.
"All of the guys she works with down at the laboratory."
"She never mentioned anything about working around men to me."
"Oh, I'm sorry. I thought you knew about Ronald."
"Who?!" Angel asked, in a harsh tone.
"Ronald, her boss. He calls once in awhile and checks on her."
"Oh, yeah, Ronald, huh?"
"He even gave her a raise a few weeks ago and suggested she change professions. She said he was a real nice man."
"Oh, yeah", Angel said, taking a seat on the couch.
"He's black, too, and the only other black person who works there. She loves her job", Kelly smiled.
"I see why. After I take a shower and get dressed, can I borrow your car?"
"Sure", Kelly said, watching Angel get up and walk into the bedroom.

Philadelphia, PA...

Parked inside a black Ford Explorer Jeep, F.B.I. Special Agent Stan Reynolds and his partner, Mitch Sanders, were talking.
"We have all the information we need now. That black, white, whatever he is, motherfucker is going down", Stan said, smiling.
"He can run but he can't hide", Mitch added.
"We traced his cell phone to a house in Atlanta", Stan smirked.

"Are you going to contact the F.B.I. in Atlanta to arrest him?"

"No, he'll be back. He can't stay away from Philly for long. I can't wait for the day his ass is sitting in his own cell. The info we got from our special witness will bury him. And not even his green eyes will be able to save him. His uncle was murdered before we could get him, but Angel will pay dearly. Hopefully with his life", Stan smirked again.

"Once we cut off the head, the body will crumble. And the rest of his young thugs will all blame him. What a country!"

Taking out a black and white picture of Angel, Stan crossed an X on his face. "It's over, Mr. McDaniel. It's all over", he said, driving away.

That afternoon...

Inside the Pharmacy of Scientific Laboratories where Alexis worked, she and Ronald were separating different pills and putting them into their respective containers.

"What's this one, Ron?" Alexis asked, picking up a small white pill.

"What does it say?"

"Nothing. It just has a capital 'C' on it."

"It's cyanide. That little pill can kill a thousand men."

"Whoa!" Alexis said, putting it inside the small container with the rest of them.

"The 1000 mg of Motrin goes there", Ronald said, pointing to a small brown container.

"I need a few for myself. This shoulder is still killing me from playing basketball the other day", he continued.

"You're getting too old, Ronald. Stop trying to be like Mike", Alexis said, smiling.

"I'm serious, Alexis. I'm gonna have to take a few days off."

"Is it really that bad? Let me see", Alexis said, as she stood behind him checking.

"I see a little knot. All you need is a few Motrin and a good massage."

"A massage won't help me. I need more than that. My shoulder is killing me."

Putting both of her hands softly around Ronald's neck, Alexis began to massage his hurting shoulder.

"How does that feel?" Alexis asked, digging her soft hands deep into his flesh.

"Not bad!" Ronald smiled. "I had better."

"Just give me a minute", Alexis said, playfully. "I only do this for my man, so be grateful."

At the same time, Angel had just entered the lobby of the laboratory and approached the front desk.

"Yes, may I please help you?" a short older white woman asked.

"Yes, does an Alexis Lambert work here?"

"Yes, and who may I tell her you are?"

"Her fiancé. My name is Angel."

"Oh, you're Angel. She's right down the hall, first door on the left", the lady said, pointing down a hallway.

"She told me if you came to just let you in."

"Thank you very much", Angel said as he started walking down the hall.

As Angel approached the door, he could hear Ronald's voice on the other side. "Oh, that feels a lot better, Alexis. Girl, you are one of a kind." In a mad rage, Angel burst into the room. Seeing Alexis' hands down Ronald's back, Angel quickly grabbed Ronald and threw him to the ground. Before the shocked Alexis could say a word, Angel was punching Ronald in his face with hard fierce blows. Even Alexis' screams couldn't stop Angel from brutally beating Ronald down like he stole something. Angel continued to deliver blow after blow to a dazed and bloody Ronald as he tried to shield himself.

"Angel, stop! Please! You're gonna kill him!!" Alexis screamed out.

Finally, seeing Alexis tearfully crying and screaming, Angel stopped. As Ronald's brutalized body slumped to the floor, Alexis continued to scream.

"What were you doing massaging his back?" Angel yelled.

"It's not what you think! It was nothing. He's only a friend."

"Yeah, okay, do I look stupid to you? Do I look like a fuckin' fool, Alexis?"

"Angel, leave now. I'll talk to you later when I get home."

"Fuck you, bitch!" Angel shouted out in frustration.

With all of her strength, Alexis smacked Angel across his face, leaving a bright red mark.

"Angel, leave, just leave!" she said as a cascade of tears began falling from her eyes. "Is this how it is?" Angel said, looking into Alexis' watery brown eyes.

"Just leave. I said I'll talk to you later", Alexis said, walking over to help Ronald. "Ronald, are you okay?" Alexis asked in a concerned voice.

Standing there looking at Alexis holding the bloody Ronald in her arms, Angel walked away, slamming the door behind him.

"I'm fine", Ronald said, wiping the blood from his mouth.

"I'm so sorry, Ronald. I don't know what got into him."

"I'm alright, Alexis. Don't worry about it. I understand how he felt. We were in an awkward position", Ronald said, trying to smile through his pain.

"Are you sure you're okay?"

"I'm fine, just a busted lip. I'll manage", Ronald said, standing up.

"I feel so embarrassed. Everything just happened so fast", Alexis said, helping Ronald to a seat.

"Its love, that's all", Ronald said.

"If that's love, then I don't ever want to see his pain", Alexis said, shaking her head.

"Me either", Ronald said. "I've never seen a man that jealous before."

"I swear Angel never acts like that."

"Maybe you've just never seen it."

"Well...when we were very young, but we were kids then."

"Some people never change, Alexis. We just overlook their faults. Sometimes love blocks our vision", Ronald said, walking into the bathroom.

"I'll talk to him later when I get off. We need to have a serious talk today."

"Yes, do that. Next time might be much different", Ronald said, closing the door behind him. Standing there with a confused look on her face, Alexis couldn't believe what had just taken place. As she wiped away her tears, inside her heart she was still crying.

THIRTY-5
Thirty minutes later...

Walking back into the apartment, Angel sat down on the couch. Looking at his fist, he noticed it was cut and bleeding. Coming from the kitchen, Kelly saw Angel holding his bloody hand and quickly ran to his side.

"What happened? Are you okay?"

"I'm fine. I got into a little fight", Angel said.

"With who?"

"Alexis' friend at her job."

"What! With Ronald?"

"Yeah, him. I think she's been cheating on me", Angel said.

"Don't worry about it. Everything will work itself out."

"No, no, I don't think so. She crossed me, she lost me", Angel said.

"What happened to your face?"

"Alexis smacked me."

"She smacked you. Why?"

"Showing off for that nigga. I'm outta here. I'm going back to Philly."

"You just chill for a minute and first let me take care of that hand", Kelly said, getting up and running into the bathroom.

When she came out, Kelly held a wet white washcloth in her hand. "Give me your hand", she said. Angel held his hand out to Kelly who gently started wiping away the blood. Running back into the bathroom, she rinsed out the washcloth and hurried back to Angel's side. With the cold cloth, she began gently wiping it across his face.

"Oh, this is a pretty bad mark on your face."

"I'm alright. I just have to get out of here and get back to Philly before I fuck around and kill something."

"Calm down. It's not that bad. Alexis loves you."

"Yeah, me and who else?" Angel sarcastically said.

"Hold up one minute. I have something that will help calm you down", Kelly said, running into her bedroom.

Moments later, Kelly walked back out holding a lit joint in her hand and two unlit joints in the other hand.

"You smoke weed?"

"Not really. Once in a while", Angel answered.

"Here, just try it. It will calm you down, trust me", Kelly said, passing the lit joint to Angel. Taking a strong puff of the joint, Angel sat back and let his mind enjoy the high. Lighting up another joint, Kelly sat back next to him and began smoking her own joint. "Feel better?" she asked. "A little. This is some good weed", Angel said, taking another strong puff, letting it smoothly flow through his lungs.

"Yeah, I needed that."

"Girl, you're full of surprises", Angel said as he finished smoking his joint.

"So you feel better now?"

"Yup, too good", Angel said, standing up and walking towards the bedroom.

"Where are you going?"

"To lay down. That weed got me feeling too good."

Walking into the bedroom, Angel took off his sneakers and lay across the bed. Moments later, Kelly entered the room. Looking up, Angel noticed Kelly standing there in front of him totally naked.

"Whoa!" Angel said, starring at Kelly's gorgeous naked body. "Just chill and don't say a word", Kelly said, pulling down his sweat shorts. "Hold up! I can't do this. You're Alexis' friend", Angel said.

Paying his words no mind, Kelly reached out and grabbed Angel's rock hard dick with her hands, then inserted all of Angel's hardness into her wet warm mouth. "Oh, shit" Angel said as Kelly slowly began sucking him non-stop. Even if Angel wanted to, the feeling was just too enjoyable to stop her. The combination of the weed and the blowjob was overwhelming. Closing his eyes, Angel firmly gave in and let both aphrodisiacs do their job, the wonderful weed and Kelly's soft juicy warm lips. Feeling Angel was ready to release, Kelly gripped her lips tightly. As Angel released, Kelly swallowed every single bit of him without letting a drop get away.

"Oh, my God!" Angel yelled as Kelly continued to swallow him whole. As Angel lay motionless on the bed, Kelly finally released her deadly lips and slowly began to climb on top of Angel's still hard dick. Inserting every inch inside of her soaking wet pussy, Kelly began to ride Angel like he had never been ridden before. Up and down she went as Angel guided her thriving hips with both hands. "Oh, Angel, this dick feels so good!" Kelly screamed out. "Yes! Yes!" she yelled.

But Angel remained silent. The feeling was too good to comment on. He was only thinking of two things as he was being pleased by this gorgeous woman. One, how well she could fuck and two, she lied about being a virgin. As the two of them continued to indulge in their sexual activity, neither of them heard Alexis enter the apartment.

Walking into her bedroom, Alexis' heart dropped a thousand feet seeing her man and girlfriend having untamed and intense sex. Her loud scream quickly interrupted both of them. If her tears could talk, that moment they would have asked to die. Seeing the only man she had ever loved having sex with another woman was worse than death.

"Angel, how could you do this to me?!" she screamed out. "How could you?" Pushing Kelly to the side, Angel quickly grabbed his shorts and put them on. As Alexis fell to her knees crying, Kelly quickly ran into the other room.

"I'm sorry, baby! Please forgive me! I don't know what I was thinking" Angel said, kneeling down to her side. "I don't believe you, Angel", Alexis said. "I thought I could trust you. How could you?" she yelled. "I'm sorry, baby. I just wasn't thinking straight", Angel sadly said.

Looking into Angel's eyes, Alexis could tell he had been smoking weed. The smell of the marijuana was still lingering throughout the apartment. "I can't believe you're in my apartment smoking weed and fucking my girlfriend. Do you have any respect for me at all? Do you?" Putting his arms around Alexis, Angel tried to comfort his grieving and heartbroken girlfriend.

"Get your fuckin' hands off me!" Alexis screamed. "Get away from me! Get out! Please, just leave me alone!"

"Alexis, I'm sorry, baby. Don't do this!" Angel begged.

"You did this, Angel! You did it", Alexis said as she stood up and sat at the foot of her bed.

"Angel, please, just leave, please!" Alexis said as her tears continued to fall from her eyes.

"I love you, Alexis. Why are you doing this? You're all I've got left in this world."

"I was all that you had left, but now you have nothing! Nothing!"

"You don't mean that."

"Right now, Angel, I do", Alexis said as she took off her diamond engagement ring and threw it at Angel's feet.

"Please, just leave me alone" she yelled.

After taking a long deep breath, Angel stood up and walked to the door.

"So it's over?" Angel asked.

Staring at Angel with her brown watery eyes, Alexis remained silent.

"Is it over, Alexis? Just tell me."

Still Alexis said nothing.

"Is it the fuck over, I said?"

"It's over, Angel. It's over", Alexis finally said, putting her head down.

After grabbing a pair of jeans and a shirt from off of the dresser, Angel put on his sneakers, looked at Alexis one last time and walked away. Upon hearing the front door shut, Alexis started crying like a lost child, knowing she had just lost the only man she had ever loved.

THIRTY-6
Two days later...

Inside his plush condo, Angel, Pooda, and Rodney were all talking. A few moments earlier, Tisha had dropped off a half million dollars in cash inside a black briefcase, then left.

"You still haven't heard from Alexis?" Pooda asked.

"No, she hasn't called", Angel answered in a sad voice.

"Don't worry about it, man. She'll be calling you soon", Rodney said.

"Yeah, Angel, she's just upset, that's all", Pooda added, trying to cheer his friend up.

"Not this time. She's worse than just upset", Angel said.

"Stop stressing, dawg. She'll be back", Pooda said with a smile.

"Whatever comes of this, it's definitely been a learning experience", Angel said.

"What did you learn?" Rodney asked, wondering.

"I learned that lust isn't anything but the devil. And love is heaven. That's why in order to get to heaven we must conquer lust first."

"What's lust?" Rodney asked.

"Money, greed, sex, women, power, and the list goes on", Angel said.

"How could you ever conquer all of that?" Pooda asked.

"With love. Love can conquer anything", Angel said, looking at a picture that hung on the wall of him and Alexis when they were both kids.

Hearing the phone ring, Angel quickly answered.

"Hello."

"Yo, it's me, A.L. I'm downstairs in the lobby. Buzz me in."

On Everything I Love

"Okay", Angel said, pressing a button on the phone.

"Who's that?" Rodney asked.

"A.L.", Angel said as he continued to stare at the picture on the wall.

"Can he ever be on time?" Pooda laughed.

"Nope, that boy will be late to his own funeral", Rodney said jokingly.

Hearing a knock at the door, Rodney walked over and opened the door for A.L.

"What's up, fellas?" A.L. said, walking in holding a large briefcase.

"Here, Angel, one million. It's all there", he said, sitting the briefcase next to three other similar black briefcases situated in front of Angel's feet.

"That's all the money people owed you while you were out of town...my $200,000, Pooda's $200,000, Tisha's $500,000, and A.L.'s $100,000. One million dollars!" Rodney said, adding everything up.

"We told everybody things would be shut down for a while also", Pooda said.

"Angel, do you hear me?" Pooda asked.

"I hear you, Pooda", Angel said, waking from his momentary daze. With one million dollars in cash sitting at his feet; still all he could think about was Alexis.

"What's wrong with you, man?" A.L. asked, seeing Angel with a withdrawn expression on his face.

"My girl", Angel said in a sad voice.

"What's wrong with Alexis?" Is she okay?" he asked.

"We broke up a few days ago!"

"What! How? What happened? I know you're joking, right?"

"Nope! I'm serious as a heart attack."

"Damn, dawg, y'all will work it out", A.L. said.

"I don't know, man. I really don't know."

"What happened?"

"I got caught fucking one of her girlfriends in her apartment when I went to visit her."

"What! Nigga, you crazy? Was it one of her college girlfriends?"
"No, one of her girlfriends from Philly who was visiting her. Her name is Kelly."
"Kelly?! What does she look like?" A.L. said.
"She's pretty, light brown skinned, big titties, about 5'6", and she's from West Philly."
"Oh, shit I don't believe that girl", A.L. said.
"What are you talking about A.L.?"
"Remember that time I had that Toyota 4-Runner with those girls inside?"
"Yeah", Angel said. "I remember. Last year."
"Well, remember the girl who wanted to meet you real bad, but you found out they all went to Central High School with Alexis, so you said never mind?"
"Yeah, so what?" Angel said.
"That was Kelly. She said she was going to get you, but I didn't know she was a fatal attraction bitch."
"Oh, shit! I knew I saw her face somewhere. She said that she didn't know me."
"She's lying. She's been trying to get you for years."
"She set me up!" Angel shouted. "That no-good bitch! And she had the nerve to say she was still a virgin!"
"A virgin?! What?! Man, half of the football team fucked her", A.L. laughed. "She was a cheerleader. You never paid her no mind 'cuz you never took your eyes off Alexis."
"'Cuz, that's my girl! I gotta keep an eye on her."
"It's okay to keep an eye on your girl, Angel, but keep the other eye on the snakes and predators that are lurking around", A.L. said.
"That bitch set me up! She had me smoking weed and all types of foul shit!"
"Smoking weed?!" Rodney said.
"Yeah, I was trippin'. Damn! I fucked up big time", Angel said, shaking his head in disbelief.

"I could kill that bitch", Angel shouted.

"Cool *out,* man!" Pooda said.

"I don't like anybody playing me like a sucker, especially some no-good ass bitch!"

"Let it go, Angel. Just let it go", Pooda said.

"I lost my girl over that whore!"

"Angel, I'm sorry, but you can't just blame her", Pooda said. "You're just as much to blame."

"But I was set up!"

"But you still fucked her. You could have just said no", Pooda counter attacked. "I'm pretty sure you knew that girl liked you. You've never been stupid, so don't play dumb now."

Looking at Pooda, a smile came to Angel's face.

"Yeah, y'all right. I knew from the moment we met she was on me, and was going to be trouble. I caught her looking at me a few times and just played it off. In the front of my mind, no woman could make me cross my girl, but in the back of my mind...who knows."

"I'm sorry about you and Alexis, homeboy, but if it's true love like it's been since y'all were both children in the same crib, then it will last till the grave. No woman can destroy that", Pooda said.

"Yeah, man, give her some time. She'll be back", A.L. said.

"She's probably going through it, too", Rodney added.

"I hope she's smart enough to see that Kelly isn't any good", Angel said.

"Alexis is smart. She will. I'm sure she knows now", A.L. said.

"I hope so, 'cuz I don't want Alexis around any she-devil like that."

"Anyway, what about this money?" Pooda said, changing the subject.

"Tisha will be back here in about an hour. We are taking a trip down to Virginia Beach to drop this money off at my Aunt Vanessa's house. We'll be back tomorrow afternoon. I'll call y'all and let y'all know when I'm back."

Everyone got up and shook Angel's hand and gave warm hugs.

"I'll see you tomorrow", Pooda said, walking out of the apartment.

"Me too", A.L. said. "And I won't be late", he added, laughing.

"Me too", Rodney said, walking out the door and shutting it behind them.

Now sitting alone, Angel continued to stare at the picture of him and Alexis as he silently prayed to God to bring him back the love of his life.

THIRTY-7
Later that night...

    Inside Angel's white 500SL Mercedes Benz, he and Tisha sat talking. "What's wrong with you, Tisha?" Angel asked, seeing the unsociable look on her face.

"Nothing!" Tisha answered quickly.

"I know when something is wrong with you. Now stop lying. What is it?"

"I'm scared, Angel!" Tisha said, looking into Angel's eyes.

"What! What are you scared of?"

"Something just isn't right."

"What are you talking about, Tisha?"

"Everything, Angel. Every fucking thing!" Tisha screamed out loud.

"Will you talk to me and stop talking in riddles", Angel said.

"Angel, shit is all fucked up! And you've been too blind to see what's going on around you."

"What are you talking about, girl?" a confused Angel asked.

"I'm talking about the damn Feds! The murders! My Uncle Howard! And this fucking blood money, Angel!" Tisha said, pointing to the million dollars in cash that was inside the black briefcase she was holding.

"What?"

"You heard me, Angel. My Uncle Howard loved you like his own son. He wanted you to be better than he could ever be. He groomed you to take what he had and turn it into something positive. Something unbreakable. You were his protégé, his soldier. But you changed, Angel. You changed."

    With a lost look on his face, Angel continued to listen.

"When Uncle Howard was alive, everything was well organized. Now look. Look at us, Angel. We're nothing but low-life drug dealers. Drug dealers who kill to have it all. Tell me, Angel, is it worth it? I killed my first love for this shit! And that shit scares the hell out of me!!" Tisha yelled.

"Why are you so scared, Tisha? Nobody knows."

"Because Angel, maybe you don't realize it, but one day we'll be judged. We have to answer to someone, too! Even with all the money I have, all of the cars and clothes, I still feel like nothing! Nothing! Nobody! Remember when my uncle would tell us this was a game that nobody wins in, so get in, get rich, and get out?"

"Yeah, I remember", Angel said, as he thought back to that time.

"Well, all we got was caught up", Tisha said.

"So Tish what are you saying?"

"I'm saying, Angel, I'm afraid something will happen to you. That some crazy jealous motherfucker will shoot you or something. Or that you'll go to jail and never get out. And I'd rather see you dead than suffering inside a cold lonely cell by yourself."

"Tisha, you don't have to worry about that. I'm okay", Angel said as he continued to drive.

"My uncle thought that! Kevin thought that, too. Lucky thought that, also. Your teacher even thought that! You're not God! You're only an angel! Stop thinking that you're untouchable!" Tisha shouted.

"I'm only telling you this because I love you, boy", Tisha continued, as her eyes released tears of anguish. "I always loved you, and I can't stand the thought of anything ever happening to you."

"Tisha, I'll be alright. Stop worrying yourself. But if anything ever did happen to me, I want you to know everything is yours."

"I'd rather have you here than any amount of money in the world."

"I know, Tisha, but I'm just saying what's true. If I ever get caught up in any type of shit, remember, everything is all yours, Tisha. But I'll be okay."

Tisha remained silent as Angel pulled into the driveway of his aunt's beautiful beach house. Holding the briefcase full of cash, Tisha along with Angel got out of the car and went inside.

Inside the F.B.I. Headquarters in Philadelphia...

Stan Reynolds sat all alone looking at pictures of Angel and his crew. Crossed out were the faces of Howard, Kevin, and Shiz.

"A few more to go! You've been lucky so far, Angel, but your luck has finally run out, buddy", he mumbled to himself. "I will personally make sure that you get the death penalty for what you've done", he said, picking up Angel's picture. "Finally, I have someone who can take you down, Angel. And unlike the other witnesses, this one you can't do anything about. It's over, pretty boy! It's over!" Stan said, putting all of the pictures back inside a brown folder.

Walking out of his office, Stan saw a tall white man who appeared to be a doctor of some type walking down the stairs.

"George, did you check it again?" Stan said, catching up to him. "Yes, Stan, it's official. 99.9 percent. Nothing's changed. It's totally unbelievable, but it's true", George said, shaking his head. "Thank you, George. Thank you and your staff for everything."

"You're welcome, Stan. Now please go home and rest. This case is killing you. You can't stay here forever. You have to go home sometime, Stan."

"I'll go home and rest tonight now that I have what I needed", Stan smiled. "99.9 percent" Stan said as he and George both exited the back of the building and into the parking lot, where both of their cars were waiting.

As George watched Stan get into his Ford Explorer and drive off, he thought about his friend and how obsessed he was with solving the case, a case that would destroy so many people's lives. But he also knew if Stan didn't win the case, it would destroy his own career and his life.

THIRTY-8

After Angel dropped off the million dollars, he and Tisha began their long trip back to Philadelphia. While in Virginia, Angel was excited about seeing his Aunt Vanessa and his two younger cousins. Although his visits were brief, Angel would go visit his family at least once a month, and with every visit, he would bring with him a briefcase full of money. Only three people knew about Angel's large sums of money, Tisha, Aunt Vanessa and Angel. No one else knew this 18-year-old man had millions of dollars locked safely inside his late uncle's steel safe in a secret compartment he had made under his aunt's basement.

Early the next morning...

After dropping Tisha off at home, Angel called his crew and asked them to meet him at his condominium. After about an hour, the first to arrive was Pooda. Ten minutes later, Rodney showed up. After having asked everyone to meet him there at 9:30 a.m., at ten o'clock, Angel found they were still waiting for A.L. to arrive, who was bringing another $100,000 and a box of brand new 9mm's with him. "Where is that nigga?" Angel said, looking at his platinum Rolex watch.
"Its five after ten now! What's wrong with the boy?" Angel said.
"You know A.L., Angel. He is never gonna be on time", Pooda said.
"He has these new guns I bought, a whole box of nines." Angel said.
"He'll be here. He's probably getting some gas or something", Rodney responded.

"Anyway, like I was saying", Angel said, changing the subject. "Tisha and I were talking last night and she made a lot of sense. We don't have to hustle anymore, fellas. We made it. We're all out of the ghetto and all of our families are well taken care of. Who would have ever thought that a bunch of young Philly boys would be young millionaires before they turned twenty-one years old? Tell me, who? All from drug money. We all have nice cars and plenty of paper. What's left?"

"Angel, are you trying to tell us something?" Rodney asked.

"Yeah, it sounds like you're trying to say something", Pooda said.

"I am! I've really been thinking a lot, ya'll. A whole lot. I've been thinking about all of y'all, your families, my family, my uncle's legacy, my woman who I haven't spoken to in days, and my own life, also."

"What is it then?" Pooda asked.

Looking into Pooda's eyes, Angel took a long deep breath.

"I'm tired of killing our own people. I just can't do it anymore, y'all! I'm tired of seeing so many of God's original people slowly dying from the evils of their own brothers."

"But aren't you the one who said winners never quit and quitters never win?" Rodney said, waiting for an answer.

"Yes, Rodney, I did say that, but we've won already! We've won! If yesterday you were poor and today you're rich, then tomorrow you enjoy your rides. I did all I set out to do. My goals have been conquered. I'm eighteen years old and I would like to live to be a hundred and eighteen, God willing. In a few more months, I'll be nineteen. I've got to start enjoying my life with those who truly care and love me."

"We love you, dawg!" Pooda said.

"And I love y'all. All of y'all. That's why I want us all to walk away before we're all carried away", Angel said sadly.

Hearing the phone ring, Angel quickly answered.

"Hello."

"It's me. Buzz me in", A.L. said from the downstairs lobby.

After buzzing A.L., Angel hung up the phone. "That's A.L. I'm gonna tell him what I told y'all", Angel said.

Inside the elevator, A.L. never paid any attention to the two undercover F.B.I. agents that were dressed in janitor uniforms holding brooms and mops in their hands. As they all got off on the same floor, another two men dressed in the same janitor uniforms and a black female who had on a maid's outfit were all talking.

Holding a black briefcase full of money in one hand and another box full of brand new 9mm handguns in the other, A.L. calmly walked down the hall. Walking by the attractive black female, A.L. winked his eye at her and smiled. As she smiled back, A.L. never knew he had just flirted with an undercover F.B.I. special agent. Reaching for the door handle, he walked inside.

"What's up, fellas?" He greeted them and sat the box of guns on a large glass table.

"Here you go" he said, passing Angel the briefcase full of money.

"Why does everybody look so sad?" A.L. said.

"What took you so long, man?" Angel asked.

"I'm here now. That's all that matters", A.L. said, smiling.

"Man, that maid y'all have is one pretty woman" he continued.

"What maid?" Angel asked.

"The black chick who works here", A.L. responded. "She's out in the hallway talking to two white janitors. You know all of them white dudes want to fuck a sister", he said as everyone except Angel started laughing.

"What are you talking about, A.L. The janitor up here is an old Spanish man named Mr. Sanchez. And the maid is Spanish, too, and she only works on the weekends", Angel said.

"Well, they must have fired him, 'cuz I saw about four or five janitors walking around. And like I said, the maid is a pretty black sister."

Quickly standing up, Angel grabbed the box of guns from the glass table.

"What's wrong?" Pooda asked.

"They're not janitors or maids. They're the fuckin'..."

Hearing a loud crash at the door, Angel knew who it was without finishing his sentence. Four white undercover F.B.I. agents along with a black F.B.I. female agent rushed in holding loaded guns and demanding everyone to get on the floor, which everyone quickly did.

"The Feds!" A.L. said, realizing he had seen these same individuals who were on the elevator with him. Looking up at the female who had a gun pointed at him, he shook his head in disbelief. "Bitch", he mumbled. Dressed in a janitor's uniform, Agent Stan Reynolds knelt down. Looking into Angels' open eyes with a smirk on his face, he began speaking.

"Mr. Angel McDaniel, you have been indicted by a federal grand jury for the double murder of a Mr. Peter Smith and a Mr. John Williams. You have the right to remain silent. Anything you say will be held against you in a court of law. You have the right to an attorney and a fair trial." As Agent Reynolds continued to read Angel his Miranda rights,

Pooda, Rodney, and A.L. remained silent and at the same time very scared. While Agent Reynolds cuffed Angel, another one of the F.B.I. agents opened up the brown box that was lying next to Angel's head. "Oh, shit! What do we have here?" he said, taking out one of the brand new guns from inside the box. "A box of illegal handguns." He smiled as he passed the box to Agent Reynolds. "Now everyone is going downtown", Reynolds smiled. "Why? It's all mine! Those are my guns, all of them. Let them go", Angel yelled. "Shut up!" Stan ordered. "Handcuff them all", he told his agents. "And what's this?" Stan asked, picking up the black briefcase. "It's my money!" Angel shouted.

Opening up the briefcase, Stan's eyes almost popped out of their sockets upon seeing the large stacks of hundreds all neatly packed inside. "Whoa! I think we hit the jackpot with this one", he said. Passing the box of guns to one of his agents, Stan said he would hold the money to make sure it was used for evidence. After everyone was handcuffed and read their rights they were taken outside and put inside a waiting black F.B.I. van. Everyone, that is, except Angel who was placed in the back of Stan Reynolds' car.

"It's over, Angel", he said, pulling out of the parking lot and driving away. "Your uncle was lucky, but you're not", he smiled.
"I don't know what you're talking about", Angel said calmly.
"Oh you know so you can stop playin' games now."
"I don't know shit!" Angel shouted.
"You fuckin' liar! You know exactly what I'm talking about!" Stan screamed. "I know you had something to do with your teacher's husband murder! And I know you also played a part in Lucky and our informant being murdered as well. You can't fool me, motherfucker! I know your type. I've been watching

your every move for over a year. You're nothing like your uncle. You're nothing but a murderer who thinks he owns the world. I don't know how you pulled it off but I know you did it. I just know."

Angel remained silent as Agent Reynolds continued on.

"You're trash! If I could, I would kill you right now, you dirty son of a bitch! Ever since I was young, guys like you have always been getting over, thinking y'all are above the law. The looks, the money, the fame. I lost the only woman that I ever loved over some guy like you. For all of my misery, you'll pay! When they sentence you to death I hope I'm granted permission to be the one who'll strap you in the chair! Your uncle only escaped us because he was killed in New York. But there's no way out for you. You can't escape!"

Angel said nothing as he remained calm and quiet. Even though he realized this man had something very personal against his Uncle Howard and was taking it all out on him. Angel also realized something that was buried much deeper. He realized this man was full of so much hatred because everything he had ever loved was taken away from him. Now his only love was his job. And his only happiness was seeing men like Angel being taken off the streets to either a cell or a grave...with his preference being the latter of the two.

THIRTY-9
Three days later
Inside the County Jailhouse...

Angel sat calmly inside a small room having a conversation with his high-priced lawyer. Anthony Rozzetti was his name, and he was considered one of Philadelphia's top attorneys for beating homicides and beating the Feds. Just one year earlier, he had gotten three men from the South Philadelphia mob acquitted on murder, racketeering, and drug distribution, making the federal government very upset with him. But no one disliked him more than F.B.I. Special Agent Stan Reynolds, the man who had investigated all three men for more than two years and frustratingly watched all three men walk away scot free. From that day on, Stan had a dislike for defense attorneys, but none more than Anthony Rozzetti.

In his long orange jumpsuit, Angel sat quietly across from his lawyer. Anthony Rozzetti was a tall, slim, dark-haired man with a soft voice and a smooth style.

"The grand jury has indicted you on two counts of conspiring to murder and murder. But that's not our problem, Angel."

"It's not?" Angel said in a totally surprised voice.

"No, our problem is much bigger", Anthony said, closing his briefcase.

"What can be much bigger than murder?" Angel asked.

"Revenge! Revenge, Angel, and his name is Stan Reynolds", Anthony said.

"The crazy cop who locked me up?" Angel asked, sounding confused.

"Yes, him. He's been mad at me ever since I got three men acquitted. Three men that he investigated for two years. It's very personal with him. He'll do anything he has to do to win this case. And I mean anything!"

"I don't care. I still want you to represent me, Tony. You're the best in the city. You're my only chance and my only choice."

With a grin on his face, Anthony agreeably shook his head.

"How have they been treating you in here?" Anthony asked.

"I'm cool, the food is some shit. A nurse came by to take some blood today."

"For what?"

"She said that they take blood samples from all of the new inmates."

"Oh I guess it's for some type of health require-ment", Tony said.

"Tony, if it's more money you need, I'll get Tisha to bring you another $150,000."

"Whoa! Slow down. One hundred fifty thousand was enough."

"How come they won't give me bail?"

"They think you are a flight risk. The government knows that you're a very rich young man."

"So what does that have to do with anything?" Angel shouted.

"A lot. They are afraid you might leave the country."

"I'm tired of being here, being in these clothes. This shit is depressing, Tony!"

"I understand, Angel. Believe me, I do, but until trial starts, you're gonna have to be here. The good thing is that you are separated from all the other inmates because of the status of this case. So, you'll have plenty of time to think about what's important to you."

"How long will it be till trial?"

On Everything I Love

"Soon. The government seems to think they have an open and shut case. They were prepared for a trial."
"So how long?"
"Maybe a month, somewhere around mid-October."
"That's a long time to be here", Angel said, sounding distressed.
"You'll make it."
"So what do you think, Tony? Seriously!"
"I'd rather not say, Angel, but I'll try my best to win this case. You can count on that. I'm also thinking about bringing in another lawyer to help me. It's gonna be one helluva trial."
"Who do you have in mind?"
"I have a few people who called to help me with this case. Smart, bright, intelligent attorneys, especially one who contacted me yesterday with very high credentials", Anthony smiled.
"Well, whatever they want to help you, I'll pay them up to $75,000.
"Angel, slow down, first things first. I have a lot of work to do, pretrial motions and getting ready for trial. You'll be the first to know if I choose to use another lawyer. I'll try my best to get this trial started as soon as possible. This is not a piece of cake, Angel. You're being charged with a double homicide", Anthony said, standing up.
"I'll be back here in a few days. I've got so much paperwork to do, and I plan on meeting the other lawyer sometime this week to talk about your case. This has been a stressful couple of days. Just getting your three friends released was a headache. Even though the Feds had nothing on them, Stan made sure everything was difficult for me. Getting the guns thrown out will be easy, but beating this double murder will take all that I've got."
"What about the money they got?"
"The government is holding the $80,000 for evidence. You'll have to wait."

"Eighty thousand! It was $100,000 in the briefcase", Angel said.

"Well $80,000 is what was reported in the F.B.I. statements."

"Those no good motherfuckers!" Angel shouted, shaking his head in disbelief.

"They are known to do much worse, my friend", Anthony said. "Anyway, I have an important meeting this afternoon, and tomorrow morning I have to meet with the Federal U.S. Prosecutor. You take care, my friend", Anthony said, shaking Angel's hand and walking out of the small room. Moments later, an armed guard walked in and escorted Angel back upstairs to his cold, lonely cell.

~~~

Inside Tisha's apartment, she and A.L. were talking.

"Do you think he's gonna beat it, Tish?"

"I don't know, A.L. I seriously don't know", Tisha said, wiping the falling tears from her face.

"We just had this talk. I knew something was gonna happen" she said.

"Why didn't they give him bail?"

"I don't know why they didn't. His lawyer didn't say why."

"How was he yesterday when you went to see him?"

"He's holding up. You know Angel is alright and can handle himself."

"I know he's going through it, and missing the hell out of Alexis. Did you   talk to her?"

"Yeah, I talked to her today. She's still very upset with him for some strange reason."

"Oh, you don't know what happened?" A.L. asked.

"What are you talking about, A.L.?"

"They broke up because of some chick!"

"What chick?"

261

"Some girl named Kelly who was on him and set him up. She went to high school with Alexis and had secretly liked Angel for years. When Angel went down to Atlanta, she was there visiting Alexis and the two of them had..."

"Sex!" Tisha said.

"Yeah, but she told Angel lies about Alexis and her boss, and had him and Alexis arguing and all types of shit."

"Why didn't he tell me this?"

"Maybe he didn't want you to know, Tisha."

"So that's why he was so sad and kept asking me did I hear from Alexis."

"Probably so. They haven't talked in over a week or longer. It's killing Angel inside."

"Do you know where this girl lives, A.L.?"

"Yeah, she lives in West Philly. Why?"

"Don't ask questions, just come on", Tisha said, grabbing her car keys from the coffee table.

"What is it? Why do you want to meet her?"

"You'll see. Now come on, boy."

Tisha quickly rushed out the door with A.L. closely behind her. After getting inside her new 1998 yellow convertible Mercedes Benz, Tisha and A.L. headed to West Philly.

FORTY
An hour later...

Tisha and A.L. pulled up in front of Kelly's house. Sitting inside her car, Tisha remained quiet. At the same time, A.L. spotted Kelly walking down the street holding a brown shopping bag in her hand.

"There she is, right there", A.L. said, pointing at Kelly who never saw them sitting inside the car. "You sure that's her?" Tisha asked, grabbing her small black purse from under the seat. "Yeah, that's her. I'm sure" he said. "Ride around the block. I'll be right back", Tisha said as she quickly got out of the car and walked towards Kelly. A.L. slid over behind the wheel and drove down the street as Tisha had ordered.

Tisha walked up to Kelly, opened her small purse and pulled out a brand new shiny chrome .380 handgun.

"Bitch, you better not scream!" Tisha said pushing Kelly in between two parked cars so no one could see what was going on. Nervously shaking, Kelly didn't utter a word. Looking into Tisha's eyes, she knew she was in some deep shit and one false move could end her life.

"Bitch, do you know why I'm here?" Tisha said aggressively.

"Are you Rico's girlfriend?" Kelly nervously said.

"No, bitch, try again."

"Paul? I didn't know he had a girlfriend. I swear we only had sex one time."

"No, you fucking slut. I'm not Rico or Paul's girlfriend."

On Everything I Love

With a dumb look on her face, Kelly wondered whose man she had been fucking and forgotten about.

"Do you know Angel?" Tisha asked, pushing the gun harder into her stomach.

"Angel! Green eyes?" Kelly asked.

Kelly knew if she lied she would pay severely.

"Bitch, I said do you know Angel? Don't make me ask you again!"

"Yeah, I know him" Kelly answered, shaking so badly her teeth chattered.

Grabbing Kelly by her shirt collar, Tisha began pressing the gun deeper into her flesh. "Bitch, if you don't call Alexis and tell her everything you did and how you set him up, I swear on everything I love that I'm gonna hunt you down and personally kill your ass myself. I know where you live and I know where you go to school. You've got twenty-four hours to tell Alexis everything you did. And I mean everything. The crush you had on him, the weed, everything, bitch, you hear me?"

"Yes, I hear you, just don't shoot me", Kelly begged as the tears began falling down her frightened face. "Twenty-four hours and not a second more or I'll be back", Tisha said.

Seeing her car parked down the block, Tisha put her gun back inside her purse and calmly walked away. With piss running down her legs, Kelly sat on the bumper of one of the cars. Still scared to death, she put down the bag of groceries and thought about what had just taken place and what had to be done in twenty-three hours and fifty-five minutes.

Getting inside her car, A.L. quickly pulled off. "What happened?"

"I told that bitch to call Alexis and tell her everything she did."

"Oh shit you're crazy, Tisha!" A.L. laughed.

"I'll call Alexis tomorrow and find out if she called her."

"What if she doesn't do it?"

"She will, or she'll wish she had", Tisha said bluntly. After putting her black purse back under the seat, Tisha sat back and closed her eyes as A.L. drove them back to North Philly.

The next few weeks...

Angel and his lawyer had gone over everything involving the case. Both sides were now ready for battle in what was definitely being talked about as the trial of the city.

The local media had been covering the story since day one. It even made the front page of the *Philadelphia Daily News*. Angel and his lawyer also discovered other things about the case they were both unaware of. Still, both were prepared for the Federal Government and their agency's trickery and deceitful tactics.

After three long weeks, Angel still hadn't heard from Alexis. Even though Kelly called Alexis and told her everything she did to spoil their relationship, Alexis was still very upset with Angel. She told Tisha her heart would take some time to heal. Tisha understood how she felt because she too was regrouping from a healing heart that had been hurting for over a year.

Aunt Vanessa came back to Philadelphia to give all of the support she could to her nephew. She was staying at Angel's condominium until the trial was over. All charges were dropped on Pooda, Rodney, and A.L. for possession of the guns because the government had no search warrant for the property, only an arrest warrant for Angel.

On Everything I Love

Inside the U.S. Prosecutor's Office...

Angel's lawyer and Stan Reynolds were on opposite sides of a long black table. Also seated was U.S. Prosecutor David Stillman, who represented the Eastern District of Pennsylvania.

"Tony, you should have taken the twenty years", Dave said.

"Dave, I believe my client can beat this. I've done it before."

"Stop kidding yourself, Tony. There's too much evidence against Mr. McDaniel."

"Well, we'll let a jury decide", Tony said. "O.J. did it!"

"I'm serious, Tony. This is a young man's life we're talking about. The kid is only eighteen."

"My client and I both believe we can win this, Dave, and neither you nor your people can make us change our minds. Your allegations are bullshit and you know it."

"Alright, alright, if that's how you want it, fine", Dave said as he walked out of his office very upset.

Standing up and leaning over the table, Stan Reynolds pointed his finger at Anthony's forehead. "You're going down, you and that murdering motherfucker. I promise you won't win this case", Stan said, walking away.

Anthony closed his briefcase and walked out of the office. Seeing the hard look on Stan's face and the hatred in his eyes had kind of shaken him up. He knew exactly how the government played -- by any means necessary to win. Anthony also knew Stan wasn't playing with a full deck and meant every word he said, because he was still very bitter about the case he had lost last year.

After Anthony got inside his car, a blue Ford pickup truck pulled up behind him so he couldn't back out of his parking space. Seconds later, a black Ford Explorer pulled beside him and rolled down the tinted window. Still shaken from the conversation, Anthony was even more terrified seeing Stan Reynolds pointing a loaded .357 Magnum at his head.

"Just like that it could be over and won't nobody know shit!" he said angrily. Anthony was speechless and very scared, as Stan rolled up the window and both trucks drove away. Sitting back in his car, Anthony realized this case was much more than what it seemed to be. Not only was Angel fighting to save his life, but so was he.

FORTY-1
Tuesday, October 24th,
Two days before trial...

Once his aunt and Tisha left after a brief visit, Angel returned to his lonely and cold cell. Looking through the stack of mail that was on his cot, he was shocked to see a letter from Alexis. Immediately opening the letter, Angel sat on his cot and began reading it to himself.

Dear Angel,

It has taken me some time to get over the pain you inflicted on my heart. I would never hurt you like you did me, never. I finally found out the whole truth about Kelly, and I realize that I was just as much of the blame. I should have seen her evil ways a long time ago. And for missing it, it caused this painful separation between us.

I know how much you love me, but I still don't think you know how much I love you. A long time ago, when we were both kids, I told you, "Love isn't to be told, it's to be shown." I never did anything to hurt you and I never will. Still, I must forgive and forget in order to move on. My love for you is real and will always be real. Believe me it hurts me like hell to be away from you while you're going through this tragic time. But how can I help heal you when I need healing myself? I just want you to know that I'll be back in Philly very soon, and I have a very big surprise for you! I want you to know something. You fell into this large pit you dug, but you are not alone. And that's on everything I love.

Love always and eternally,
Your fiancé, Alexis

P.S. Read Psalm 30:5

Angel reached under his pillow and grabbed his Holy Bible. Going through the Bible, he finally came across the pages he was looking for and began to read.

"For his anger lasts only a moment, but his favor lasts a lifetime; weeping may remain for a night, but rejoicing comes in the morning."

After reading the touching verse, a lonely tear fell from one of Angel's watery green eyes. Receiving Alexis' letter had finally brought joy back into his sad and lonely heart.

Downtown Philadelphia...

Inside his law office, Anthony Rozzetti was talking on the phone. "This won't be a piece of cake", he said into the phone.
"I know, but I'm ready", a voice responded.
"The government wants his head on a golden platter."
"Like every other black man in the country", the voice said.
"And like I told you, Stan Reynolds plays by his own rules."
"I'm not afraid of him."
"Okay, I'm glad to have you on the team. I'll see you soon."
"Bye, bye, Tony", the voice said, hanging up the phone.

~~~

On Everything I Love

On the other side of town, inside Angel's condominium, Aunt Vanessa and Tisha were talking about the upcoming trial.

"I'm afraid, Auntie", Tisha said, looking at a family photo of her, Angel, Aunt Vanessa and her late Uncle Howard.

"I'm afraid, too, Tisha, but we are gonna have to be strong for Angel."

"This is really stressing me out. I can hardly sleep at night and now since the trial will begin in two more days, I'm stressing even more."

"Well, how do you think Angel feels? Being away from all of his loved ones, especially Alexis, he's probably going through it. He has never been locked up before. This is all new to him."

"What if he's convicted?" Tisha sadly said.

"I don't know what I would do if they convict him, but I couldn't stand around seeing Angel suffer in prison all his life. I know Angel. He would rather die than suffer behind bars."

"That's what he told me one time, that he couldn't spend the rest of his life behind bars", Tisha said.

"It's nothing but a slow death. Torture!" she continued.

"I talked to Alexis yesterday. She'll be here for Angel's trial. She's not going back to school until it's all over", Aunt Vanessa said.

"How's she holding up?" Tisha asked in a concerned voice.

"She's scared! Very scared. She said she couldn't see herself living in this world without Angel here beside her. That girl loves that boy."

"She always has, and he's always loved her", Tisha said.

"I pray that if he beats this case he'll get his life in order. He has a family who loves him and a woman who would die for him. I hope he sees that and knows he's a lucky man. Alexis told me she has a big surprise for me."

"What do you think it is?"

"I don't know, but she was very excited about it, whatever it is."

"I hope it can help cheer things up around here", Tisha said.

"She was one of her school's top students. One day, she's gonna be a helluva lawyer."

"I talked to her mother and father. They'll be at the trial, too."

"Angel will be so pleased to see us all sitting together supporting him. To see Alexis sitting next to me and you, will help ease some of his pain", Aunt Vanessa said.

"To see Alexis period will help ease his pain", Tisha said, as they both smiled trying to be strong for one another.

FORTY-2
Thursday, October 26, 1998
The Trial...

UNITED STATES OF AMERICA
VS.
ANGEL REGGIE MCDANIELS
Case number: 98-00954-01

The Federal Courthouse was packed with family, friends, and the local Philadelphia media. A few armed guards stood outside the crowded courtroom controlling the enthusiastic crowd. Inside the courtroom, Aunt Vanessa sat next to Tisha, behind where Angel would be seated. A few seats back, Sandy and her husband sat together. On the opposite side of the room, Pooda and Rodney were seated with an empty chair for A.L. once he showed up.

Finally, Angel appeared, being escorted by an armed officer and his lawyer, Anthony Rozzetti. They both took a seat on the defendant's side of the courtroom. Opening up a large briefcase, Anthony took out a few pieces of paper, and he and Angel began whispering into each other's ears. On the opposite side of them, U.S. prosecutor David Stillman sat with two of his associates discussing strategy for the trial. Not too far behind them, F.B.I. Special Agent Stan Reynolds and his partner, Mitch Sanders, calmly sat next to each other with hard looks on their faces and cold stares for Angel and his lawyer.

As the judge entered the crowded courtroom, the bailiff ordered everyone to stand. The judge, whose name was Arthur Libberman, was a short, skinny man in his early 50's. He was known around Philadelphia as a fair judge by his peers, but was very hard on murderers and rapists who entered his courtroom.

After everyone had taken their seats, the bailiff began speaking. "Case number: 98-00954-01, UNITED STATES OF AMERICA versus ANGEL REGGIE MCDANIELS", he yelled into the crowded courtroom.

"Prosecutor, are you ready to present your opening argument?" the judge asked. "Yes your Honor", David Stillman said, standing up and walking over in front of the twelve men and women of the jury. "You may begin", the judge stated. Rushing through the crowded courtroom, Alexis, dressed in a black Versace suit and matching briefcase, walked up and whispered in Anthony's ear.

"Is everything alright, counselor?" the judge asked. "Yes your Honor, I just wanted the court to know that Miss Alexis Lambert will be my assistant throughout the length of this trial."

"What?" Angel said, looking at both of them in total disbelief.

Everyone's faces were filled with surprise after hearing the announcement.

"You think I would let you fight this alone?" she said, smiling at Angel.

Looking at the prosecutor, the judge asked, "Prosecutor, do you have a problem with this?"

"No, your Honor, the defense can choose to have anyone they like", he answered.

"You may proceed then", the judge said.

Everyone was shocked to see Alexis, but none more than Angel who still couldn't believe his fiancé would be assisting his lawyer in his federal trial.

"That's the surprise!" Aunt Vanessa whispered in Tisha's ear.

"You think you're ready?" Angel asked.

"I was born ready." Taking a seat next to Angel, Alexis tightly grabbed Angel's hand under the wooden table.

"It's me and you all the way baby", she smiled.

"All the way?" Angel asked.

"All the way!" Alexis said.

Looking up, Angel and Alexis watched as the prosecutor began his opening argument and the stenographer recorded every word.

"On Thursday, May 28, 1997, just one week after Mr. McDaniel visited his childhood friend by the name of Sean Perry, who was an inmate at the C.F.C.F Institution for men located in Northeast Philadelphia on State Road, two men by the name of Peter Smith and John Williams were both brutally murdered inside their cells. Each stabbed repeatedly until they both died from numerous stab wounds. We have evidence and witnesses to show the jury and the people of this courtroom that Mr. Angel McDaniel paid inmates inside to have both these men killed. Once this evidence is shown to be true, the prosecutor's office would like the harshest penalty to apply to this defendant, and that's life in prison with no parole", the prosecutor said, sitting back down in his seat.

As Anthony whispered in Alexis' ear, the judge asked him if he was ready for his opening statement. "Yes your Honor", Anthony said, walking in front of the on-looking jury and the very eager crowd.

"On Thursday, May 28, 1997, my client, Mr. Angel McDaniel did in fact visit the C.F.C.F. correctional facility on State Road. My client", Anthony stated, pointing to Angel, "was simply visiting a friend of his to show him some support for his upcoming trial. Records will show my client visited this same individual five other times, each time putting money onto his prisoner's account. My client has always been a model citizen of Philadelphia. Not once has he even been arrested before this incident occurred. Not even a parking ticket! My client was simply visiting a dear friend of his who needed a shoulder to lean on. So he gave his. These accusations are all false that the government and its agencies made up to convict my client for something he knows nothing about. As this trial proceeds, my assistant and I will prove to this jury and the citizens of this beautiful city that my client, Mr. Angel McDaniel should be acquitted on all these false charges. Thank you", Anthony said, walking back to his seat.

"That was good", Alexis said to Anthony.

"It's only the beginning, Alexis. They seem too calm over there, like they've got something up their sleeves. I know Dave pretty well, and he never puts all of his cards out on the table. He always keeps one hidden up his sleeve. Hey, do you have the paperwork I asked you to get for me?"

"Yes", Alexis said, reaching into her briefcase and pulling out a small folder. "Thank you, Alexis", Anthony said as he took the folder from her hand.

As the judge was talking to the bailiff and his clerk, everyone in the courtroom patiently waited for him to continue.

"Go in my pocket", Alexis whispered to Angel.

"What?" Angel said confused.

"Go in my pocket", she said, nodding her head.

Reaching into Alexis' pocket, Angel pulled out the diamond engagement that he had bought her. "I want you to put it back on my finger", she said, smiling. "I wasn't gonna wear it again unless you put it back on my finger." Grabbing Alexis' hand, Angel placed the ring back on her finger where it belonged. "Don't take it off anymore", he whispered. "I

275

won't. Now come on, we have a case to win", she said.

"Prosecutor, are you ready to present the government's case?" the judge asked.

"Yes, your Honor, we're ready", David said, standing up once again in front of the on-looking jury.

"You may begin", the judge said.

"As I said earlier in my opening argument, on May 28, 1997, Peter Smith and John Williams were brutally stabbed to death inside their cells. One week earlier, jail records will show that Mr. McDaniel deposited one thousand dollars in Sean Perry's prison account. You may ask yourself what one has to do with the other. Money is put on prisoner's books all the time from family and friends. And you'd be exactly right. But ladies and gentlemen of the jury, there's so much more to this story, more than any one person in here could ever imagine. Through a thorough investigation by our Federal agencies we discovered tons of evidence that all points to one man. And that man is Mr. Angel McDaniel. Don't be fooled by his looks and charm, ladies and gentlemen. He's nothing but a young man with power, who does whatever to whomever he wants to do it to. Even if its murder.

Mr. Peter Smith and Mr. John Williams were two former mental patients at the Mercy Mental Hospital located in West Philadelphia. These two unstable men were investigated by Philadelphia undercover police officers, and then later charged with the murders of nine young women. I know everyone is still wondering what all of this has to do with Mr. McDaniel. Well, ladies and gentlemen, in time you'll see why, and just like I was, you will all be shocked by what will be exposed in this trial.

First, your Honor, I would like to call up the first of the government's three witnesses in this case", David said, pointing to the armed sheriff who was waiting by a side door. The sheriff then walked inside the room and shut the door."

"What does he mean by three witnesses?" Alexis asked Anthony.

"We only know about two. Who is the other?" she whispered.

"I'm not sure what David's trying to do", Anthony replied.

Moments later, the sheriff walked back with a tall heavy-set black man garbed in prison clothes.

"Ladies and gentlemen of the Court, I would like to introduce my first witness, Mr. Ralph Spinner", David said as the large heavy-set man approached the stand.

"Do you swear to tell the truth, the whole truth, and nothing but the truth so help you God?"

"Yes, I do", Ralph quickly answered.

"On Thursday, May 28, 1997, do you remember where you were on that day?"

"Yes, I was an inmate at C.F.C.F. on State Road", Ralph said in a deep bass-like voice.

"Do you know a Mr. Sean Perry?"

"Yes. We were on the same block. He lived a few cells down from me."

"Would you say the two of you were friends?"

"Yes, we were pretty tight."

"And what would you call pretty tight?" David asked as he slowly paced back and forth.

"I mean we played cards and basketball together. We talked sometimes."

"Did you ever see these two men before?" David asked, holding up two large black and white photos of Peter Smith and John Williams.

"Yes, I did. I saw them both when they first came in."

"Do you know who killed these two men?" David asked.

"Yes sir."

"And who killed them, Mr. Spinner?"

"Sean Perry and Leon Pittman!" Ralph shouted into the microphone.

"And how do you know this?"

"I was paid to look out and make sure no cops were around."

"You were paid?"

"Yes. Sean Perry gave me two hundred and fifty dollars' worth of commissary to make sure nobody saw anything."

"So you're saying that Sean Perry and Leon Pittman murdered these two men?"

"Yes sir. I was there."

"Do you know why they killed these two men?"

"Sean never said anything, but one day while I was talking to Leon, he told me somebody had put a lot of money on Sean's books and wanted those two men dead."

"Thank you, Mr. Spinner. Thank you very much."

"Is the defense ready for their cross-examination?" the judge asked.

"Yes your Honor", Anthony said, standing up and walking over to the witness.

Ready for battle, Angel sat up in his seat as his lawyer began his turn to question the witness.

"Mr. Spinner, you said that you were the lookout man, right?" Anthony asked.

"Yes, that's what I was paid for."

"So you are an accessory to the murders, also. That's what you're saying, right? You're no better than the two men who you claim killed these two men."

"I just watched the door. I didn't kill anybody", Ralph nervously replied.

"Mr. Spinner, weren't you convicted of murdering your boss in 1996 at the steel plant where you worked?"

"Yes."

"And weren't you sentenced to life in prison for that murder?"

"Yes", Ralph mumbled.

"Did the government make a deal with you to get your first degree murder conviction lowered to twenty years for your testimony?"

"Objection, your Honor!" David shouted.

"Objection overruled", the judge shouted back. "Answer the question, Mr. Spinner. Did the government offer you a deal?"

"Yes. If I told them all that I know, they said they would help me."

"Therefore, you're doing this to give some time back, huh?"

"I'm doing it because it's the right thing to *do*", Ralph said.

"The right thing to do, huh? Well, our records show that since you were 15 years old, Mr. Spinner, you've been arrested over 123 times for robbery, burglary, et cetera. You name it and you've done it. Now you want to do the right thing", Anthony said, shaking his head.

Seeing Alexis call for him, Anthony walked over to her.

"Are you sure?!" Anthony asked as Alexis whispered in his ear.

"Yes, I'm positive", she said.

"Counselor, is everything alright? Are you finished with the witness?" the judge asked.

"No, your Honor. My associate, Miss Alexis Lambert, will continue with the cross-examination of this witness."

"Well, let's go", the judge said impatiently as Alexis rose from her seat and approached the witness stand.

"What's going on, Tony?" Angel asked.

"Alexis said she thinks he's lying and can prove it. So I'm giving her a chance."

"She's not ready for this, Tony!"

"I think she is, Angel. Just give her a chance."

Everyone in the crowd nervously looked on as Alexis began.

"Mr. Spinner, how tall are you?" Alexis asked in a sweet voice.

"I'm 6'3".

"And how much do you weigh, sir?"

"Around 265 pounds."

"Our records show that Mr. Sean Perry weighs 155 pounds and Mr. Leon Pittman weighs 167 pounds. And both these men are 5'8" in height. After Mr. Rozzetti and I further investigated this case, we learned that both of the men who died had to have been held down by two men while the third individual did the stabbing."

"Objection, objection!" David yelled.

"Objection overruled!" the judge said.

"It was just Sean and Leon, nobody else", Ralph said as the sweat began to pour from his forehead.

"The doctors who performed the autopsy said that both men were held down while someone else savagely stabbed them to death.

"I want the jury and the Court to know that Mr. Peter Smith's height and weight before he was murdered was 5'10" and 185 pounds. Mr. John Williams was 6'3", 220 pounds. Both men were much bigger than the two men who Mr. Spinner claims killed them. After talking with Dr. Kennan Lee at the Philadelphia Medical Examiner's Office, he said it would have been almost impossible for two small men to carry out this double murder alone. Someone much bigger and stronger would have been needed to hold these individuals down while another person did the stabbing."

"I just watched that's all! That's all I did!" Ralph said, shaken.

"You keep claiming that all you did was watch, nothing more. Do you expect me, the jury, and the judge to believe you...? Mr. Spinner, you were the biggest man around and your own record shows you to be the most violent...and you simply watched?"

"Objection, your Honor. She's trying to lead the witness", David said.

"Objection overruled. You may continue", he told Alexis.

"Tell me then, Mr. Spinner, what did you see if you claim that's all you did was watch?"

Nervously looking at David, Ralph took a deep breath, then began.

"That night, when everybody was asleep, Sean, Leon, and I went inside of Mr. Peter Smith's cell that was open. They grabbed him while he slept and I ran back to look out for the C.O.'s who had just taken a smoke break. It was kinda dark inside the cell. I really didn't see who was the one stabbing the man, plus I had to keep a look out. After we realized

Mr. Smith was dead, the three of us went down the hall to Mr. John Williams' cell and the same thing took place. I don't know which one was doing the stabbing that time either. I was too busy looking out for the C.O.'s", Ralph said, apparently nervous.

"You said when they grabbed him while he slept, you ran back to look out for the C.O.'s, right?" Alexis asked.

"No, I meant..."

"Please, Mr. Spinner, remember you're under oath. Why did you run back if all you had to do was watch out for the C.O.'s? Are you the one who grabbed these men while they both slept?"

"No, no, I just watched!" Ralph shouted.

"Are you the one who stabbed both these men to death?"

"No, it wasn't me! It was them!"

"But you said it was dark. You couldn't see who stabbed these two men."

"It was dark."

"So you don't know who the real killers are then?"

"Sean and Leon did it!"

"No, Mr. Spinner. I believe you did it. You and one of these men held them down and someone else stabbed them."

"Objection, your Honor!" David yelled, jumping up.

"That will be all, your Honor", Alexis said, walking back and taking a seat.

"Wonderful job!" Anthony said, smiling.

"Did you like that, baby?" she asked Angel who still couldn't believe what he had just witnessed.

"Did I?!" was all Angel could say.

After the witness was escorted from the stand by the sheriff, the judge asked for a one-hour recess. Everyone left the courtroom to stretch, make phone calls, or go to the bathroom. Angel was taken back to his holding room along with Alexis and his lawyer. The government still had another witness to take the stand and a surprise witness that Anthony or Alexis had never known existed until today. Each side was happy with the first part of the trial. And both sides were looking forward to the rest of the trial. Anthony was satisfied with his new protégée, Alexis, who shocked him like she had done the whole courtroom with her cross-examination. For it being her first time ever working on a real trial, she was very mature and more than ready, he thought to himself. And seeing their daughter representing Angel brought tears to both Alexis' parents' eyes, as it did Tisha and Aunt Vanessa, too.

After everyone had taken their recess and handled their business, it was time for the second half of the trial to begin. Everyone sat back in their seats as Angel and his lawyers re-entered the courtroom. A.L. finally showed up and took a seat next to Pooda and Rodney.

FORTY-4

"Ladies and gentlemen please stand for the Honorable Judge Arthur Libberman", the bailiff announced. Everyone in the courtroom stood.

"You may be seated", he said as everyone took their seats.

"Prosecutor, are you ready?" the judge asked.

"Yes, your Honor, we're ready whenever the defense is ready", David said, looking through a folder.

"Are you ready, counselor?" the judge asked Anthony.

"Yes your Honor."

"Prosecutor, you may begin", he said.

"I would like to bring our second witness to the stand", David said.

"Would the sheriff please bring in Mr. Mark Smith?"

Leaving through the side door of the courtroom, the sheriff returned with Mark Smith by his side. Angel just shook his head in disbelief, realizing that Tisha was right when she told him to never trust a cop. But now it was too late.

"That snake!" Angel mumbled.

"Don't worry, baby. I got this", Alexis said, smiling.

"His testimony could be very damaging. This is the government's top witness", Anthony said.

"What about the other witness they have? They said they have three", Angel whispered.

"I doubt it. Dave will try his best to bluff and throw us off."

Angel stared penetratingly at Mark as he took the stand.

"Don't worry, it's his word against yours, baby", Alexis said, grabbing his hand under the table.

"We've been ready for this", she said.

Walking up to the witness stand, David Stillman began.

"Can you please state your full name for the Court?"

"Mark Smith", he shouted into the microphone.

"Mr. Smith, do you know these two men?" Dave asked, holding up pictures of Peter Smith and John Williams.

"Yes, I do."

"From where do you know these two men?"

"From my job."

"And where did you work?"

"At the C.F.C.F., a facility for men on State Road."

"And what was your job there?"

"I was a correctional officer for six-and-a-half years."

"Do you know Mr. Sean Perry, Mr. Leon Pittman, and Mr. Ralph Spinner?"

"Yes, I know all of them", Mark said confidently.

"And how is it that you know these three individuals so well?"

"They were all inmates on the floor that I worked on."

"Which floor?"

"G-block."

"Did you have any connections with any of these men in any way?"

"Yes, sir."

"Can you explain it to the Court?"

"I was asked by Mr. Sean Perry if I wanted to make a thousand dollars."

"For what?" David asked.

"To leave the cells of Peter Smith and John Williams open one night during my night shift."

"And what did you say?"

"I said sure I would, just tell me the night to do it."

"How did you get paid, Mr. Smith?"

"When Mr. McDaniel visited Sean, he placed the money inside of Sean's pockets. When I checked

Sean after the visit was terminated, the thousand dollars was there for me. I was paid to leave Sean, Ralph, and Leon's cell's door unlocked, too."

"Is that all?" David asked sarcastically.

"No, there's more."

"Will you please finish?"

"After I came back from my smoke break, I went inside the inmate's bathroom and got the bloody clothes these men had on. Once I got the clothes, I placed them inside a green trash bag and threw them away. Afterwards, I went by each man's cell and locked all of the ones I had left open. My partner never paid me any mind. He thought I was just checking up on the inmates like I would usually do."

"You said that one thousand dollars was put inside of Sean Perry's pockets for you by Mr. McDaniel?"

"Yes."

"And Sean Perry, who is a close friend of Mr. McDaniel, asked you to leave his and two other inmates' cells open?"

"Yes."

"Do you remember seeing Mr. McDaniel in the visiting room?"

"Yes. He looked very upset when he was talking to Sean."

"Do you know why?"

"No, but I heard it had something to do with his mother."

"Thank you, Mr. Smith", David said, smiling as he took his seat.

"Counselor, are you ready to cross-examine the witness?" the judge asked Anthony.

"Yes, your Honor", Anthony said, approaching the witness stand.

"Mr. Smith, why were you fired from your job?"

"I was indicted after a federal investigation."

"On what charges?"

"Conspiring to murder."

"How much time does a person get for that if he's found guilty?"

"Life!"

"Did the government offer you a deal for fifteen years if you testified today?"

"Objection!" David shouted.

"Objection overruled!" the judge said.

"Yes. If I told them the truth, I would receive a deal."

"For fifteen years instead of life, right?"

"Yes", Mark mumbled.

"Please speak up", Anthony said.

"Yes! Yes! Yes!"

"Did you see my client, Mr. McDaniel, give any money to Sean Perry?"

"No, but it was there. How else could he have gotten it?"

"Did you ever talk to my client before?"

"No."

"Do you know a young woman by the name of Vikki Smith?"

Mark's eyes widened from the unexpected question. As the sweat started to pour down his face, he remained quiet.

"Can you please answer the question?" Anthony said loudly. Nervously shaken, Mark lowered his head toward the floor.

"Oh, shit!" David mumbled to one of his associates sitting next to him.

"Please answer the question, Mr. Smith", the judge ordered.

"Yes, I know her", Mark finally answered.

"Where do you know her from?" Anthony asked.

"She's my niece!" he yelled.

"And what happened to your niece?"

"She was murdered a few years ago", Mark said.

"Murdered by whom?"

"She was murdered by the two men on the pictures."

"By Mr. Peter Smith and Mr. John Williams?"

"Yes, they were both charged with my niece's murder."

"These same two men who killed your niece coincidentally became prisoners where you worked, huh?"

"Yes."

"Wasn't your niece found raped and stabbed over fifty times?"

"Yes", Mark said tearfully.

"Murdered just like those two men who were inmates on your block at C.F.C.F. Did you know the two men who killed your niece were on your floor?"

"No, I didn't know who they were until I read the paper."

"At which time you found out they were your niece's killers?"

"Yeah, you can say that."

"So you had a very strong motive to have these men killed?"

"Objection, your Honor!" David shouted.

"Overruled!" the judge yelled.

"They murdered my little niece and eight other young women. They both deserved what they got!"

"And you made sure of that, huh?"

"I didn't know those two men were gonna be killed."

"Why did you leave their cells open?"

"I thought maybe they were faggots and wanted to have sex. I've done it before for inmates who were gay."

"So you're saying you only opened these two men's cells so the other men could have sex with them?"

"Yeah, that's it."

"Not to revenge your niece's murder?"

"No. I didn't know about anybody being killed."

"Do you hate the two men who killed your niece?"

"Yes, I do."

"If you could get away with killing both these men, would you?"

"I don't know", Mark said, wiping the tears from his face.

"Thank you, Mr. Smith, you've been very helpful", Anthony said, returning to his seat.

"Will that be it for cross-examination of the witness?"

"No, your Honor", Alexis said, standing up.

"Alexis, we've got them", Anthony whispered in her ear.

"Just a few more questions, Anthony", she begged.

"Okay, but don't mess this up."

"I won't", Alexis said, approaching the witness stand.

"What is she doing now?" Angel asked Anthony.

"I don't know, Angel. We'll both have to wait and see."

Everyone looked on as Alexis began questioning the witness. After seeing how Anthony broke the witness on the stand, giving the defense almost a sure victory, everyone wondered what this smart, attractive young law student had up her Versace sleeves.

FORTY-5

"Mr. Smith, what did you do with the bloody clothes that you got out of the bathroom?"

"I put them in a trash bag and threw them away."

"Isn't it prison policy that if an inmate is bleeding or cut he must be seen by the medical staff?"

"Yes."

"How did you know that bloody clothes would be in the bathroom?"

Once the question had been presented to him, Mark began shaking nervously on the stand.

"Can you answer the question please? Cat got your tongue?" Alexis said as everyone started laughing. "Never mind, you don't have to answer the question." Alexis smiled confidently. "What were the clothes that you found in the bathroom, shirts or pants?"

"Shirts", Mark answered.

"How many shirts, if you remember?"

"Three shirts, I remember", Mark said, wiping the sweat from his brows.

"Did all three shirts have blood on them?"

"Two of them did...the triple X and one of the smaller ones."

"So would you say that the 3X large shirt would have had to be worn by a much larger individual?"

"Objection, your Honor!" David nervously shouted.

"Objection overruled! Proceed counselor", the judge said.

"Do you think the bloody 3X large shirt was worn by a large man?"

"Probably so, it was real big."

"You stated earlier under oath that you knew nothing at all about any murders that were taking place on your shift at work, right?"

"Yeah", Mark mumbled, not sounding too convincing.

"That you thought these three inmates and the other two inmates who incidentally are the killers of your own niece were all just a bunch of gay men, right?"

"Yeah", Mark said as he began fidgeting in his chair on the stand.

"Mr. Smith, I think you are lying and knew all about the plot to kill the two men who murdered your niece", Alexis said.

"It's the truth! Everything I said was the truth!" Mark screamed into the microphone.

"Isn't it just too much of a coincidence that the two men who murdered your niece were both found dead on your shift at the prison. You, yourself, said that you were paid one thousand dollars to leave certain cells unlocked. You also said that you went into the bathroom and found three shirts, two covered with blood. And when asked earlier by Mr. Rozzetti if you would murder the two men who killed your niece if you could get away with it, your answer was 'I don't know.' Not no, but I don't know!"

"I didn't know that anyone was going to be killed!" Mark shouted.

"That will be all, Judge. We're finished cross-examining this witness", Alexis said, walking back over to her seat and sitting down.

Everyone was impressed with Alexis' cross-examination tactics. But none more than Angel who couldn't believe how good Alexis was and how she and Anthony were slowly winning his case. After Alexis caught both government witnesses in numerous lies, it was almost an open and shut case for the defense. Even the twelve men and women of the jury were impressed with the calmness of Alexis and her mentor, Anthony Rozzetti. The Philadelphia media were also impressed as its reporters had their stories already prepared about how the young gifted law student was taking down the big, bad government. One reporter's headline read, "Government KO'd by Alexis!"

After both sides were finished with their witnesses and cross-examinations, the judge decided to continue the trial at 10:00 a.m. the next morning. Angel was taken back to the county jail, and Anthony Rozzetti returned to his office to prepare for the next day of the trial while Alexis went back to the condominium with Angel's aunt Vanessa.

Stan Reynolds and David Stillman showed no signs of defeat. Both men remained confident and arrogant about the trial that many thought they had already lost. In fact, everyone thought the government had lost the case already. Everyone, that is, except Stan Reynolds and David Stillman who still had something up their sleeves.

Later that night...

Inside Angel's condo, Alexis was talking with Angel, who had just called on the phone.
"Where's Mama?"
"She's asleep in your bedroom", Alexis said, closing her briefcase.
"What were you doing?" Angel asked.
"I just finished going over some more stuff for the trial tomorrow."
"You know I'm proud of you, right?" Angel said.
"I know, baby, I'm just glad you realize how much I love you."
"I always knew how much you loved me, Alexis."
"No, I don't think you really know."
"Well, tell me then."

Jimmy DaSaint

"I can't. I can only show you my love. Remember what I told you? Anyone can say it out of their mouth, but not many can show it."
"What do you think of the trial so far?" Angel asked, changing the subject.
"It would almost take a miracle for us to lose this trial. Both government witnesses committed perjury on the stand. The government still hasn't proven why you would want those two men dead. The correction officer looks guiltier than anybody. I'm almost 99.9 percent sure we'll win this case, baby."
"Why not one hundred percent?"
"I always say, 'never be too confident or too cocky.' Though only a miracle can save the government right now."
"They're probably running around crazy by now", Angel smiled.
"To be honest, they seem calm. Too calm, like they didn't have any worries. For them to be losing this case, they were very relaxed."
"Maybe they realize they can't win", Angel said.
"Maybe you're right. Tomorrow we'll find out, and hopefully, we'll get it all over with."
"Yeah, and I can take you away for a few days."
"No, your birthday is Monday. I'll take you away for a few days."
"Oh, you remember, huh?" Angel said.
"Did I ever forget?"
"Nope!"
"Well, stop playing then. You know I know when your birthday is."
"I love you, Alexis."
"I love you, too, baby. Make sure you get on your knees tonight before bed."
"I will."
"Bye, Angel. I'll see you in the morning."
"Bye, Alexis", Angel said, hanging up the phone.

293

On Everything I Love

Once again, friends, relatives and reporters filled the large Federal Court-room. The judge and prosecutors along with Angel and his lawyers were all ready to begin. Everyone took the same seats as they had the day before. Rumors were floating around that the jury had already made its decision in favor of Angel and his team of lawyers. Everyone was all set for an acquittal for Angel once the jury had deliberated. Alexis had done herself well catching the government witnesses in numerous lies.

Gathering around in a small circle, Anthony began whispering.

"I think we should put Angel on the stand", he said. "What?" No, I don't think that would be a very wise move Anthony. We got 'em where we want them. Why risk it? Alexis asked.

"Alexis, look over your shoulder at the twelve men and women on the jury. Do you honestly believe that every one of those people is convinced that Angel's innocent? They need to hear him speak. They must know the man whose life is on the line. I've seen it happen so many times - a case that should've won- but even with all of the evidence and law behind the case, the jury still comes up with a guilty verdict."

"He's right, Alexis. I ain't got nuthin to hide", Angel said, confidently.

"Are you sure baby? These people are the worst kind. They search and dig until they find something. And even if they don't find anything they'll lie about it. I can see that Stan Reynolds has something personal against you, so why take the chance?" Alexis asked.

"Baby, it will be alright. Anthony, what do you really think?"

"It's really up to you Angel. However, I think putting you on the stand would be the icing on the cake. Then the government can kiss this bogus case against you goodbye."

"Okay, I'll do it! I'm ready", Angel said as he moved to an upright position in the chair.

Dressed in a dark gray Salvatore Ferragamo suit, Angel crossed his arms and nodded his head at Anthony to proceed.

"Yeah, let's do this!" Angel said as he held Alexis' hand.

"Counselor, are you ready to begin?" the judge asked.

"Yes, your Honor", Anthony said as he got up from his seat.

"Your Honor, I would like to call my client, Mr. Angel McDaniel to the stand."

The onlookers as well as the judge and the jury were stunned that Angel's attorney would put him on the stand. The courtroom became a buzz at the announcement, and the judge had to quickly silence everyone. Angel walked to stand and calmly sat down.

"Do you swear to tell the whole truth, nothing but the truth so help you God?" the bailiff asked, with Angel's right hand on the Holy Bible.

"I do" Angel said, as he looked at the sea of people staring at him.

"You may begin counselor", the judge said.

"Mr. McDaniel, is it okay if I call you Angel?" Anthony asked.

"Yes, that's what everyone calls me." Angel smiled, showing his pearly whites.

"Mr. Mc .... I mean Angel. Prior to this frivolous charge, have you ever been in any kind of trouble before?"

"No! Never!"

"So you've never, not once been in any trouble with the law? Anthony inquired.

"Never", Angel said shaking his head no.

"Not even a parking ticket?"

"Nope, I make sure I put the right amount in the meter", Angel responded, and the courtroom erupted in laughter.

"No speeding ticket, fights, or anything else, huh?"

"Nothing. This is the first time I've ever been inside a courtroom. My Mama taught me to always respect others if you want the same respect returned."

Angel spotted his Aunt Vanessa and saw a smile on her face.

"I've got a copy of your high school records." Anthony said as he waved a small brown folder in front of the court room. He proceeded to open it. "I see from the 9th grade to your senior year you received high marks, A's and B's. All of your teachers had nothing but good things to say about you. It seems as though you were very popular and a well-liked young man in school. Is that true?"

"I just wanted to set an example for all of the younger kids under me. You don't have to be an entertainer or an athlete to be a role model. I figured if they saw me doing well, they would also want to follow suit and do the same", Angel replied.

"That's a good attitude to have. Not many young men your age think that way."

Angel interjected.

"Well, I had two good role models. My mama, and my Uncle Howard who passed away."

"So Angel, how long have you known Sean Perry?" Anthony asked.

"I've known Sean since we were kids. He is one of my closest friends. We were both in boy scouts together and we played on the same baseball and basketball teams. We are very close. I love him like a brother."

"Is that why you went to see him and put the money on his books?" Anthony asked.

"Yes, I just wanted to show him some support. Let him know that he still has a friend out here who loves him. I always went to see him and gave him money."

"Is it also true that every summer you give a community cookout for your neighborhood?"

"Yes. My Uncle Howard started the custom, and when he died I continued his tradition. My uncle loved the community and all the people who lived there. He always told me that it's good to show people the light some time. That no one should stay in darkness...even if everything around us is pitch-black. Most times a little light is all a person really needs to shine."

"Is that all you do for your community, Angel?" Anthony asked as he quickly surveyed his attentive audience.

"No, I also give out turkeys for Thanksgiving and toys to the less fortunate children the day before Christmas."

"So, let me get this straight, Angel. You've never been arrested before. You were an exceptional student in high school. You care very deeply for your family and close friends and you give back to your community. I see you were giving the perfect name." Anthony said, stirring laughter from the crowd in the courtroom. However, Stan and David did not find the humor.

"Do you know anything at all about these two men you're accused of having murdered?"

"No, I have no reason to kill anyone. I never saw those two men in my life." Angel responded.

"Ladies and gentleman of the court and jury-only a man who has nothing to hide and who is telling the truth would risk getting up on this stand..."

"Objection, your Honor!" David shouted.

"Objection overruled" the judge said, banging his gavel.

Anthony continued. "My client is a law abiding citizen of Philadelphia, who has never been arrested for anything in his entire life before this bogus charge was brought against him by the government. He's well respected throughout his community, and loved by all of those that he comes across. All of these accusations from the government witnesses are false. These are people who would do and say anything to cover their own hides. I'm through your Honor" Anthony said, returning to his seat.

Stan Reynolds sat alone in a corner with a devious smirk on his pale white face. Both Stan Reynolds and David Stillman had information no one else was privy to, and each of them had been waiting for this moment to finally happen. Their wish to have Angel on the stand had been granted. "Prosecutor, you may begin your cross examination", the judge said. Removing himself from his seat, David smiled as he cracked his knuckles and stretched his arms to loosen up as if preparing for a brawl. Approaching the stand, David looked directly into Angel's green eyes. He paused for effect.

"I want to cut right through to the chase, Mr. McDaniel. Did you have anything at all to do with Mr. Peter Smith or Mr. John Williams being murdered at the C.F.C.F on State Road?"

"No", Angel said confidently.

"Did you pay Mr. Mark Smith one thousand dollars at any time?"

"No."

"Did you visit your friend, Sean Perry, at C.F.C.F?"

"Yes."

"Mr. McDaniel, who raised you as a child?"

"My Aunt Vanessa and my Uncle Howard", Angel said.

"Is this the same Howard Johnson that was murdered last year in New York City?"

"Yes, that's him", Angel answered in a calmly.

"Why did your Aunt Vanessa have to raise you and not your real mother?"

"Because my mother died when she had me", Angel said.

"So why didn't you go stay with your father then?" David asked, as a sneaky grin appeared on his face.

"I don't know who my father is."

"I believe you do. I believe you're not telling the people of this court the truth."

"I don't know my father. I never met him."

"What is this all about?" Alexis asked Anthony.

"I don't know, Alexis, but it doesn't look good", he said.

"So you don't have a clue in the world as to who your father is?" David continued.

"I said no!" Angel said, now visibly frustrated.

At that moment, Aunt Vanessa sadly put her head down.

"What's wrong, Auntie?" Tisha asked.

"Everything is bad now. I can't believe this!" she said as her tears began to pour down her face. At that moment Aunt Vanessa realized what Angel had done, knowing he had done it all for her happiness.

"What's bad now?" Tisha asked, unaware of what was going on. But Aunt Vanessa could say nothing. All she could do was pray and cry.

"Is there any reason at all why you would want these two men dead?" David asked.

"No", Angel answered.

"Not even if these two men raped your mother?!" David said.

As the crowd became loud and stunned, the judge asked everyone to calm down.

"What did he say?" Alexis asked Anthony.

"It doesn't look good, Alexis. It doesn't look good", Anthony said, now becoming very worried.

"That will be all with Mr. McDaniel, Judge", David said.

As Angel got off the stand and sat back down, Alexis asked him what was going on.

"Nothing, Alexis. They're trying to play head games."

"Something is going on! What are they talking about, Angel?" Don't lie to me!"

"I don't know, Alexis", Angel said. "I don't know."

"Your Honor, the government would like to bring up its final witness" David yelled into the crowded courtroom.

"The government would like to call up Mr..."

Everyone in the courtroom nervously waited to hear who the government's final witness was to help with their case.

"Mr. Peter Smith."

"Peter Smith!" Anthony said to Alexis. "He's dead!"

No one in the courtroom could believe what they had just heard. Even Aunt Vanessa and Angel had disorganized looks on their faces. Everyone except David Stillman and Stan Reynolds were confused. Walking through the crowd, a tall white man with a folder and two small white capsules of blood got on the stand.

"Ladies and gentlemen of the court, I'm sure you are all wondering how Mr. Peter Smith could possibly be here when he was one of the two men who were stabbed to death in jail. This here is Dr. George Moffet with the F.B.I. criminal laboratories in Washington, D.C. He's also one of the nation's leading analysts on DNA research, and he'll be representing the deceased Mr. Peter Smith."

After the bailiff had once again finished swearing him in, David began.

"Mr. Moffet, how long have you been working for the government?"

"Seventeen years next month", he said.

"And how long have you been doing DNA research?"

"Ten years."

"So then, one would say that you're a pro at this?"

"I guess one could say that", he smiled.

"Can you please explain to me what's in your hand?"

"It's blood! Two capsules of blood."

"Of whose blood?"

"Mr. Peter Smith and Mr. Angel McDaniel."

"Why both of theirs?"

"I was asked by the F.B.I. to check both men's blood types a few weeks ago."

"Did anything strange happen?" David asked, smiling.

"Yes, very strange."

"And what was that?"

"Both these men's blood types and samples were identical!" he said.

Everyone's eyes lit up when they heard the connection. Angel put his head down in disbelief. And so did Aunt Vanessa.

"Excuse me, but can you repeat that?"

"They are both identical. Those two people are related."

"And how sure are you on that?"

"I'm 99.9percent positive that Mr. Peter Smith is Mr. Angel McDaniel's father!"

Aunt Vanessa would have fainted to the floor if it were not for Tisha catching her. Alexis shook her head as her heart dropped a million feet. Pooda, Rodney, and A.L. couldn't believe what they had all just heard. Stan Reynolds displayed a victorious smile.

"I have a copy of a report from both men before they were killed. It's a report which lists all the women they had raped and murdered. One particular woman stood out more than anyone else, and that was the girl who got away. Both these men told F.B.I. agents and Philadelphia Police about the one girl who they had raped but spared her precious life, leaving her lying on a cold dark alley. Both said this incident occurred about sometime in March of '79 in West Philadelphia.

After a six-month investigation, we found out that in March of 1979 Penny, Vanessa and their paralyzed mother all lived just a few blocks away from the Mercy Medical Hospital where Peter Smith and John Williams were patients, right where these two men said they had raped their second victim - a young black girl - and let her live. Seven months later, Miss Penny McDaniel gave birth to a mulato baby boy and later died from labor complications. Ladies and gentlemen of the jury, that child whose young mother died while having him and whose blood sample matches the late Peter Smith is none other than Mr. Angel McDaniel, the gentleman who is sitting in this courtroom now. We believe that Mr. McDaniel found out the truth about his father and personally plotted this double murder. He set out to revenge his mother's death by killing the men who had raped her, even though one of them was his own father," David said, now holding up a large color picture of Peter-and you could see that Angel inherited his father's green eyes.

"Ladies and gentlemen of the jury, Angel McDaniel is a cold-hearted killer. He's a liar and he should be given the harshest penalty for this savage and brutal crime that he orchestrated. You have just seen scientific proof from one of the country's top doctors on DNA research that showed this courtroom the real truth and mystery surrounding Mr. Angel McDaniel. Thank you very much" David said, taking his seat and excusing Dr. Moffet from the stand.

The courtroom was blown away with this new information. A trial that seemed to be a guaranteed victory for the defense had now turned its favor for the government. All Tisha and Aunt Vanessa could do was cry. Even Anthony didn't know what to do now. The press immediately began changing their headlines for the next day's papers, but no one was more in pain than Alexis, who just grabbed her briefcase and tearfully ran out of the courtroom.

The judge continued the trial for Monday, October 30th at 10:00 a.m., where Angel's fate would lay in the hands of the jury.

FORTY-6
Later that night...

Angel and Aunt Vanessa were talking on the phone.

"I'm sorry, Mama", Angel said.

"It's not all your fault, Angel. I'm also part of the blame. I know you did it for me."

"Where's Alexis?"

"She flew back to Atlanta!"

"What for?"

"She said she had something very important to get. She's very scared, Angel."

"Why did she go back to Atlanta? She knows that my case will resume on Monday."

"She said she'll be back by Monday."

"You don't know why she left, huh?"

"No, Angel, she just told me and Tisha it was very important that she hurry up back to Atlanta to get something. She'll be back. She knows what she's doing."

"I know I hurt her. I'm so sorry, Mama."

"It isn't over, baby. God hasn't made his decision yet! That's all that matters. I can't see you going to prison for all of your life. I can't see you suffering in that place."

"I'd rather be dead than locked up all my life!" Angel said.

"I don't think Alexis can stand to see you locked up either, Angel. Nobody can!" Aunt Vanessa tearfully said.

"I'm so sorry, Mama, for disappointing you."

"Angel, you never disappointed me, and don't you ever say that again. Everything will be alright, baby. God has a way to fix the worst things."

"I love you, Mama", Angel said.

"I love you, too, baby. Bye, bye", she said, hanging up.

After hanging up the phone, Angel was taken back to his cold lonely cell where he would wait until Monday for the final decision of his young life.

~~~

Inside David Stillman's office, he and Stan Reynolds were talking.

"It's over, David! It's all over. They're done!"

"Yes, it's definitely over, Stan. There's no way a jury will acquit him now."

"I've finally beaten that bastard Rozzetti...him and his client!"

"Angel will definitely receive no less than life in prison. I told Rozzetti to take the deal. I know he's smacking himself in the head now", David said.

"I can't wait to see that scared, little pretty-boy finally get what he deserves, a life sentence in federal prison. Today, I'm a very happy man. He can't get out of this one. His uncle died on me before I could get him indicted and sentenced to life, but he'll pay for them both. I can't wait to see their scared faces on Monday, him and his little girlfriend", Stan said.

"She put up a good fight", David smiled.

"Not good enough", Stan said, smiling back as both men happily shook hands and walked out of the office.

~~~

The weekend was the longest in Angel's life, as he prayed to God to help him through this painful period of his young life. At the same time, Alexis was doing the same in Atlanta. After getting what she had come to Atlanta for, Alexis quickly got on the first flight back to Philadelphia.

On Everything I Love

Inside the packed courtroom, relatives and the press had once again filled the large courtroom. After the defense had presented their final argument to the jury, the prosecutor's final cross-examination was even stronger now with all of the evidence they had on Angel. After both sides had finished their closing arguments, the judge then charged the case to the jury who was ready to deliberate and come with its verdict.

As the jury was inside a room deliberating, Angel, Alexis and Anthony all sat nervously quiet. The entire courtroom was on the edge of their sweaty seats. The longer the jury took, the more nervous everyone seemed to get.

Finally, after forty minutes of deliberation, the twelve men and women of the jury emerged from the room and took their seats. The judge then asked Angel and his lawyers to stand as well as the government prosecutors. Alexis stood nervously holding her black briefcase.

"Will the foreman of the jury please stand", the clerk of the court said.

All eyes were now on the short, fat, bald white man, dressed in a black double-breasted suit. "Please answer the next question yes or no. Members of the jury, have you reached a verdict on which at least ten of you have agreed?"

"Yes, we have", the foreman answered nervously.

"Members of the jury, do you find Mr. Angel McDaniel guilty or not guilty as charged?"

Total silence was now in the courtroom. Sitting on the opposite side of the courtroom, Stan Reynolds confidently looked on. Clearing his throat, the foreman began.

"We, the jury, find the defendant, Mr. Angel Reggie McDaniel, guilty of conspiracy in the double murders of Mr. Peter Smith and Mr. John Williams."

The crowded courtroom immediately burst out of control. "No! No!" Tisha screamed as Aunt Vanessa grabbed her and tried to calm her down. Pooda, Rodney, and A.L. couldn't believe their ears as they began shedding tears. Alexis stood calmly but shook her head knowing the sentence would be worse. The judge called for silence in his courtroom and everyone did their best to regain their composure as they once again took their seats.

Looking at Angel, the judge finally spoke. "Mr. McDaniel, you have been found guilty of the murders of Mr. Peter Smith and Mr. John Williams by a jury of your peers. The sentence prescribed by law for this charge is life in prison without the possibility of parole. Court's adjourned", he said, banging his gavel.

The sheriff quickly escorted Angel and his lawyers through a side door. Closely following them was David Stillman and Stan Reynolds. Alexis suddenly whispered in Angel's ear and grabbed his hand as they all went inside a small room.

"You have a few minutes, counselor", the sheriff said to Anthony.

Outside the door, Stan Reynolds and David Stillman happily stood around waiting to talk with Anthony and Alexis. The sheriff then closed the door behind him and waited outside the door to take Angel back to the county jail. Inside the small room Anthony was talking.

"I'll appeal this. It's not over, Angel!"

"Thanks for everything, but I'll be okay, Tony", Angel said calmly.

"Everything is fine, Tony. You did a wonderful job", Alexis said.

On Everything I Love

"Is everything alright with you two?" Anthony asked, confused at how calm they were.

"We're fine", they both said in unison.

"Anthony, can you please just give us five minutes alone?" Alexis politely asked.

"Sure, I'll tell the sheriff you'll be ready in a few more minutes",

Anthony said, walking out of the small room and shutting the door behind him. Stan and David were both surprised to see Anthony walk out of the room alone.

"He's giving the love birds a final few minutes. She can save that mess for when she visits him in prison", Stan laughed.

"A few more minutes", the sheriff said to Anthony, who waited outside till Alexis was finished.

Sitting at the small round table inside the room, Alexis reached over and grabbed both of Angel's hands.

"I can't live without you, Angel. I can't stand to see you go to prison for the rest of your life", she said as the flow of tears began to fall from her face.

"I feel the same way, baby", Angel said, reaching over and wiping away her tears.

"On Everything I Love, you are my world, my life, my source!

 On Everything I Love, you mean so much to me!

 On Everything I Love, you are my tomorrows!

 On Everything I Love, you are my reasons! And without you around, Angel, there's no me. No us!

On Everything I Love, I've been yours since I was put in your crib!

On Everything I Love, you complete me, and I'm incomplete without you!

 On Everything I Love, I love you, Angel!

Every woman has a man that she treasures...and **On Everything I Love,** you're mine!" Alexis said.

"You mean it? Angel said.

"On Everything I Love" Alexis smiled.

Opening up her briefcase, Alexis took out two small bottles of spring water and a small brown pill container.

"Along time ago, somebody told me that dying is easy, it's living that's hard. They were right!" Alexis said, opening up the small brown pill container.

"Do you see what the container says?" Alexis asked.

"Yes! I read it", Angel smiled.

"Are you ready to go?" Alexis said with a smile on her face, as well.

"Yes, baby, I'm ready to go together", Angel said as they both opened up their bottled spring water.

Outside the door, Stan wondered what was taking Alexis and Angel so long inside the quiet room. "Can you tell her to come on?" Stan said to the sheriff who was standing by the door. Turning the doorknob, the sheriff realized that the door had been locked from the inside. "It's locked!" he said to Stan. Stan, David, and Anthony all walked over to the door.

"What do you mean it's locked?" Stan said as he began banging on the door.

"Open the damn door!" he shouted.

"Open the goddamn door, Alexis!" David yelled, also.

"I know you hear us. Open the door!" Stan shouted as he continued to bang harder.

As they desperately tried to gain access to the room, neither of them heard a word from the other side of the door.

"You can't get out of going to prison, Angel!" Stan shouted. "It's all over!"

Finally kicking the door down, Stan and the other three men quickly entered the room. "No, no, no!!!" Stan screamed out as he looked at the bodies of Angel and Alexis both lying next to each other on the floor. "No, not again!" Stan yelled out loud as he fell to his knees in disbelief.

Picking up the small brown container from the table, David couldn't believe it. "Cyanide!!" he said, shaking his head and seeing the opened bottles of spring water spilled on the floor. "No! No!" Stan continued to cry out as the sheriff ran off to get some medical help. But Stan already knew that they were both gone and nothing could bring them back. Knowing once again he was beaten and just like Howard, he would never see Angel behind bars either.

"Happy birthday, Angel", Anthony mumbled to himself. Looking inside Alexis' open briefcase, David saw a small handwritten letter and began reading it.

Dear Mama,

Please give everything that I own to Tisha and $500,000 a piece to Pooda, Rodney, A.L. and Sean. I'm sorry for all I've taken you through, but I would do it all over again for your happiness. Alexis and I love each other. And everyone has always known this. We'll both be okay, Mama, so be happy for us. And remember that nothing can separate true love...not even death.

Love always,
Your Angel

Jimmy's concluding words...

This book is dedicated to all of my people. We were born to love, but something happened along the way. I beg y'all to get on the right track before God comes back! It's real, y'all! Life is real. As death waits for us all, I pray that everyone finds their purpose in life, their meaning for existence! Believe me we all have a meaning for existence.

When I was shot ten times and survived, I knew there was a meaning for my existence. And when I was sentenced to serve time in federal prison, I first became confused about my existence. Then, one day, I picked up a pencil and began writing. And just like that, I knew the meaning for my existence. I knew that God wanted me to write and touch people with His words. I say His words because I write from my heart. And my heart only knows love. And God is love! My stories are your realities. Everyone has a story, but everyone can't write it down. So I write for all of those who can't. I was blessed with a God-given talent to touch souls with my writing. Hopefully, you've been touched!

Just remember there are three things that we are born to do. We are born to love, find the meaning of our existence, and one day die. So, for every poverty-stricken person who is living in a ghetto, don't be fooled. Everything around us is a test. Many will pass, but more will fail.

Remember, your life is what you make it, so find your meaning for existence.

Love,
Jimmy DaSaint

Psalm 30:5

"For his anger lasts only a moment, but his favor lasts a lifetime; weeping may remain for a night, but rejoicing comes in the morning".

"If I Should Die Today"

If I should die today, who will remember me **tomorrow?**
Who will pray for my sins and feel my **sorrow?**
Tell me, who will miss me and take my death **hard?**
Tell me, who really loves me, no matter if I'm small or **large?**
If I should die today, who will cry? Who will **laugh?**
Who will say, *"Oh* that's a shame", or, "The hell with his **black ass?"**
If I should die today, who will throw my name **around?**
Stab me in my back while I'm six feet **underground.**
Disgrace all of the mistakes I made, just to move in-to my **place.**
Cry a river of false tears, and then smile once the dirt hits my **face.**
Who will call me all types of bad names, like "That no-good fucking **bastard?"**
Then jump for joy like a kid with a new toy when they finally close my **casket.**
All I have to say is real love will stay **true,**
And we all must die one day, so what you do to me will happen to **you.**

Bye,
Jimmy DaSaint

DASAINT ENTERTAINMENT ORDER FORM

Ordering Books
Please visit www.dasaintentertainment.com to place online orders.
Or
You can fill out this form and send it to:

DaSaint Entertainment
PO Box 97
Bala Cynwyd, PA 19004

Title	Price	QTY
Black Scarface	$15.00	_____
Black Scarface II	$15.00	_____
Young Rich & Dangerous	$15.00	_____
The Underworld	$15.00	_____
A Rose Among Thorns	$15.00	_____
Contract Killer	$15.00	_____
On Everything I Love	$15.00	_____
Money Desires & Regrets	$15.00	_____
What Every Woman Wants	$15.00	_____
Ain't No Sunshine	$14.99	_____

Make Checks or Money Orders out to:
DaSaint Entertainment
Name: _____
Address: _____
_____
City:_____State:_____ Zip:____
Telephone:_____
Email:_____

Add $4.00 for shipping and handling
$2.50 for each additional book
($5.00 for Expedited Shipping
Plus $2.50 for each additional book)
WE SHIP TO PRISONS!!!

34423140R00177

Made in the USA
Middletown, DE
21 August 2016